"I'm so sorry. It se ~~causing you a problem.~~

For some silly reason the words caught in her throat and wobbled.

Nate clasped her shoulders and looked into her face as if searching every corner of her mind. "You are not a problem to me."

Louise told herself it was only words, perhaps for the benefit of those who couldn't help but overhear. Despite her arguments to the contrary, she believed him. For the moment, she'd allow herself to be comforted by his admission.

She nodded, the book clutched to her chest.

He reached past her to get the title he'd chosen, and they returned to the table to sit side by side.

She read the words and turned the pages, but couldn't have said what the story entailed. Her thoughts wouldn't settle. It was merely worry, she told herself, about getting to Eden Valley Ranch before the baby came. Concern for the safety of the little life she carried. But in a moment of honesty she admitted that her predominant thought centered on Nate. Why was he being so nice to her? Treating her as though he really cared when they both knew he was only doing this out of a sense of obligation.

Linda Ford lives on a ranch in Alberta, Canada, near enough to the Rocky Mountains that she can enjoy them on a daily basis. She and her husband raised fourteen children—four homemade, ten adopted. She currently shares her home and life with her husband, a grown son, a live-in paraplegic client and a continual (and welcome) stream of kids, kids-in-law, grandkids, and assorted friends and relatives.

Books by Linda Ford

Love Inspired Historical

Christmas in Eden Valley

A Daddy for Christmas
A Baby for Christmas

Journey West

Wagon Train Reunion

Montana Marriages

Big Sky Cowboy
Big Sky Daddy
Big Sky Homecoming

Cowboys of Eden Valley

The Cowboy's Surprise Bride
The Cowboy's Unexpected Family
The Cowboy's Convenient Proposal
Claiming the Cowboy's Heart
Winning Over the Wrangler
Falling for the Rancher Father

Visit the Author Profile page at Harlequin.com for more titles.

LINDA FORD

A Baby for Christmas

HARLEQUIN® LOVE INSPIRED® HISTORICAL

Recycling programs for this product may not exist in your area.

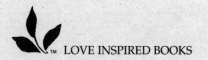 LOVE INSPIRED BOOKS

ISBN-13: 978-0-373-28334-7

A Baby for Christmas

www.Harlequin.com

Printed in U.S.A.

For unto us a child is born, unto us a son is given: and the government shall be upon his shoulder: and his name shall be called Wonderful, Counsellor, the mighty God, the everlasting Father, the Prince of Peace.

—Isaiah 9:6

Chapter One

Twenty-year-old Louise Porter cupped her hands to her rounded belly. How was she to protect this baby, as well as herself and her eighteen-year-old sister-in-law? Where could she go? Where could she find help?

No answer came to mind, but she must get away from that vile man who grew bolder and bolder with his threats and advances.

She turned the corner. Without thought, she'd walked toward the church. Head down, watching her footing carefully on the rough ground, she made her way toward the spot where they'd buried her husband six months ago.

Not until she was almost there did she look up and nearly fell backward. Nate Hawkins stood at Gordie's graveside. She'd gotten a fleeting glimpse of him last year on his annual visit to his mother, but still she stared at him, taking in his rumpled dark blond hair and his blue eyes that always made her feel as if he pinned her to the spot where she stood. He'd filled out in the three years since he left, but he was still tall and slim. His muscular body spoke of hard work and strength.

"Nate, I never expected to see you." Too late she thought to pull her shawl closed to hide her belly.

Nate held his hat in his hand. "I had to come say good-bye to Gordie." His gaze skittered to her stomach and away. "You married again?"

"Hardly. This is Gordie's baby."

"Oh." He shifted from foot to foot. "Don't know if I should say sorry or congratulations."

"Don't say anything." She wouldn't tell him that she struggled with similar feelings. A baby to bring up on her own presented challenges. Some she dreaded, but that didn't mean she didn't look forward to welcoming the little one. "I'll leave you to say your goodbye." She turned back the way she'd come.

"Wait. Don't let me chase you away."

"I can come back anytime." She continued on her way, not slowing until she knew she was out of his sight. Then she paused to catch her breath. It was getting harder and harder to move about with her growing size. She patted her tummy as the baby kicked up a storm. "Not much longer, little one," she murmured. She expected the baby would be born Christmas Day. A Christmas baby. Her heart swelled with anticipated joy.

Her gaze turned over her shoulder, though she wouldn't be able to see Nate. He'd been Gordie's best friend. Hers, too.

In the past, both she and Nate had found a warm welcome in the Porter home along with the Porter children—Gordie and Missy. Nate and Louise had had their own homes, but in her case it had been unwelcoming and Nate had been mostly alone in his, so they'd spent all their free time with the Porters.

Louise's mother had left when she was little and her father had raised her on his own, usually in mining camps. When she turned thirteen and he noticed how the men began to stare at her, he had sent her to live with Aunt Bea here in Rocky Creek, Montana. Aunt Bea was… well, she didn't care to make any effort on Louise's behalf and was openly grateful that Louise spent so much time at the Porters'.

At first, Louise resented her father for sending her away, then, after she'd fallen in with Nate and the Porter family, she secretly thanked him. It was the best thing that could have happened to her. The Porters were a loving, supportive family, and Nate…well, she was more than half in love with him from the first glimpse. Puppy love only, of course.

Her idyllic life had crashed to a halt four years ago when the Porter parents were killed in a senseless accident. Their team of horses had spooked and before Mr. Porter could get the animals under control, the wagon flipped, killing them both.

Gordie was not yet eighteen and suddenly had to be the man of the house and look after Missy, his sister, only thirteen years old at the time. He resented the responsibility and the endless work. A man who hovered at the outskirts of the town's polite populace, Vic Hector, ten years older and worldly wise, had offered Gordie easier ways to make money than carrying freight and goods around for people. Most of the ways bordered on illegal. Slowly Vic and Gordie had grown more and more uncaring about staying within the bounds of the law.

That wasn't all that was despicable about Vic, though

Louise seemed to be the only one who saw how he eyed Missy and how, when he thought no one was looking, he bothered her as if he had some claim to her.

After the Porters' deaths, Nate had decided to move on and had tried to convince the trio to leave with him. When Gordie refused, Louise knew she, too, must stay and watch out for Missy.

Besides, Louise couldn't leave the only place and the only people who had ever made her feel welcome. If Nate had stuck around, perhaps he could have made Gordie realize how evil Vic was, but Nate had left them to manage on their own. He'd gone on to build his own life. A carefree one, according to his mother.

Louise had put behind her any thought that Nate had cared about her.

A year and a half ago, she'd married Gordie. She loved him in her own way, perhaps because he was a Porter. But it also gave her the hope of watching over Missy and maybe changing the direction of Gordie's life.

Oh, how she'd failed.

She waited for the tangle of anger, frustration and helplessness to unravel inside her chest. Gordie had not changed. He'd been shot to death. No one had ever been held accountable, but she suspected Vic had shot Gordie. Perhaps her husband had finally stood up to Vic and paid the ultimate price.

Since Gordie's death, Vic had grown increasingly persistent, threatening even. She rubbed the spot on her arm where he had grabbed her and held her tight just a few hours ago.

"Soon as that baby is born, I got me a job to do." He'd pressed his face close to hers and held her so she couldn't back away. "After all, Gordie and I was partners. He'd expect me to take care of his wife and little sister." As he spoke, spittle sprayed from his teeth.

She pushed aside the memory and hurried on. She had to get away. But where? Her father had already refused to have her. He said he was close to finding a rich gold strike. Besides, the tent he lived in was no place for a baby.

What was she to do?

On her way home Louise slowed her steps and recaptured her breath. Oh, to have this baby and be again able to move about as easily as she once had. A few minutes later she arrived at the Porter house—her home since marrying Gordie. If she'd hoped to again know the warmth she'd experienced there when his parents were alive, she'd soon learned it wouldn't happen. The happy home she'd grown to expect with the Porters had died along with them. As she reached for the doorknob, she heard Missy's voice raised in protest.

"Get away from me."

Anger filling her with fresh energy, Louise pushed the door open.

She'd thought Missy safe because Vic was supposed to be gone for the day. But now he had Missy in a corner, his body pressed to hers as Missy tried vainly to fend him off.

"Leave her alone." Louise grabbed the closest weapon, the broom, and beat on Vic.

He released Missy to cover his head against Louise's blows. One hand snaked out and wrenched the broom from her.

"You will soon enough discover that you belong to me. Both of you. By the way, I'm moving in so's I can keep an eye on my property." Muttering under his breath, he slammed the door behind him as he left the house.

Louise stared at his belongings stacked against the wall. She'd toss them all out into the yard except it wouldn't stop him. He wasn't a man to take no for an answer.

Missy fell into Louise's arms. "That man makes me feel dirty both inside and out."

Louise rubbed Missy's back. "I know. But don't worry. I'll find a way to make sure he doesn't bother us."

But how would she succeed in keeping her promise?

Twenty-one-year-old Nate Hawkins, known as Slim at Eden Valley Ranch where he now lived and worked, spent a few minutes at his friend's grave. "Gordie, I'm sorry I couldn't make it for your funeral." To this day, he missed his friend. Things used to be so good between them. Until Gordie's parents died and Vic entered the picture. Nate had tried to make Gordie see the foolishness of his ways, but Gordie had ignored his warnings.

After that, everything had changed.

Things always changed. His father had died when Nate was eight and Ma had moved them to Rocky Creek so she could find work to support them. She was gone long hours, so he barely saw her and had to take care of himself. He'd found a place of refuge with Gordie and his family. Louise had become part of that group when she moved in with her aunt Bea. In Nate's mind, she'd become the sunshine of the group.

And now Gordie was gone. And Louise's sunshine had turned from him.

Nothing lasted forever. Only land, he'd decided, was permanent. Which was why he had his heart set on owning a ranch.

"Goodbye, old friend." He waited until he was back on the street to put his hat on. He returned home—his ma's home, at least.

A smile curved his mouth as he thought of the home he had his eye on. A small ranch across the border in Alberta not far from Eden Valley Ranch. There he'd build a secure place of his own.

"Did you say you had a leak in your roof?" he said to Ma. He didn't wait for her reply before he grabbed a hammer and ladder and climbed up to begin repairs.

He inserted new shingles and pounded in nails.

"Nate."

He'd know that voice anywhere. Louise. Once they'd been close, but now that, too, had changed.

He'd moved on and had plans of his own. She'd stayed, married Gordie and now carried his child. She'd succeeded in holding on to the Porter family and name.

Slowly he turned to stare down at her. From this perspective, she seemed tiny and vulnerable. He half snorted. Louise had never been vulnerable. She'd always kept up with Gordie and Nate in whatever they'd tackled.

She tipped her head up, shielding her eyes from the glare. He knew their color without seeing them. Brown and challenging. Bold and demanding.

"I need to talk to you."

He backed down the ladder and faced her. "What can I do for you?"

"How long are you staying to visit your mother?"

He blinked. An odd question from a gal who'd made it clear three years ago that she didn't care if he went as far north as he could ride. He'd harbored a hope she would accompany him, but she'd quickly made him understand he would do well to pin his hopes in a different direction.

And he had, though it had taken a bit of effort. But now his hopes lay in getting his own ranch. His own land.

"I'm not staying long. A few days at the most. I need to get back and take care of some business." While out riding the herd for Eddie, owner of the Eden Valley spread, Nate had come across an empty log cabin in a pretty little valley. He'd asked about it and learned it belonged to a mountain man who had once tried ranching but found he didn't care for it. Nate hoped to catch him when he made his regular trek to town to send Christmas presents to his grown daughter. He'd learned the man only stayed long enough to visit an old friend who ran the livery barn. Nate had left a message with Rufus at the livery barn that he wanted to speak to Mountain Man Mike about buying the little ranch he had abandoned. Rufus had warned him Mike only stayed a few days. Nate couldn't afford to miss him.

"Take us with you. Me and Missy." The words tumbled from Louise's mouth. She ducked her head as if it hurt her pride to make the request, then lifted her gaze to his, and he felt her demand clear to his toes. And something more he couldn't identify and didn't try as his heart leaped at the possibility. Then reality pointed out the facts.

"Don't see how that's possible. I have one horse. You're in the family way and I'm in a hurry. I have to be back by Christmas to see a man who has a little ranch I intend to buy."

"We could ride the stagecoach."

He shrugged. "Fine. Go ahead. It's none of my business who rides it."

"It's not that simple. I don't want to travel alone with Missy."

Nate leaned into his heels. Not too many years ago

he would have welcomed her request and taken her with him. There was a time he'd do almost anything she asked of him and had enjoyed pleasing her, but that time was long gone. She'd made her choice. He'd moved on, started a new life elsewhere. There was no going back.

She ducked her head again and studied her fingers.

He looked at them, too. Saw they were white from her clutching them together. She was hiding something.

"What's going on, Louise?"

"Vic."

That's it? Nate had never cared for the man, but it seemed the others found him…what? Certainly not charming. He had all the appeal of a snake. Nate shook his head. He had never been able to understand why Louise had hung around the man. At least not until she and Gordie had married. Then it made sense.

He hated even thinking of Louise married to Gordie. But there was no denying she'd had special feelings for Nate's best friend. As much as it hurt, Nate had never let his romantic feelings toward Louise stand in the way of his two friends. Good thing he'd left when he did.

"What about Vic?" he asked her.

"He's…well, he's getting bothersome."

"In what way?" Surely now that Gordie was dead, the man had sought out another partner to do his bidding.

She wobbled her hands in a gesture that told him nothing. "Your mother says the lady at Eden Valley Ranch welcomes people who are in need of a place to stay. All I'm asking is you accompany us there, then I promise we won't bother you again."

"Louise, it's a weeklong trip. We have to stay overnight in some very tight quarters." He waited for her to realize what he meant and knew she did when pink stained her cheeks. "It wouldn't be appropriate for us to travel together that far, that long." He studied her heightened color. Even heavy with child and looking weary, she was a beautiful woman.

He'd like to help her, but her plan put both Louise's and Missy's reputation at stake. Something he wouldn't do. "You need to think of something better than this."

Louise should have known better than to expect Nate to help. Years ago he'd ridden from her life just when she'd needed someone.

Turning away, she did her best to hasten off, even though her bulk turned her hurry into an awkward waddle. He'd encouraged her to come up with a better plan? She'd do exactly that. He'd suggested she buy stagecoach tickets for herself and Missy, and she would. She'd find her way to Eden Valley Ranch with or without his help.

She returned to Aunt Bea's house where she'd taken Missy once Vic had revealed his plan to move into the Porter home. When they arrived, her aunt had inquired as to the duration of their visit.

"We won't stay long," Louise had soothed.

Aunt Bea's handkerchief had fluttered vigorously, a sure sign of her displeasure. "I thought when you married that young Porter you'd moved out. Into your own home," she'd added, as if realizing how unwelcoming she sounded.

Louise had thought so, too. In fact, about all she'd ever wanted in life was a home where she could belong. But things had changed. Vic had seen to that. Now she didn't know what she wanted. There was only one thing she was certain of. Whatever she hoped to achieve, she would have to do it on her own. No point in thinking she could count on anyone to help.

"Can I get you some tea?" Louise asked her aunt. "Or would you like me to prepare supper?"

"You'll be staying?" Aunt Bea's hands fell to her lap.

"We won't be any bother." In fact, she'd clean the house thoroughly and bake up some goodies. Aunt Bea never seemed to get around to either anymore. Not that she ever had, preferring to spend her time reading dusty old books or knitting an endless supply of blankets, scarves and thick mittens. At least Louise had never suffered from cold hands in the winter.

Aunt Bea waved toward the kitchen. "Tea would be nice."

Louise crossed to the door. "Missy, you can help me."

Missy rose to her feet quickly and almost plowed over Louise in her haste to escape Aunt Bea.

Louise chuckled. "She won't bite."

Missy leaned forward to whisper, "She scares me half to death."

"She isn't half as scary as Vic."

Missy shuddered. "What are we going to do? We can't hide here very long. Vic knows where we are."

"I have a plan. In the meantime, let's make Aunt Bea some tea and then we're going to clean this mess." How did her aunt survive amidst all the dirty dishes and the sticky floor?

Missy hustled about, filling the kettle with water, finding the teapot and tea leaves. Perhaps she was eager to put her mind to something besides where they were going to live. "So what's your plan?" she asked.

Louise considered what to say to her sister-in-law. If she revealed too much and Vic got hold of Missy, the girl might inadvertently say more than she should. "I need to work out a few details and then I'll tell you."

Missy gave her a long look. "One of these days you'll realize I'm no longer a child."

Louise patted her back. Missy was right. She'd turned eighteen two months ago, and was now a young woman. "I already do, but you can't blame me for wanting to take care of you."

Missy started sorting through the soiled dishes, preparing to wash them.

Louise waited, knowing something more troubled her.

Finally, Missy grabbed a dish towel, wiped her hands and turned to face Louise. "That house is the only home I've ever known."

"I know." There seemed no value in pointing out she'd had a home longer than Louise had ever had, as well as the surety of being wanted. The young girl had experienced loss, too, and life hadn't been easy for her, either. "But do you think we can get Vic to leave?"

Missy shook her head, sending strands of her blond hair across her cheeks. She had always been a beautiful, almost ethereal-looking child and had matured into a young woman who drew glances wherever she went. From his first look at Missy, Vic had wanted to claim her as his own.

Why he wanted Louise defied logic. Probably just to prove he could. Seemed the man always had to get what others had. Or what they said he couldn't have.

When it was steeped, they took the tea to Aunt Bea. There wasn't a biscuit or cookie or even a heel of bread in the house.

"Let's surprise Aunt Bea by making her a supper

she won't forget," Louise said. "But first, let's clean the kitchen."

They washed dishes until they both had prune-like fingers.

"I'll do the floor," Missy insisted. "You need to take it easy."

Louise wouldn't admit it, but her back ached and she was weary clear through. Too weary to make her way to the stagecoach office. She sighed. Her plans would have to wait until tomorrow.

"Thank you. I'll prepare the vegetables while you do the floor." She sat at the table to work, grateful for a chance to rest her feet. But when her gaze went to the window and she saw Vic loitering in the alley beyond the yard, her weariness vanished. Right then and there she knew what she had to do. She wouldn't say anything about his presence for fear of alarming the others, but she'd be sure to lock the house tightly tonight and sleep with a poker beside her bed.

After breakfast the next morning, Louise announced she had business to attend to. "Missy, you stay here and keep the doors locked."

"Why?" Missy asked. Then, as if she realized the reason, she took a step toward the window.

Louise caught her arm and stopped her. "He's been there a while. Don't give him the satisfaction of letting him know we know."

"He'll follow you."

"I've thought of that. And I have a plan. Why don't you open the back door and toss the dishwater out. He'll be watching you and I'll slip out the front door. He won't even know." *Please, God, make me invisible to him.*

"Be sure and lock up after I leave." She waited until Missy opened the back door, then slipped out the front and hurried down the street toward the heart of town, going directly to the stagecoach office.

"How do I get to Eden Valley Ranch?"

The bespectacled man behind the wicket stared at her. "Guess I'd have to know where it was before I could tell you that, ma'am."

She racked her brain. Had Mrs. Hawkins ever said the name of the nearest town when she'd spoken of the ranch on which her son worked? Yes. It came in a flash and brought a relieved sigh. "Edendale in Alberta, Canada."

The man tipped his nose as he studied a map on the wall to the side of the wicket. Then he brought his gaze back to her. "Well, ma'am, that's a mighty long ways off. This here stage will take you as far as Fort Macleod, but, ma'am, it's a long journey, especially for someone in your—" He turned so red his skin must have burned, and he didn't finish.

"In my condition. Yes. Yes. But isn't that up to me to decide?"

The color had begun to fade on the man's cheeks, but again intensified.

"How much will it cost?" she asked. "And when does the stage depart?"

"I can sell you a ticket to Fort Macleod. After that, you'll have to buy another to Edendale." He named a sum that made Louise cringe.

"The next stage leaves tomorrow. Early." He looked at Louise as if he thought getting up early was impossible in her condition.

"Fine. Thank you."

She left the station and headed for the bank. Within

minutes she had withdrawn enough money to buy the tickets in the morning, see them both safely to their destination and perhaps even to start a new life north of here. For a moment, her heart stalled at the idea of leaving behind the only place she'd ever felt she belonged. Perhaps she should appeal to the marshal to remove Vic from the Porter house.

Even before she finished the thought, she knew her wish was futile. Vic cared nothing for what the law demanded.

She had no choice but to proceed with her plan, and she left the bank to go back to Aunt Bea's house. She turned the corner at the end of the block and ground to a halt as Vic stepped directly into her path.

"Thought you could get away, did ya? I wasn't born yesterday."

Holding in her fear, she replied evenly, "I was taking care of a few chores."

"In the stagecoach station?" He chortled. "You thinking of taking a trip?"

She refused to answer.

"You get on that stage and I'll follow you. I'll bring you back. You will never get away from me. Not you nor Gordie's sweet little sister." He smiled benignly lest anyone be watching, but his words carried enough venom to make her skin crawl.

"I'll tell everyone we don't want to go with you."

"No one will listen when I tell them yer my wife." His eyebrows waggled in mockery.

She didn't respond. He'd do it so convincingly, everyone would believe him and see her as a rebellious wife. Some would even cheer him for coming after her. She unconsciously pressed her hands to her belly.

His gaze followed. "Seems that kid ought to be born any day now. I got plans for it."

"Plans?" What right did he have to make plans for her baby?

"Yup. Got a friend who knows people who will pay a lot of money for a baby."

She staggered back as if he'd hit her. Threatening her was one thing, but threatening her baby was quite another. She began to tremble.

Giving her a smile, Vic touched the brim of his hat as if he were a mannered gentleman. "Nice talking to ya." Anyone watching would think they'd had a friendly little chat.

They would be wrong.

Her insides rolled and tossed.

She breathed deeply, determined she would not be sick in public.

How was she to get away? How was she to make sure he didn't follow her and bring her back as his "wife"?

She could think of one thing that would stop Vic. Now all she had to do was make Nate see the reasonableness of it.

Nate remained in the alley. Vic and Louise hadn't seen him and he didn't want them to. Especially Vic.

His opinion of the man had never been a secret and it had been reinforced yet again. The man was a danger to all decent folk.

Nate had been close enough to see the expression on both Vic's and Louise's faces, and to overhear enough words to know Vic had threatened her, then threatened to sell her baby. His fists balled. This must surely be the reason for her wanting to leave. It explained why she'd used but one word to explain her fear—Vic.

Nate turned back toward his mother's house, having completely forgotten the errand that brought him into town.

Still seething, he burst into the house. But he jerked to a stop when he saw who was there.

"Louise?" She sat at the table facing his ma. "What are you doing here?"

Ma tsked. "I'm sure you don't mean to sound so unwelcoming. She said she wanted to talk to you."

Louise nodded. "There's something I want to say."

Ma got to her feet. "I'll leave you two to deal with whatever it is that's bothering the both of you." She made for the door. "It's hard to believe that you were once eager to spend time together." The door closed behind her, shutting out her words and her opinion.

Nate sank to the chair she'd vacated. Ma was right. There had been such a time. "Things change," he said. He had no desire to go back.

Louise liked to cling to what had once been, but wouldn't she soon have a baby? Didn't that mean she had to plan for the future?

He was about to say he'd seen her with Vic, when she leaned forward and started to talk.

"I want to leave. Go to Eden Valley Ranch."

He nodded. Would have said he thought it a good idea but she didn't give him an opportunity.

"I obviously can't ride a horse all that way. In my condition. I can buy us tickets on the stagecoach," she said. "I already made inquiries."

"Good."

"But—" Her head jerked up and her fierce gaze left

him speechless. She had something in mind and she meant to get it done. She lowered her gaze, enabling him to release his breath. She studied the top of the table. "If Missy and I try to go alone, I fear Vic will stop us." She lifted her head, her eyes this time filled with what he could only say was a mixture of sorrow and fear. She shuddered.

He knew she had every right to be afraid of Vic. The man would stop at nothing to get what he wanted. He wished he could offer her escape, but he didn't see how he could.

"What I need," she continued, her voice strong and steady, "is a man to protect us."

He knew from the look in her eyes she meant him. But they'd already had this discussion. Accompanying her would get her away from Vic, but it would ruin both the women's reputations. Even a widow's expecting a child.

He wished he could protect Missy and Louise. But what could he do?

"Louise, I've already told you I can't—"

She cut him off with a wave of her hand. "I have the perfect solution." She straightened in the chair and drew in a long breath. "You and I can get married."

"Married?" No other word came to his mind.

"Marry me and take us to Eden Valley Ranch."

"Marry?" Still he was capable of saying nothing else.

Her eyes narrowed. "This is the Porters' grandchild. Gordie's child. Doesn't that mean anything to you? After all they did for us? They gave us a family when our own were too busy."

She was right, but he needed to see Mountain Mike and buy his ranch. The thought of his land seemed to ground him and allowed him to think sanely again. "But the place I'm looking to buy has only a tiny cabin. Only big enough for a man. Not two women and a baby." Then again, if a man and a woman loved each other, the small quarters wouldn't be a problem. A persistent hope sprang to his mind.

"I'm only suggesting a pretend marriage until we get there. Then we can have it annulled." She widened her eyes as tears glistened in them.

A pretend marriage? Was such a thing possible?

"Must you look so shocked? Am I so unappealing?"

He managed to shake his head. Seemed the power of speech had abandoned him again. Then, seeing how she struggled to keep the pooling tears from overflowing, he started to reach for her hands. He stopped himself because he had no right. "Marriage isn't like buying a ticket for the stagecoach. It's a lifetime commitment."

Her eyes pinned him with dark fierceness. "Only real marriages are forever. You don't love me. I don't love you. We both know it's not for real."

Her words scraped through his insides. A person couldn't be much clearer than that about their feelings. Even knowing she was only asking to use him, he considered her request. Marriage gave him the right to tell Vic to leave Louise and Missy alone. He could protect her, get her to safety.

He nodded. "Very well. Let's get married."

She blinked and then blinked again. "Really?"

"You heard me."

She sprang to her feet and rushed to his side to hug him. "Thank you. Thank you. You will not regret this. I promise."

Chapter Two

Louise returned to her chair and studied Nate. He'd said yes without much of an argument. Why was he so agreeable? But she wasn't about to guess at his reasons so long as he got them safely to their destination.

A fear clawed at her brain. He was in a hurry. Would he escort them all the way or leave them in some little way station to fend for themselves? After all, he was good at leaving. Seemed all the important men in her life were. Though Pa had made her be the one to leave, and Gordie and his parents had died. Each case was different, yet in her heart she viewed them the same. She'd been left before, so it wouldn't surprise her if it happened again. Best she could do was be prepared for it.

She pressed her palms to her stomach. The funds she had would not last long and she'd have a new baby to care for besides watching over Missy. Resolve flooded her being. She could and would take care of herself. Had been since she could remember. Pa had expected it. When it got too much for him, he'd shipped her off to Aunt Bea, who likewise made it clear she didn't care to bother with Louise. Only while the Porter parents lived had she found the sort of welcome she longed for. But Eden Valley Ranch promised refuge while she sorted her life out and decided what to do next.

Would she be refused refuge at the ranch for making a mockery of the wedding vows?

Please, God, just let us get away from Vic, then I'll manage somehow. With or without Nate. Doubt again tugged at her heart. Would God refuse to help her because she meant to be untruthful about the wedding vows? As always, when doubts flared, she reminded herself of all that the Porters had taught her about God's love and faithfulness. Surely God would understand, given the circumstances.

She realized she still gawked at him. "What now?" she asked.

He laughed, his blue eyes flashing with amusement. "This was your idea. Shouldn't you be the one with things figured out?" Their gazes locked, just as their futures were soon to be bound together for a short time.

She jerked her attention to a worn spot on the table. "It's a rather new idea and I hadn't given the particulars much thought." She paused a moment. "The stage leaves tomorrow." After another hesitant beat, she added, "Early."

"Then I suggest you get on with your wedding plans." His eyes still twinkled.

"I think you're enjoying my discomfort."

He sobered. "No. But you must admit, it is a little amusing. A spur-of-the-moment wedding. The bride—" His gaze darted to her belly and he chuckled. "Some would think this is a shotgun wedding."

Heat rushed up her neck, but she would not turn from

giving him a steady look. "It's Gordie's baby. I don't expect you to take care of it."

His smile turned into a scowl. "Of course." His gaze went beyond her and grew distant.

She wondered what he was seeing. Maybe someday she'd feel comfortable enough to ask. Right now all that mattered was he'd given his word and they were to be married. All she wanted from this relationship was to get away from Vic and gain safety for herself, her baby and Missy.

She didn't expect anything more from him.

Nate got to his feet. "Seems we have a wedding to arrange. Why don't I take you to Aunt Bea's and you can tell her your plans." He held out a hand to help her to her feet.

She might have refused, but it was getting harder and harder to get up gracefully.

He squinted at her. "When is this baby due?"

She understood the question he meant to ask. Was she going to deliver on the journey? *Please, God, let me go a little longer.* One week until they reached their destination. One week of pretend marriage and then the joy of her little son or daughter. She couldn't think of a better Christmas present.

To Nate she gave a dismissive shrug. "Not for a while."

His eyebrows rose. Then he let the subject go and opened the door his mother had closed a short time ago. "Ma, I'm taking Louise home. I'll be back in a bit."

They left the house and went to Aunt Bea's house, pausing outside the door.

"I'll wait until you inform her, then take you to your house," Nate said.

"That won't be necessary. Missy and I took what we needed when we left yesterday."

He caught her shoulder and brought her around to face him. "You've left your house? Why?"

"Because Vic moved in." The words were soft, disguising the anger that burned through her at being forced from her own home.

Nate dropped his hand from her shoulder and pushed a fist into his palm. "The louse."

"Snake," she corrected. "He's a slithering snake."

"You won't have to worry about him much longer. Marriage will protect you. Listen, it's best if no one knows it's only pretend. Vic might see that as an opportunity."

"Agreed."

"Let's go tell your aunt."

She knocked. "I told Missy to bar the door when I left."

Nate's fists balled at his sides. "That will end before the day is out. He won't bother you any longer."

Good to know. Whatever lay ahead of sorrow or joy, she would at least be free of Vic.

Missy opened the door and Louise slipped in with Nate at her side. She welcomed his support. "I have good news," she said, including Aunt Bea, who sat in her customary upholstered chair. "Nate and I are getting married." Before either of the women could speak, she rushed on. "Missy and I will go north with him."

"We'll be safe?" Missy asked.

"We'll be safe." Louise patted Missy's arm as the girl let out a long gust of air.

"Well, I hate to see you go." Aunt Bea sounded as if it couldn't be too soon to suit her. "When are you planning to marry him?"

"Today." At the stunned look on Missy's face, she

choked back a giggle. Aunt Bea's eyes widened. Louise tried to think if she'd ever surprised her aunt before.

If so, she couldn't remember it.

Aunt Bea managed to get to her feet in record time. "Today? There is much to do to get ready."

Louise could think of nothing except the need to sign a document. But if Aunt Bea, with her unbending opinions of proper conduct, knew it was to be a temporary marriage, she would likely raise enough objections to create a stir, maybe even persuade the preacher to refuse to marry them.

"I'll go see to the details," Nate said. "Lock up behind me." He hurried out the door.

Louise turned the key, then faced Aunt Bea. "Tell me what I need to do."

Nate stood outside until he heard the key turn, then tested the knob. The lock held and he strode away as fast as his legs would take him. His insides burned with fury.

Vic had moved into the Porter house? Seemed he thought he owned the house and the family. Well, the family would be leaving. The family would say goodbye to their home and learn, as he had, that nothing lasts.

Not even marriage, it seemed. What they planned was only pretend. A convenience. He pushed aside the guilt stinging his thoughts.

So far as he could tell, nothing was forever, but at least he could get Missy and Louise and Gordie's unborn baby away from Vic.

He stepped into Ma's house. She stood at the stove, tending a pot of something that smelled mighty fine. "Making soup?"

"Cream of potato. Thought I'd make your favorite while you're here."

"Ma, sit down. I need to talk to you."

She pushed the pot to the side of the stove and pulled out a chair to sit. "That sounds like a warning."

He didn't know what he'd call it. Nor how to explain what he meant to do except to come right out and say it. "Ma, Louise and I are getting married."

"Good." She patted his hand. "I've always thought you two were suited to each other."

"You did? But she married Gordie."

"She was hurt and confused. The poor girl had lost so much and was trying to recapture it."

He stared at his ma. "How do you know all this?"

"I'm a mother, even though I haven't been the kind I wanted to be." Her eyes looked past him into the distance. "If only your father hadn't died." She shook her head. "So you'll be staying around a few months? That's good."

Let her believe this marriage was for real. The more who thought that, the better for them. "No, I'm leaving tomorrow."

"I see. When will you come back for the wedding?"

"We're getting married today. As soon as I can make arrangements."

Ma stared at him, her hands limp in her lap. "Today?" Her voice squeaked. "That hardly seems—"

"Proper?" He knew many would think the same, but he didn't care what anyone thought except perhaps Ma.

"No. It hardly seems enough time to plan a wedding."

"How long does it take to find the preacher, say the vows and sign the papers?" Vows. He'd be vowing before God and man to stay with her until death parted them. God did not take lightly a man making vows, then breaking them.

"Are you sure about this?" Ma asked.

No, he wasn't sure. At least not about pretending the vows. But he was sure about the reason for it. "I can't leave them here." He explained the way Vic treated Louise and Missy, and hoped she agreed the wedding had to be immediate.

"That's very noble, son, but it hardly seems enough reason to marry."

Likely it didn't to anyone but himself and Louise. "We're of a like mind." Their reasons were enough to satisfy him. "I'm going to buy a ranch and it will be nice to have a home and family, too." His insides coiled at purposely leading her to believe forever was part of their plan. He'd told her of the place he hoped to purchase. His journey home would be slowed by having to accompany Louise on the stagecoach. He wouldn't have any time to spare if he hoped to get back to Edendale in time to meet the mountain man. "You could come too, Ma."

"Thank you, but no. This is my home. I'm too old to start over again." She wiped a tear from the corner of her eye.

"You're thinking of Pa, aren't you?" Nate could barely recall his father. A man who laughed a lot, roughhoused with Nate and kissed Ma often.

"I never got over him. You are so much like him."

"In what way?" It seemed important to know, seeing as he was soon to become a husband, if only for a week.

"You look like him. He wasn't much older than you are now when he died. You are like him in other ways, too. He was ready and willing to help those who needed it."

Nate knew the story. He'd been killed helping a neighbor put up a barn. A beam had fallen and crushed him.

His mother stood up. "But enough of that. I need to get ready for a wedding." She was halfway out of the kitchen before she stopped. "Help yourself to the soup."

"Yes, Ma." He didn't have time to eat. There were details to take care of now.

"Make sure you eat. The day will be even busier as it goes along."

When he didn't move, she hustled to the stove, filled a bowl and set it before him. "Eat." She waited until he put a spoonful in his mouth.

"Mmm. Good."

"Now I must get ready. Will you come and get me when it's time?"

"Yes, I will." He ate the soup hurriedly, then trotted over to the house next to the church where he found the good preacher. A man he hadn't met before who introduced himself as Pastor Manly.

Nate took that to be his name, certainly not a description. The pastor was slight, pale and fidgety.

Nate explained he wanted to get married. "This afternoon."

"Fine. Fine. Bring your bride here." The man had thin white hair. Its thinness likely not helped by the way he ran his fingers through it.

"Is there some reason we have to get married here?" Perhaps there was some law saying where people could wed.

"It's convenient."

"Could you marry us at Miss Williams's house?" he asked, naming Aunt Bea.

Did the pastor blush? He certainly tapped the tips of his fingers together rapidly. "Yes, yes. What time?"

He hadn't asked Louise what time suited her. He'd have to guess. "Would five o'clock suit?"

"It will be fine. You will need two witnesses of legal age."

"Miss Williams and my ma, Mrs. Hawkins?"

"Yes, yes. Now, let me get ready." He waved Nate away.

Nate hurried from there to the stagecoach depot and checked on tomorrow's departure of the stage.

The agent consulted a schedule. "Be here by seven-thirty. The driver will want to be on his way by dawn. Days are short."

"Thanks." Nate didn't hang about to see what else the man had to say but hurried to Aunt Bea's to inform Louise of the time of the wedding.

At his knock, she pulled him inside and closed the door. "Vic's been hanging about out back."

"I'll take care of him." He eased Louise aside, intending to dash out the back door. Louise stopped him.

"Leave him be. What did you find out?"

He told her the arrangements for the wedding.

"I'll be ready," she said.

"You haven't changed your mind?" Seemed now was the time to do so if she wasn't sure.

"I'll do what I have to to get away from him." She jabbed her thumb over her shoulder.

He studied her, recognized the look on her face. It was the same one she used to get when he and Gordie said she couldn't join them in some activity. Didn't matter if it was playing ball, climbing a cliff or rowing a boat on the river. She always insisted she could do whatever they did even though she was a girl and a year younger.

He chuckled.

"What's so funny?"

"I remember how you always had to prove you could do whatever Gordie and I did."

Her fierce gaze didn't falter. "Seems I did it, too."

"Except rowing the boat." He chuckled again at the memory of her tipping over her boat and falling head-first into the river. "I pulled you to safety or you'd likely have drowned."

Their gazes riveted together, full of memories of a happier time. It had come to an end, of course.

She smiled. "Guess it's up to me to prove again that I can face a challenge."

He held her gaze. Or did she hold his? "I guess it's up to me to rescue you again."

He saw the protest in her eyes, but before she could voice it, the look faded to acceptance.

"You won't regret it. I promise. You'll be free as soon as we get there."

From somewhere down the hall, Missy called Louise.

"I have things to prepare." She held the door for him and locked it when he left. He stood on the step a moment, wondering how she could promise there'd be no regrets.

Then he hurried back to Ma's house.

She must have been watching for him, for she met him at the door wearing a dress he hadn't seen before. Dark blue taffeta with tiny fabric-covered buttons on the bodice. Not that he'd normally notice such things, but he was smart enough to recognize this as a special dress. Likely her best.

"When is the wedding?"

He told her the time.

"Good. That will give you time to bathe and put on your finest duds."

"Me?"

"Of course. You want to look and smell your best."

He sniffed. "Smells like you've been cooking."

"I made some goodies for tea afterward. It's customary."

He wanted to protest. After all, this was only a pretend marriage. But of course he couldn't tell his mother that. He had to go along with her plans.

"Get at it, son." She pushed him toward the kitchen.

He looked at the galvanized tub in the middle of the kitchen floor. Ma was serious about the bath. Moreover, his best shirt and trousers hung freshly ironed and waiting.

He pulled the blinds and took a quick bath.

Besides his own clothes, there was a vest in gray pinstripe that he'd never seen before. From the mothball smell, it must have been in storage. He put it on. A little short, but wearing it turned his plain white shirt into something a little fancier. Ma had also left a black tie, which he tried to knot.

"Are you decent?" Ma called, and entered at his grunted yes. "I'll do that." She quickly fixed his tie and patted his shoulders. "That vest was your pa's. He wore it for our wedding. It looks good on you."

"Thanks, Ma." He kissed her cheek, then dumped out his bathwater and put away the tub.

Ma stood ready. He took her arm and together they crossed the street to the Williams house.

He was about to take part in a marriage ceremony that was a mockery to the vows he would be asked to speak.

He could only hope and pray God would understand and forgive because Nate did it for a noble reason.

When he knocked at Bea Williams's house, Missy answered the door. Ma hurried inside and greeted Aunt Bea, then the two disappeared into the sitting room.

He hadn't seen Missy in a year. "You're all grown up." It surprised him to see she was no longer a child.

She lifted one eyebrow. "So are you. All grown up and about to marry. Sure you can handle it?"

Could he? All his life he'd wanted something to last forever. He'd planned to find that on his ranch. Yet he felt as if he was mocking the idea of forever with a pretend marriage. Could he handle the falseness of it?

Before he could argue himself out of going along with this farce, he stepped inside.

As they said on the ranch when things got tough, he'd have to cowboy up. Well, he was about to cowboy up like never before.

Chapter Three

Louise waited, all ready to wed. Aunt Bea had said she must remain out of sight until everyone had assembled. "Make Nate wait a few minutes," she'd advised. "It never hurts to make a man think you might have changed your mind."

"I'm not changing my mind." But as she waited, she wondered whether Nate would change his.

She drew in a deep breath. The last few hours had been a whirlwind. Together with Missy and Aunt Bea, she had washed the fine china and baked a cake. All necessary for a wedding, Aunt Bea had insisted. They'd dusted and tidied the parlor until it looked fit for company and was likely the cleanest it had been in a couple of decades.

When her aunt had been satisfied, she'd led Louise to her bedroom. "You won't be able to wear my mother's wedding dress. Not in your condition." Aunt Bea had looked Louise up and down.

"You have Grandmother's wedding dress?" Why hadn't Aunt Bea offered it when Louise married Gordie?

"I have her veil, too. You can wear that." Aunt Bea

had opened a musty-smelling trunk. The wedding dress lay wrapped in muslin.

Aunt Bea had pulled out the veil. "I'll press this." She'd hurried from the room, then retraced her steps. "Why are you standing there? Go get ready." She'd waved Louise toward her own bedroom, and Louise had hurried down the hall to select the only dress she could fit into that looked even halfway dressy—a gray satin with empire waistline that allowed for her girth.

"Hardly suitable for a bride," she'd murmured to herself, then realized Aunt Bea had made Louise believe for a moment this was real. Shaking her head, she reminded herself of the facts. She was expecting a baby, she was a recent widow and the marriage was only temporary.

Aunt Bea had hurried in with the fragile veil and affixed it to Louise's hair. Light as air, with sequins flashing in the sunlight, it reached to Louise's elbows and made her feel almost pretty.

Missy had stepped into the room. "You're beautiful," she'd whispered.

Just a few minutes ago, she'd heard Pastor Manly enter and speak to Aunt Bea. Aunt Bea had giggled. Louise had noted previously how her aunt got girlie and giggly when Pastor Manly was around. If she wasn't mistaken, Aunt Bea had finally found a man to her liking. Louise chuckled. Maybe Pastor Manly was responsible for Aunt Bea's sudden interest in all things wedding related.

Now she heard Mrs. Hawkins speaking to Aunt Bea, then, finally, Nate's voice, full and strong and sure. She closed her eyes. He'd come. She'd been wrong to fear that he might reconsider and ride out without a backward look.

Of course, he could still change his mind. Until the

marriage certificate was signed in black ink and blotted dry, she couldn't be sure he'd actually marry her.

"Everyone is ready." Missy stood at the door.

"You look lovely. But then you always do." She took the posy of silk pansies Aunt Bea had unearthed from her trunk, kissed her sister-in-law on the cheek, then tucked her hand into the crook of Missy's arm and marched into the sitting room.

Nate stood in front of Pastor Manly. His hair, still damp enough to be dark, was slicked down. He wore a white shirt, a gray vest and a black tie.

She moved to Nate's side. "You look nice," she whispered, then sneezed. "Sorry, it's the mothballs."

He eyed her veil. "Nice touch." His gaze caught hers, full of something she hadn't seen in a long time—strength and encouragement. "You're a beautiful bride."

Her surprise barely registered before Pastor Manly cleared his throat. "Shall we begin? Before we do, it is incumbent upon me to ask if you are both sure about this very serious step?"

Louise held her breath. Would Nate say no?

"I'm sure. How about you, Louise?" he said.

"I'm sure." The words wheezed out her tight throat.

Pastor Manly nodded and opened a black book. Only a few words registered in her brain—words of accusation. "An honorable estate not to be entered into lightly… but in the fear of God."

What they were doing was wrong in the eyes of God. Would He ever forgive her? Well, it wasn't as if He'd sent any other way of escaping Vic. And she must protect her baby at all costs.

"Face each other and hold hands. Repeat after me,"

the pastor said. "In the name of God, I, Nathaniel Hawkins—"

Nate gripped her hand so hard her knuckles cracked. His eyes were dimmed by the veil over her face, yet not enough to hide his distress. His throat worked.

She dare not breathe. *Oh, please don't refuse. I need this. I promise I won't tie you to the vows.*

"I, Nate Hawkins, take you, Louise Williams Porter, to be my wife."

She felt herself relax a bit. Still, had anyone else noticed his refusal to speak God's name in his vows? She didn't dare look at Pastor Manly, but the silence in the room echoed with the ticking of Aunt Bea's mantel clock.

"Very well, then." Pastor Manly continued, "To have and to hold from this day forward, for better or worse, for richer or poorer, in sickness and health, to love and to cherish, until death do us part."

Nate got as far as "until death do us part" and stopped.

"This is my solemn vow," the pastor prompted.

"Louise will have to take my word for it," Nate said.

"This is highly irregular, but I suppose it's acceptable." The pastor turned to Louise. "Repeat after me—"

"Excuse me, I want my vows to be the same as Nate's." She, too, would prefer to leave God's name out of them.

Pastor Manly gave them each a hard look. For a moment, Louise feared he would refuse to marry them under the circumstances. Aunt Bea leaned forward. "It's still legal, isn't it?"

"Yes, yes." He proceeded. "Rings?"

Nate shook his head. "Didn't have time."

"I shouldn't be surprised, should I? Then all you have to do is sign the papers." They did so, and after Aunt Bea and Mrs. Hawkins added their signatures, Reverend

Manly concluded the ceremony. "I now pronounce you husband and wife. You may kiss your bride."

She would have jerked her hand from Nate's, but he held tight. Slowly, he lifted her veil and smiled as he gave a little nod as if to indicate they needed to complete this charade.

She closed her eyes and lifted her face to him.

His lips brushed hers ever so softly. Quickly he drew back, but not before she felt the kiss all the way to her toes. She could almost persuade herself it had only been her imagination. Yet her lips still tingled from his tender touch.

Pastor Manly gave a tight smile. "What God has joined together let no man put asunder."

Heat pooled in the pit of Louise's stomach. Oh, why had he said that? She tried to swallow away the burning. It was only heartburn, she told herself, not guilt. Wouldn't God expect her to do what she must in order to protect those in her care? She cradled her arms around her stomach.

Missy hugged her and kissed her cheek. Aunt Bea patted her arm. Mrs. Hawkins squeezed her hands. "Welcome to the family. I know you'll make my Nate a happy man."

Her gaze sought and found Nate. *Help*, she cried silently. She hadn't expected to feel so guilty over this.

He met her eyes over Aunt Bea's head as her aunt shook his hand. Did she imagine he looked as flummoxed as she felt?

She allowed herself to be led into the kitchen where the good china had been set out to welcome the guests. She and Nate were given the place of honor at the head of the table. His mother set a layered cake before them. "Congratulations! You may cut the cake." She handed

Louise the knife. "Nate, you put your hand over hers. It means you will support her and take care of her, and for Louise, it means she will take care of you and your children."

Children? Louise almost choked. But she must do as instructed, as must Nate. He cupped his hand over hers and they cut a generous slice of cake.

Mrs. Hawkins clapped her hands together in glee. "The bigger the piece, the larger the family, and it looks like you are going to be blessed with lots of children."

Aunt Bea shook her head. "I always thought it meant a long marriage."

Why didn't she know this? It wasn't as if this was her first wedding. But she and Gordie had gone away to get married in a nearby town and come back as Mr. and Mrs. Porter with little fanfare. The church ladies had offered to hold a tea after the service to honor them, but she knew Gordie wouldn't likely have agreed to come, so she'd declined.

Nate still held her hand and squeezed as if to encourage her to remain calm.

Aunt Bea and Mrs. Hawkins served tea and sandwiches. Where had they come from? Nate's mother must have brought them. Aunt Bea cut pieces of cake for everyone and chatted on and on about the kind of marriage Nate and Louise would have. Even Missy added her comments.

Louise couldn't choke down a single bite and pushed her plate aside to cup her hands around the teacup, seeking the warmth it offered. She would have gulped down the liquid but feared her hand would shake and she'd slosh the tea everywhere.

Pastor Manly seemed to be in no hurry to leave. He

asked Aunt Bea about a book he was reading and they entered into a long discussion that was only noise in Louise's head. The room shifted and swayed. She needed to breathe before she fainted, and concentrated on filling her lungs then releasing the air slowly.

Nate rubbed her back and the faintness passed.

"Feel better now?" Nate whispered, his mouth close enough to her ear that no one else heard.

She slowly brought her gaze round to his. "I didn't think anyone noticed," she whispered.

His smile flooded his blue eyes with warmth. "I did. Are you okay?"

"Good as can be expected." Her words were full of resignation.

He chuckled. "We'll survive. We're good at that."

She nodded. "We do what we must do."

His gaze held hers. She couldn't find the strength to turn away.

Still looking into his eyes, she leaned closer to whisper in his ear, "That's a vow I can make honestly."

The smile fled from his eyes.

She almost wished she hadn't reminded him of the dishonesty they'd engaged in…vowing before God to something they didn't mean to do. But they both understood the step they had taken together.

He patted her hand as if he wanted her to forget that part of the day.

"I must be on my way." Pastor Manly wished Louise and Nate all the best before Aunt Bea escorted him to the door.

As soon as she returned, Nate spoke loud enough for the others to hear. "I have things to attend to."

"You'll be back. You'll want to stay with your new

wife." Aunt Bea turned pink as a summer rose. "Louise, show him your room." Poor Aunt Bea could hardly choke the words out.

"What about Missy?" Louise found herself as choked as Aunt Bea. She had to think of a way to refuse.

It was the most uncomfortable moment in her life.

Nate had things to attend to, but he couldn't seem to budge from his chair as Aunt Bea's words blared through his head. She expected them to stay in the same room. Of course she would. They were now man and wife. In the sight of God.

Poor Louise had looked about to faint more than once throughout the long afternoon. Who cared about cake and what it meant? Why couldn't they all just get on with their business?

But stay the night in the same room? That was taking this pretend marriage too far. "We'll wait until the baby is born," he announced.

Aunt Bea made a protesting noise.

He noticed Louise's shoulders rise, as if she was trying to hide from her aunt and his ma who were about to unleash protests.

Nate's knee had started to bob up and down and he pressed his free hand to it, his other still clutching Louise's on the tabletop next to the uneaten piece of cake. Neither of them had touched it after the startling predictions of a long wedded life and a large family. He would release her hand, but he felt the tension in every finger and suspected she might bolt from the table. Perhaps from the house. He couldn't allow that, not when he'd caught glimpses of Vic wandering past the yard. No doubt wondering what was going on that required Pastor Manly's presence.

Or did he hold tight to Louise for fear his own legs would bolt for the door, knocking over chairs and perhaps breaking to pieces the flowered teacups made of such fine china that they were almost transparent? The little handles were surely designed to make a man feel as clumsy as an ox.

His ma spoke up, ending the echoing silence. "Are you coming home, Nate? You're welcome to bring Louise."

Louise's hand spasmed beneath his. He had to force himself to remain calm and refrain from squeezing her fingers any tighter.

"Ma, we leave on the stagecoach tomorrow morning. I have to get things organized. If Aunt Bea will allow it, I'll sleep on the sofa here so we can get going early." It wasn't that early and Louise didn't need any help getting herself ready, but it would enable him to be close by, should Vic grow more troublesome.

"Of course," Aunt Bea said.

"Then I must get at the preparations. Ma, would you like me to escort you home?"

"I'm ready."

Aunt Bea gathered up the dishes Ma had brought and held them while Ma pulled on her woolen shawl and winter gloves.

Vic ducked out of sight around the end of the block as Nate stepped from the house. He would confront the man later.

Behind him, the key turned in the lock. Good. Louise hadn't forgotten to take precautions.

At home he packed his few belongings. In truth, he had little preparation to do. In the morning, he'd take

Missy and Louise with him to the depot. He'd ride his horse beside the stage when they left. But despite having made all the arrangements he could for now, he was in no hurry to return to Louise and their pretend marriage.

And he had one necessary thing to do. He left the house and crossed to Aunt Bea's house, suspecting he'd find Vic lingering nearby.

The man must have seen him approach, for he ducked behind a building. Nate strode in that direction.

Vic pressed against the wall of a back shed, but at Nate's approach he straightened, jammed his hand to his hips and gave Nate one of his dark scowls.

Nate paid the scowl no mind. He stopped a few feet from Vic. "Thought you'd like to know that Louise and I got married this afternoon."

Vic's expression didn't change one iota. The man was an expert at hiding his feelings. "That baby ain't yours."

"That's not what the law says." He knew that the wife's husband was the legal father to any of her children, even though Louise had been clear about this being Gordie's baby, lest he get the idea he should care about the little one.

Vic's scowl turned to a leer. "How about that sweet little Missy?"

Nate narrowed his eyes. Other than that, he would not give the man the satisfaction of seeing how his question riled him. "She's now my sister-in-law." It wasn't accurate, but close enough. "And I will protect her, just as I will protect my wife and her child."

Vic gave a mirthless laugh. "My, ain't you all righteous and noble? But you ain't got no claim to Missy. I been waiting a long time for her. Someday she'll be mine."

"When the sun falls from the sky and lands at your

feet, maybe." He widened his stance, leaned back on his heels and crossed his arms as if he was in complete control of the situation. He could only hope and pray he was. But would God listen to the prayers of a man who made vows invoking God's name with no intention of fulfilling those vows?

"Be careful." Nate's voice was low, but he made sure every syllable carried a warning. "You bother them again and you won't be facing two helpless women." Not that they were entirely helpless, but what chance did they stand before a ruthless man like Vic?

Vic snorted. "You think I'm ascared of you?"

"I suggest you should be." He stalked away without waiting for the man to answer. If Vic should threaten Louise or Missy in any way, Nate would make sure he regretted it to the depths of his heart.

It was dark before he went back to Aunt Bea's house and knocked. The key turned and Louise pulled the door open.

"I wondered if you'd left without us."

"Nope. What kind of groom would leave his bride on their wedding night?" He didn't succeed in keeping the teasing from his voice.

"A pretend one." She stepped back to let him enter, then locked the door behind him.

"If I didn't mean to take you with me, why would I bother with a pretend marriage that involved vows made before God and man?" It still bothered him to swear falsely.

"It plagues my conscience, too, you know. But Vic threatened to sell my baby." Her arms cradled her stomach, protecting the unborn one. "I don't doubt he would."

Nate took his time about hanging his hat and coat.

Done, his insides somewhat calmed, he turned to Louise and rested his hands on her shoulders. At the trembling beneath his palms, he pulled her closer, till only an inch separated them. He bowed his head over her hair. "I will protect you and your baby. I will see you get safely to Eden Valley Ranch where you will be given shelter for as long as you need it."

"That is so good to know." She stepped back and went to the sitting room, waving her hand for him to follow.

He wished he knew if she meant it was good to know he would protect her or good to know she would be welcome at the ranch.

A pile of blankets rested on a chair, reminding them both that the future would be different from anything they'd known.

He shifted his gaze from the blankets to Louise. She chewed on her bottom lip. "You still worried about Vic? Don't be."

She quirked an eyebrow. "I'll stop worrying when we reach the ranch. Maybe."

He wouldn't mention his conversation with Vic earlier, nor the man's insistence about wanting Missy. She'd be safe at Eden Valley Ranch. It wouldn't be the first time someone had come after a woman there and ended up facing more than he figured on. The whole crew would protect Missy and Louise. He'd not say that now, though. It would only give Louise reason to think she couldn't outrun Vic.

"We'll be on our way tomorrow." And he'd be keeping a sharp eye out for any trouble Vic might present.

"You hungry?" she asked. "I am. I couldn't eat after the wedding."

"Me neither. Do you suppose that piece of cake is still there?"

She smiled. "You mean the one that indicated we would have a long marriage?"

It was good to see her relax, and he chuckled. "And many children."

She laughed softly.

"Where're Aunt Bea and Missy?"

"They thought we might like some privacy, so they went to bed early." She dipped her head, then lifted her eyes. "Seems we're the only ones who remember this." She patted her rounded stomach. While he tried to think of an answer, she said, "I'm going to find that cake. Come on." He followed her into the kitchen.

A piece of cake and a handful of little sandwiches were on a plate under a glass dome. She poured a glass of milk for each of them and placed the plate of food on the table.

They sat kitty-corner from each other, eating the cheese sandwiches. When they were gone, she cut the cake and they each had a piece.

She grinned at him. "Aunt Bea was really into the wedding stuff. Do you know she has my grandmother's wedding dress in a trunk in her bedroom? I think she's still hoping to wear it."

"Your aunt Bea? That's a surprise."

"I know. But she and Pastor Manly seem to have an interest in each other." She sobered. "I don't suppose I'll get to see her in a wedding dress."

Nate hadn't thought about all she was losing in her flight north. The home she'd known for seven years, her friends, all the memories she'd made in this place. But she had no choice. "I guess you'll take your memories with you."

"And my baby."

"And Missy."

"I haven't forgotten." She pushed from the table, gathered the dishes, carried them to the basin and poured hot water over them.

He saw she was about to wash them. Saw weariness in the way she moved. He sprang to his feet. "You sit and I'll take care of the dishes."

She opened her mouth to refuse, but he took her by the shoulders and guided her back to the table and eased her down into the chair. She let out a sigh of relief.

As he washed the few dishes and dried them, he talked to her. "We have to be at the depot at seven-thirty tomorrow morning."

"Not a problem. We'll be ready to go."

He dried the last dish and hung the towel on the rack by the stove. "Is there anything you need me to do?"

Her eyebrows came up. "You mean, besides marry me?"

He tipped his head in acknowledgment. "Do you need me to bring a trunk from the attic or…" He had no idea what she might need.

"I'm packed and ready to go." She patted his arm. "Missy and I have been on our own for a while Nate. We won't be a nuisance. I promise." She rested her hand on the top of her tummy bulge. "All we need is the protection of marriage so Vic can't convince strangers I'm a runaway wife."

"Vic won't bother you again. I promise." He hoped his words were not another pretend vow.

Chapter Four

Louise was awake long before it was time to rise. The baby kicked as if excited about the journey. *Just stay where you are for a few more days.*

She lifted her head from her pillow. Did she hear a tapping at the door? A chill wove around her spine. Not Vic! She'd locked the doors solidly. But she knew that wouldn't prove enough barrier to stop the man.

"Louise, are you awake?" Nate whispered from the other side of the bedroom door. He'd spent the night in the parlor, which should have made her sleep a lot better than it did.

Her lungs emptied in a whoosh and she rose gingerly from bed, donned a wrap and cracked the door open. "Yes?"

"I'm going to get a wagon. Lock the door after me."

She waited until he went outside to move down the hall as fast as she could and turn the key.

Missy had begged to sleep in the room with Louise last night, saying she was afraid to be alone, afraid Vic would find her. She sat up as Louise returned to the bedroom. "Today we start our great adventures." She lifted her hands over her head and laughed. With an ease Louise could barely remember, Missy scurried from bed and began to dress.

"Remember to wear your warmest clothes." Although the weather had been mild, it was December and the temperatures could drop anytime.

Missy chattered as they dressed. "I've always wanted to see what was north of here. But more than anything, I want to get away from that vile Vic."

"You're about to get your wish." Louise put the last of her things in her valise. She wouldn't need much for the journey. Everything else was in a small trunk—baby things, some outfits for after she'd had the baby and a few mementos of her mother.

She paused a moment to let regrets at what she was about to leave waft through her, combined with wishes for what might have been if her mother had stayed.

Aunt Bea had told her the truth about Louise's mother. Not that she died and that was why Louise and her pa were on their own, as Pa always said, but that she'd left Pa because she couldn't stand the mining camps. Aunt Bea said she thought Ma had tried to take Louise, but Pa wouldn't allow it. Louise thought Aunt Bea only wanted to remove the look of shock from Louise's face. Ma had died of consumption three years after leaving them.

Louise reached into the trunk for an item.

"I have something of your mother's," Aunt Bea had once said, and brought out a painting of a young child. The painting she now held in her hands.

"Is that me?" Louise had fingered the frame.

Her aunt had nodded. "Your mother was a talented artist. The picture is now yours."

"Thank you." The painting had been her most cherished possession ever since. In it she was sure she saw love. But love had not been enough to make her mother stay. Because of that thought she'd never display the picture. For a moment she mused on a thought. What was enough to make any person stay? If not love, then what?

She'd considered the question many times and had never found an answer. Nor did she expect to today, either. She put the picture into the trunk, closed the latches, then went to the kitchen.

They ate a hurried breakfast. Aunt Bea insisted they take an abundant lunch for the journey, most of which was the remainders of meals Louise had prepared in the past two days.

A wagon rattled up to the house and Nate knocked.

She unlocked the door and stepped back to let him in.

"Where's the luggage?" he asked.

Louise directed him to the two trunks—hers and Missy's, and he hoisted one to his shoulder and trotted to the wagon. She and Missy carried their smaller bags. In minutes, he had both aboard and stood at the door. "Are you ready?"

Louise and Missy pulled on their warmest outer clothing. Aunt Bea pressed a gray woolen blanket into each of their arms.

"Stay safe. Let me know when you arrive." She hugged Louise.

Tears stung Louise's eyes. Aunt Bea had only twice before hugged her. Once when she told her about her mother and the other time when Gordie was killed.

"I'll send a letter," she promised Aunt Bea, then let Nate lead her to the wagon and help her aboard. He had to practically lift her.

"I'm sorry," she said. "I'm such a size right now."

"For better or worse," Aunt Bea reminded them.

Louise met Nate's gaze, as full of secret and regret as hers. He acknowledged the moment with a little nod of his head and a barely there smile before he turned to assist Missy.

They rattled down the street to the depot. He helped them alight and, with his arm around Louise's shoulders, led them inside where it was marginally warmer than outside. It would be warmer if the door was closed, but the ticket man had it propped open.

She sat on the narrow wooden bench and Nate unfolded the blanket Aunt Bea had provided and draped it over her lap. A person could get used to being taken care of. She buried the thought. Best not get used to it. This was temporary. She must stand on her own for her sake, as well as that of her unborn child.

"Wait here," he said. "While I take care of the wagon." He rushed out. Seemed he was as impatient to start this journey as Missy, who wriggled on the bench beside her. Louise tried to decide what she felt. Certainly not the excitement Missy showed. Truth was, she was worried. Not so much about Vic anymore, though she'd never quite believe he was out of her life. But the baby had been more active lately. *Please, God, don't let it be born before we reach Eden Valley Ranch. Let it be a Christmas baby.* But would God even hear her? Or listen if He did? So many times in the past she had felt abandoned by God, though she did her best to believe He loved her, as the Porters had so fervently taught her.

If the baby came on the trip, it would slow them down, and Nate had made it clear he wouldn't let them hinder him from getting back to Edendale in time to see a man about buying a ranch. She drove steel into her spine. If he left them somewhere, she would simply continue the journey at her own speed.

What if the stagecoach left them, too?

She would not contemplate all the things that could go wrong.

A shadow crossed the floor. She looked up and there stood Vic leaning against the door frame.

"Going someplace?" He drawled the words.

"Away from here." Louise's reply carried a full dose of her dislike for the man. *Away from you.*

"Hear you and Nate got hitched. You figger you can tie that cowboy down, do ya?"

She figured no such thing. "I fail to see how that's any of your business."

The man behind the ticket wicket watched them. The room was small enough he could hear every word. She didn't care. She and Nate were legally married. That's all anyone had to know.

Vic strode over and sat beside Missy.

Louise moved down the bench so Missy could put space between herself and Vic. He simply moved down until Louise balanced on the end.

The ticket man cleared his throat.

Vic ignored the subtle warning. "Missy, you don't have to go with Louise."

"I'm going because I want to."

Louise had to give the girl credit. She never let on how much Vic frightened her.

"You sure? Hear it's real primitive up there. No decent town for miles. Mostly Indians and buffalo roaming about. You might get tired of nobody who can show you a good time." He pushed closer to Missy.

Louise pushed back to keep from being bumped to the floor.

The ticket man cleared his throat most loudly. "Ladies, is this man bothering you?"

As if that wasn't obvious. But Vic had a reputation throughout the town, and Louise didn't blame the ticket man for being cautious.

Vic scowled at the poor man. "This ain't none of yer business."

"It is mine." Nate blasted through the door, yanked Vic to his feet and rushed him outside.

Vic fought to free himself from Nate's hold as he scrambled to keep his feet under him.

Nate shoved him from the building and released him on the sidewalk.

Vic splayed his arms to stay upright.

"Leave my wife and sister-in-law alone. You hear?" Nate stood tall, his fists on his hips, and glowered at Vic, who picked up his hat and dusted it off before smashing it back on his head.

"You done made a mistake." He stalked away.

Louise didn't know whether to be shocked at Nate's actions or amused at Vic's blustering.

Missy chuckled. "Someone should have warned Vic not to mess with Nate. He never did take kindly to unfairness."

Louise let those words simmer in her brain. She'd forgotten how Nate sprang to the defense of others.

The ticket man stared at Louise.

"That's right," she said calmly. "Nate and I are married now." She felt a sense of pride in saying those words, even if it was only pretend.

She could hear the man gasp clear across the room.

The stagecoach rattled to a stop and Nate helped put the trunks on top.

Louise pushed to her feet and followed Missy, who practically danced out to the sidewalk.

Louise made it as far as the door and stopped. It was too late to change her mind. She'd burned her bridges yesterday when she married Nate. The baby kicked her hard as if to remind her that she had no choice. Vic was too dangerous. Yet she couldn't make her feet move. She didn't like change. Going meant leaving…leaving her life, her friends. She glanced to the right and left. None of her friends had come to bid her farewell. But then, they didn't know she was leaving. Any more than they knew she was married again.

Nate stood in front of her, his expression quietly concerned. He touched her arm. "Is something wrong?"

His touch, his words, filled her with strength and resolve. "Everything is fine. I was just saying a mental goodbye."

He nodded. "Do you want me to give you a moment?"

He had always had this gentle consideration for the needs of others—spoken or otherwise. Another thing she'd forgotten. Encouraged by that memory, she smiled. "I'm done. I'm ready."

He bent his elbow for her to hold as she crossed the wooden walkway and escorted her down the wooden steps to the ground. Grateful for his help, she turned to face him. "Thank you. I'm sorry I'm so awkward right now."

"As your husband, I am more than willing to help you."

Her heart beat a rapid rhythm as wild wishes for forever tangled with regret and reality.

He flashed a smile so unexpectedly warming that she could only stare. He leaned closer to whisper, "We might as well enjoy this while it lasts. I, for one, fully intend to."

"How can you think that's possible?"

He chuckled. "We were friends in the past. Let's see if we can remember what that was like."

A relieved smile curved her mouth. See, he truly wasn't Vic nor like Vic in any way.

"Folks, I'd like to get on the road soon as possible." The driver's urging made it impossible to do more than nod her agreement to Nate.

He steadied her as she climbed into the stage and sat next to Missy. Facing them was a woman whose expression was full of curiosity. No doubt she'd strained to hear every word. She shifted and a pained look came to her face, perhaps from sharing the space of the man on the other end of her bench—a weathered old man who ought to have shaved and bathed. Clean clothes would have been nice, too. Between the two, a cowboy in rumpled clothes leaned forward on the leather-covered seat as if uncomfortable at being pressed so close to the others.

At least Louise and Missy weren't crowded together with a stranger. Unless they picked up more passengers on the way.

The smell of the one man permeated the coach and made Louise's stomach roll. Perhaps when they got moving, fresh air would help.

With a crack of the whip and a call to giddyap, the journey began.

Her heart lurched along with the coach. Where was Nate? Had he abandoned her already?

She glanced out the window. He sat astride his horse, riding beside them. Was that how he planned to make the trip to Fort Macleod? Or did he plan on leaving them before they arrived at their destination? Riding out there, he could leave at any moment, and then what would she do?

Her lips pressed tight. If he left, she'd have to manage. At least they were going away from Vic.

If Nate left, would he look her up later and arrange to dissolve their marriage?

She sat back. Oh, how upset Aunt Bea would be if she knew the falseness of her marriage vows. How often had she warned Louise to do what was right even when it was difficult? Aunt Bea never came right out and said so, but Louise understood her to mean Louise shouldn't be like her mother. In Aunt Bea's opinion, Ma ought to have honored her wedding vows.

The baby kicked against Louise's ribs.

She relaxed as much as was possible in the swaying coach. She was doing this for the right reasons—to protect her baby.

Missy poked her head out the window on her side. "We're almost out of town. We're on our way." She laughed from sheer joy.

Louise took one more look out the window, glancing back. Why couldn't things stay the same? People left or died. Things changed. Just once she'd like to think she could hold on to something, or someone.

Instead, she was leaving the place that had been her home for many years. She was heading into an uncertain future as part of a very temporary marriage.

Seemed forever was always going to be out of her reach.

We used to be friends?

Nate grinned as he thought of Louise's surprised expression when he said those words. She had looked so worried, frightened even. Guess he couldn't blame her. She was a widow, about to become a mother, and now leaving her home for a place she'd never seen.

He chuckled softly and ducked his head, lest anyone see and wonder why he was so amused. She was also a new bride. No wonder she wore such a tense expression.

At that moment he had decided to try to make the journey enjoyable, though he'd ridden in a stagecoach once and wondered if it was possible to find any pleasure in the ride. But he would do his best to help her through the next few days. Not only because he was her temporary husband, but because of Gordie. And also because of the past they shared, a happier time, to be sure. He had no desire to go back. The future beckoned. He'd always thought of Louise as part of his past, but now she was part of his present. Just not his future. Even so, it wouldn't hurt to help her. He didn't find the prospect distasteful, which alarmed him. Still, it was only a few days out of his life, seven or eight at the most. Might as well make the best of it.

They left the town behind them. In a few miles they turned toward Fort Benton. From there they would follow the Whoop-Up Trail north.

He'd decided to ride his horse rather than be cooped up in the coach, but now he wished he was inside so he could point out different landmarks to Louise.

It was cold but clear. No threat of snow or rain. Dust rolled up from the horses' hooves and the wheels. Some of it drifted into the coach. Was she comfortable enough?

He'd have to wait until their first way station to ask.

He settled back into the saddle and drank his fill of the scenery. It felt good to be in the open again, riding horseback. That was his life now—a free-and-easy cowboy about to start his own ranch. It would mean lots of work. Hours of riding. Cattle to buy and move. Horses to break. Meat to hunt.

And no one to worry about but himself. He liked that. Back in Rocky Creek he was reminded of the futility of worrying about others. He'd asked around for details on Gordie's death. No one had been charged with his death, even though it seemed likely he'd been murdered. The last person seen with him had been Vic. It was enough to convince Nate that Vic had something to do with Gordie's death. Nate had worried when his friend had joined up with Vic. He'd tried to convince Gordie it wasn't wise. Rather than continue to argue with his friend, he'd left. Every year when he visited, he'd sought out Gordie and tried again to persuade him to leave, to follow him to Eden Valley Ranch and get work.

Every year he'd failed and left. All his worry and concern had achieved nothing. Better to be free and easy. To move forward, not back, not even glance over his shoulder at what might have been.

The stage hit a hole in the trail and jolted from one side to the other. The occupants clutched at the leather handholds to keep from being tossed from their seats. Sure didn't look comfortable to Nate. He'd sooner ride a horse any day.

He'd taught Louise to ride. Not that she'd never been on horseback before she moved to Rocky Creek, but she'd never ridden astride at full gallop across a field.

Ma had heard of it and scolded Nate royally. "She's a young lady. Have some regard for her safety and reputation."

It was a warning he meant to heed but Louise had

ideas of her own and had continued to follow him and Gordie around, insisting she could do anything they did. Mostly she could.

No longer. She could barely waddle. Wouldn't she pitch a fit if he pointed it out to her?

At least he was doing what he could to protect her reputation with this pretend marriage, and at the same time keep her safe from Vic.

He glanced around, studying every bush and boulder, looking for someone lurking after them. He saw no one. Had Vic given up on his quest to have Louise and Missy? And the baby? Nate's jaw protested at how hard he clamped down on his teeth. Imagine selling a baby! The mere thought made his insides twist. Best for Vic if he stayed away.

But would Vic give up so easily? One part of Nate thought Vic would move on to easier prey, especially after Nate had tossed him into the street. But another part thought Vic didn't like to admit defeat.

Nate rode around a rut dug in the trail by wagon wheels during a rain. The stage wasn't able to miss it and lurched from side to side again.

Nate fell back and to the side. From his position, he could see Louise without her noticing unless she looked over her shoulder.

Her face was pinched and pale, her eyes closed, her mouth a thin line.

The ride had to be most uncomfortable in her condition. Maybe she was regretting this decision.

He kept his position as they continued, watching with growing concern. He might have lost his right to ask God for favors by vowing falsely, but somehow he knew that wasn't true. How many talks had Bertie given back at the ranch as they gathered in the cookhouse for Sunday services? He'd said God never gave up on people. *God, don't give up on me. I know what I did was wrong, marrying with no intention of staying married. But I did it for Missy, Louise and her baby. I'm still concerned about them. Please help me get them safely to the ranch.*

They came to the first way station to change horses.

The driver called, "Folks, time for a quick break, but be late getting aboard and be left behind."

The threat of being left behind in this desolate place would make all of them hurry. There was only a crude barn, a set of corrals for the horses and a dugout home for the bewhiskered man who sauntered over to help with the animals.

Nate dismounted, led his horse to water, then made haste to help the ladies down.

Missy hurried to the well to drink her fill of water.

Nate pulled Louise's hand around his elbow to rest on his arm. When she leaned heavily on him, he dipped his head to study her face. Was she gritting her teeth? "Are you okay?"

She nodded, then worked her jaw loose. "I need a drink and to stretch my legs."

He filled a dipper and she gulped back three swallows, then stopped and handed the dipper back with a word of thanks. He again pulled her hand around his arm as they walked along the dusty path.

She stopped at the corner of the corrals and leaned on a post.

"You sure you're okay? It's not too late to change your mind."

She turned on him, pierced him with a sharp look. "Are you suggesting I go back? And do what? Fight Vic? Do you really think I'd stand a chance against someone so despicable and sneaky?"

"I was only thinking of you. We've just been gone a few hours and you already look exhausted."

She drew herself upright, no longer leaning on the post. All hint of tiredness had been erased from her demeanor. "I am only thinking of my baby."

Their gazes held, hers full of fury and determination, his, he supposed, full of resignation. "Put that way, I guess you have no choice but to cowboy up."

"Cowboy up?"

"Means you do what is hard instead of moaning about it."

She nodded. "Exactly what I mean to do."

He grinned. "Awfully good to see there is some spark left in you."

She rumbled her lips. "I might lose my spark, but I'll never lose my fight." Her hands pressed to her stomach and he understood she would fight whatever enemy threatened her baby.

"You won't fight alone." Although she'd made it clear this was Gordie's baby, he felt more than a little concern for the little one's safety. "I'll make sure all three of you get to Eden Valley Ranch."

Her gaze burned a path through his thoughts as if she didn't believe him. Didn't trust him.

Why would she think that? He'd never done anything to give her reason to doubt his word. "You don't trust me. Why?"

Her reply was cut off by the coach driver. "Folks, get aboard unless you want to stay here."

Louise hurried back to the coach with Nate on her heels. He knew he wasn't wrong in thinking she was grateful she didn't get a chance to answer his question.

Chapter Five

Louise sat in the coach wishing it didn't have to move. The constant swaying made her seasick. The jolting from side to side brought on spasms in her stomach muscles. But with a gentle bounce they were on their way once again. She hung on to the leather strap and tried to think of something besides her stomach.

Nate was right. She didn't trust him. But what purpose would be served in admitting it? As to her reasons, they were too numerous and too convoluted to tell. Throughout her life she'd had no evidence she could trust anyone.

Not even God? her conscience accused her.

There were times she trusted Him. Like when she'd told Gordie they were going to have a baby. She'd been thrilled at the thought of another little Porter in the family. Gordie had seemed to enjoy the idea, too.

But then Gordie had been killed. It was hard to trust after that.

They jerked over another hole in the trail and she bit her bottom lip to keep from crying out a protest.

You don't need to trust when everything is going ac-

*cording to your wishes. It's when things are difficult and
hard to understand, you need to trust.*

She recalled hearing the words in a soft, gentle voice.
Not Aunt Bea. They seldom talked about such things. It
was Mrs. Porter who had said them. And Louise did her
best to believe them. But there were days she wanted
things to be easier. Then it would be easy to trust.

They swayed hard to the right and she could do little but think about keeping from crying out against the
pain in her ribs.

"That young man is keeping a close eye on you," the
lady across from her said. "Allow me to introduce myself. My name is Miss Rowena Rolfe."

Louise and Missy introduced themselves.

The three women looked toward the men awaiting
their introductions.

The cowboy said, "Sam."

The other man grinned, revealing stubs of yellowed
teeth. "Sparky George."

No one asked if George was his first or last name, and
after a minute he settled back.

Miss Rolfe continued, "I'm journeying to Fort Macleod
to join my brother." She leaned closer and whispered, "He
tells me there are ten men to every marriageable woman."
She blushed and lowered her gaze.

The two men to her left slanted looks in her direction.
The cowboy turned away quickly, but Sparky George
studied Miss Rolfe several seconds.

Miss Rolfe looked out the window at Nate. "If that is
a sample of what's available, I believe my decision to go
to Fort Macleod will be a wise one."

Missy chuckled. "He's married to her." She jerked her
thumb toward Louise, then pointedly nodded her head

toward the men beside Miss Rolfe as if to suggest they might be available.

Miss Rolfe shrank into her corner, clearly not liking the possibilities one man in particular on this ride offered.

Missy grinned widely.

"How far are you going?" Miss Rolfe asked.

Seemed she had a need to pass the time with conversation, while all Louise wanted to do was close her eyes and pray for the day to end. Yes, she'd pray. Things couldn't get much more difficult or hard to understand, so it seemed like a perfect time to start trusting God. *I know I've not been faithful. I lied before the preacher and before You. I hope You can forgive me for that. But please, if You care about me at all, help me make it to Eden Valley Ranch.* After a silent groan, she added, *Help the baby to stay where he is until we get there.*

She closed her eyes and rested her head on the back of her bench as Miss Rolfe and Missy continued to talk. All she had to do was survive another mile and after that another mile, another hour, and another stop to change horses until they stopped for the night. Then repeat it all the next day and the next until they reached their destination.

A day might as well have been a lifetime the way she felt at the moment.

At the next stop, Nate came toward her as she walked about trying to get the cramps out of her legs and back. Not wanting to talk to him, she turned and retraced her steps.

He followed. "Did you get water?"

She shook her head. Sparky stood by the pump and she wanted fresh air more than she needed water.

Nate trotted over, filled a dipper and brought it back to her.

She grabbed the handle and drank sparingly. There would be no stops along the way for a pregnant lady needing to empty her bladder.

"We'll soon be at Fort Benton," Nate said. "We'll stop there for the night."

"Good."

"You'll be okay?"

"I'm fine." As fine as could be expected, but she'd spare him the details. Her discomfort was temporary. Getting to safety at the ranch was all that mattered.

She returned to her seat to endure the rest of the journey. She half dozed, lulled by the sway of the coach and the murmur of conversation around her.

"Louise." Missy's frantic whisper brought her fully alert. "Look."

She followed the direction Missy pointed. From the trees rode two men with bandannas pulled up over their faces. She grabbed Missy's hand. "Vic?" Not waiting for an answer, she jerked down the leather curtain. Missy did the same on her side.

Sparky leaned forward, saw the men and jerked the curtain down on his side. "Ma'am, pull down the curtain," he ordered Miss Rolfe. She peeked out the window, let out a squeak and jerked the leather covering down.

Louise lifted a corner on her window to look for Nate. She couldn't see him. Where had he gone? He was about to be tested on his promise to get her to safety.

One of the men rode to the side of the driver and leveled his gun on the man. "This is a holdup."

Louise almost laughed. Did the robber think the driver

might mistake him for someone wanting to get passage on the stage?

"Whoa. Whoa." The stage jerked to a halt.

"Throw down the strongbox."

There was a strongbox? Was there one on every stage? Louise had never had any need to know.

A metal box hit the ground beside her, the thud racing along her nerves.

"You passengers get out."

Louise looked at Missy. If one of the men was Vic, could they expect to hide inside? Again she looked for Nate. Had the robbers found and shot him? Tears welled up behind her eyes but before she could explain them to herself the door yanked open and one of the robbers aimed his gun toward Miss Rolfe. "Out."

She scrambled past him.

Sam was ordered out next. He took his time about climbing out until the robber hit him on the side of the head, then he hurried up.

"Old man, yer next."

Sparky muttered under his breath and earned himself a smack on the side of the head, as well.

Louise gasped as blood oozed from the wound. Finally she could see that this man wasn't Vic, but he was every bit as evil. She measured the distance from her foot to the hand that held the gun. But before she could put her thought into action and kick the gun away, the robber turned to Missy.

"Well, well, lookee what we got here. Sid, you ought to see this. Well, I guess you will."

Sid! Not Vic! Louise could almost feel relief that his partner was not the man she feared. Except this pair was equally dangerous.

The gunman reached for Missy. She shrank back and kicked her feet, landing a blow to the man's arm.

He laughed. "I like 'em with a little spit."

Missy showed him a little spit all right. She spat right in his face.

He climbed the steps and grabbed her by the hair and yanked her out.

Louise held on to Missy's arm until the man jerked them free of each other.

Louise swallowed back a cry. She would not show fear before these scoundrels. No matter what. Perhaps they'd leave her alone, given her condition.

Missy continued to fight the man, kicking and clawing, which only seemed to excite him further. Louise would not stay here while they bothered her sister-in-law. She couldn't move fast, but that didn't mean she had to sit idly by while Missy struggled. She edged forward, intending to jump on the man's back when the opportunity presented itself.

"Anyone else in there?" the second robber asked.

"One more lady."

"Get her out."

The gunman pushed Missy to the ground and returned to the stage.

Louise was on her feet waiting for him, so when he returned, she kicked him in the face. The gun fell to his feet as he grabbed her and yanked her headfirst from the coach.

She landed on her hands and knees. *Thank God. Thank God.* If she'd landed on her belly...

The outlaw headed toward Louise.

She tried to scramble away.

"Leave her alone." Appearing from the bushes, Nate

sprang forward and punched the man in the nose. Blood spurted from beneath his bandanna and he fell to the dirt, clutching his nose.

The robber growled and Louise heard a gunshot ring out.

Right in front of her, Nate fell to the ground. His eyes were wide and it seemed he had stopped breathing.

Louise's heart froze within her. Was Nate dead? She began to tremble and had to rein herself in from rushing to his side, but the man on horseback still wielded the gun. Had she been the cause of Nate's death, and only one day into their journey?

Then she sucked in air and looked at his shoulder. A hole in his coat indicated where he'd been shot.

Despite the danger to herself, and still on her hands and knees, she crawled to his side. "Nate? Nate?"

Before she could determine whether he was alive or dead, she heard another blast of gunfire and a barked order. "Throw down your weapons." She looked up and saw the driver holding a shotgun, aimed at the man on horseback.

With a curse, he threw his gun to the ground.

Sam gathered up both guns.

The driver threw down rope and the pair were soon trussed up.

She saw it all out of the corner of her eye while she knelt at Nate's side. She looked down at him and realized for the first time that he was breathing. Only now did she think herself capable of drawing in a breath of her own.

"I'm okay," he said. "The bullet only grazed me. When I saw them approaching, I took to the trees, hoping to waylay them. They got around me. I tried to get here sooner but didn't want them to hear my approach."

"Stop talking." He'd been nearby all the time. The thought made her feel better. "You're bleeding." A dark stain had spread around the hole in his coat, and it was growing larger. "Let me look at it." She started to unbutton his coat, but he grabbed her hands.

"Never mind me. You took a bad tumble. Are you okay?"

She looked into his eyes. Felt herself sinking into the concern she saw there. He brought his free hand up and cupped the side of her head.

"Are you hurt?" he asked.

He sounded as if he cared. As if it mattered to him. More than just keeping his promise to get her safely to the ranch. Her throat thickened. "I'm okay." Realizing her thoughts were foolish and impossible, she turned back to his coat and worked on his buttons. "Let me look at that wound."

He sat up, undid the buttons on his own, but let her pull the coat from his injured arm. She tore the shirt to expose the wound. "I'll mend it for you later."

She wiped the blood away with her white hankie, the one she'd been tempted to press to her nose all day. "You're right. It's only a graze. But I expect it hurts like all get out."

"No cowboy cries over a flesh wound." He pulled his coat back on and stood, reaching out to help her to her feet.

She hurt in places she hadn't known existed, but she would not complain.

Sam grinned. "We're a tough lot."

She didn't know if he meant her, but then he looked at her and she felt included.

"Let's get this rig on the road again," the driver called.

"Put that pair on their horses. We'll take them to Fort Benton."

Sam pushed them into their saddles. When Nate reached for his horse, Sam said, "I'll escort them. Why don't you ride inside."

"I'm riding up top," Sparky said. "Feel better being in the open."

Louise wondered if Nate would refuse Sam's offer, but after a pause, he nodded. "Thanks."

In a moment they were all back inside. Missy and Miss Rolfe sat side by side. Louise and Nate sat facing them.

Several times as they continued on their way, she felt his gaze on her, and when she turned to meet his look, he smiled—mostly with his eyes.

Was he worried about her? Well, no more so than she was about him. He'd been shot defending her. She couldn't say what it meant except it felt good. And right.

She turned to stare out the window. Right? Everything about them was wrong.

Pretend. Lies. And yet, for just a little while, she'd felt as if she mattered to someone. Enough for that person to do something to protect her.

It was a new feeling and she liked it.

Even though she knew it was only temporary.

Nate's pulse still thundered in his ears. Almost as loud as it had when he'd seen the road agents approach. He'd expected Vic to be one of the men, and he knew he'd shoot the man before he'd allow him to take Missy and Louise. Trouble was, he didn't wear a sidearm. His pistol was in his saddlebag, and by the time he could get it out, he knew the robbers would be upon them. He'd turned into the trees, keeping out of sight as he pulled out his gun. They had reached the stagecoach before he could stop them.

It hadn't been Vic and an accomplice, but men every bit as bad. When one of them yanked Missy out and then Louise, not even allowing her to get her feet under her, a feral growl had come from his throat and he'd sprung forward, acting out of sheer instinct.

He would not let them hurt his wife.

His wife.

When had he started thinking of her in those terms? They were married, but she wasn't his wife. She was his best friend's wife carrying his best friend's baby. He would see her to safety, then his obligation, his duty to the past, would be over and done with. As it should have been years ago.

He'd tried for the past three years to put the past behind him. But it was impossible to dismiss a friendship such as he and Gordie had enjoyed, equally impossible to forget he owed the Porter family for opening their door to him. Taking care of Louise and the baby would be payback for their kindness.

But getting Louise to Eden Valley Ranch in one piece was becoming more of a challenge than he'd anticipated. Not only had she confronted some bad men, he had seen the strain in her face and understood travel was very uncomfortable for her. He'd asked when the baby would be born and she'd assured him it wouldn't be for a while.

He could only hope she was right and they'd make it to the ranch before that event.

They reached Fort Benton late in the afternoon. The dusty frontier town bustled with activity, and the aroma of several thousand oxen and mules assaulted them with every breath. Few of the bull trains would be ferrying freight north during the winter. Instead, the animals were corralled in town.

The stage pulled up in front of the Overland Hotel. He sprang from the coach and helped the women down, making Louise wait until last so he could pull her to his side. He led them inside and registered Louise and Missy into a room. He would sleep in the stables or the empty warehouse he'd slept in on his way down.

The proprietor handed them a key. "Dinner will be served in half an hour. Gives you time to wash up. I suggest you get there right off or the men will clean up every bite."

"Louise, I'll take you upstairs to your room," Nate said.

She turned. "Nate, you look terrible. Go wash up. Maybe sit down before you fall down." And with that, she turned and lumbered up the stairs, Missy right behind her.

"I'll be back in half an hour," he called.

"Fine." Her voice drifted down the stairs.

She couldn't be feeling too bad if she could still be bossy, he realized. Hiding a pleased smile, he trotted out to his horse outside the jail where Sam had taken the robbers.

Nate took the animal to the stable and brushed it down, ignoring the sting in his injured arm. Only after he fed and watered his mount did he wash himself and find a shirt without blood soaking the sleeve. He looked at the wound. It was only a graze, not worth taking note of even. Hardly hurt at all. Nevertheless, he tied a clean neckerchief around it so it wouldn't ooze blood onto his shirtsleeve. He donned his clean shirt and hurried back to the hotel, knowing the half hour had come and gone.

The proprietor looked up when he entered the lobby.

"The ladies are in the dining room." He waved in the general direction of the double doors that stood open. "The dark-haired one told me to say they couldn't wait. They were hungry."

"Thanks." At noon, Louise had barely nibbled the lunch they'd brought, so hearing she was hungry raised his spirits considerably. Chuckling, he stepped into the room and glanced around, finding her seated with Missy and Miss Rolfe. Sam and Sparky had joined a table full of men. He returned Sam's friendly wave but ignored the invitation to join them.

He would eat with his wife.

"You're looking better," she said when he took a seat across from her.

"So are you."

She squinted at him. "I wasn't shot."

"Nope." But she'd endured a rough ride for more hours than he cared to contemplate.

A man wearing a soiled apron set a plate of food before him and he dug in. The three ladies had already cleaned their plates. "Food's good," he murmured after a bit.

Missy chuckled. Miss Rolfe watched, wide-eyed. Louise rested her chin on elbow-supported hands and grinned.

"What?" He looked around the table. What were they all staring at?

Louise answered. "We were wondering when you'd come up for air."

He cleaned his plate with a slice of bread and sat back with a sigh. "A man gets hungry, you know. Besides, this might be the last decent meal we see until we reach Fort Macleod."

At the way her eyes widened and her mouth pulled

into a worried frown, he wished he'd kept that bit of information to himself.

Seeing he was finished, the ladies pushed back from the table. He sprang to his feet to assist Louise.

"Thank you," she said, but her eyes filled with warning.

"What? I'm only being polite."

"I see."

But she obviously didn't. Was she so determined to remind him this arrangement was only temporary?

"I'm going to my room," Miss Rolfe said.

Missy glanced around, saw nothing to hold her interest. "I have a book to read. Are you coming, Louise?"

Louise sighed. "I feel the need to move about."

"Would you like to see Fort Benton?" Nate asked. It was dusky out, but there would be lots of activity yet.

She brightened. "Why, yes, I would. Give me a minute to get my coat." There was a time she would have flown up the stairs, but not now. She held the handrail and labored to the top. In minutes, she reappeared and as carefully made her way down to his side.

He wisely kept any comment to himself and pulled her arm through his. Outside, he led her across the street to the waterfront. "The stern-wheeler brings freight and goods and people up the Missouri to here, then wagons go in every direction like spokes in a wheel."

"It's busy." She watched men hurrying to and fro. One carried a box on his shoulders, another pushed a handcart loaded high enough to block the man's view, causing the pedestrians approaching him to dart out of the way.

"Why do some of the men have red sashes about their waists?"

He was pleased he could explain. "They're French Canadians. They use the sashes around their coats. I hear they're useful for a number of other things, too, like a saddle blanket, rope or towel."

"It's nice to see the color."

As they walked, he kept close to the river and away from the many saloons, though tinny music reached them. "It's getting cold. Do you want to go back?"

"In a minute." They were in front of a hardware store with lantern light falling from the window to a bench on the sidewalk. "Let's sit for a spell."

She waited until they were both comfortably seated to speak again. "I've never gotten a chance to thank you for agreeing to marry me for as long as it takes to get to Eden Valley Ranch."

He thought to tell her that her continual reminders, whether subtle or obvious, as this one was, weren't necessary. He hadn't forgotten the temporary state of their marriage and was quite sure she'd never let him. "Gordie was my best friend. His parents opened their home to me when I felt alone." More like abandoned, he amended silently. Pa had died and Ma had had to work long hours. Nate had hated being alone at their new house.

"To me, as well."

"Do you remember—"

She spoke at the same time. "Do you think—"

They both stopped.

He lifted his hand to indicate he would stop. "You go ahead."

"No, you go first."

"Very well. Do you remember when they took us to the circus in town?"

She made a sound, half laugh, half sigh. "It was exciting. The elephants, the clowns, the tightrope walker. What did you like best?"

"The cowboys riding and roping."

"Is that when you decided you wanted to be a cowboy?"

He shook his head. "Before my pa died, we lived on a ranch of sorts. It was small. But we had cows and horses and other animals. We had a mare due to foal and Pa had said the foal was to be mine. But he died of pneumonia and Ma sold everything, including the mare and my unborn foal." He drew in a deep breath. "Why am I telling you this? It's the past."

She squeezed his hand. "I never knew that. You never said."

"Because there is no point in regretting what is gone. A man needs to look ahead not back."

"I'm sorry. But aren't you soon going to get what you lost back then?"

He turned to her, his eyebrows raised in question.

"Your own ranch. Surely you'll have foals now."

He nodded. Was he unknowingly trying to replace what he'd lost?

"Mr. Porter gave us each a nickel at the circus," she reminded him.

He readily let his thoughts return to those happy times. "I bought cotton candy with mine."

"You shared it with me. Remember?"

He turned to her, met her eyes, felt drawn into their shared memories. "I'd forgotten." Their look went on and on, searching, remembering, perhaps regretting all they'd lost.

"What were you going to say?" he asked her.

She turned from him to study her hands in her lap.

"Do you think God is angry with us?" she whispered. "For making vows we have no intention of keeping?"

"I wondered the same thing, then I recalled something Bertie said to us."

"Bertie? Who is that?"

"Bertie and Cookie run the cookhouse at the Eden Valley Ranch. There isn't a church nearby yet, though the building is almost finished in Edendale. In the meantime, we've had Sunday services in the cookhouse. Bertie always gives a little talk rather than a sermon. What he says makes a lot of sense."

"And he said something that made it okay to lie to God?" Her voice revealed a healthy dose of skepticism.

"No, but perhaps God understands we didn't have a choice. I remember Bertie saying, 'He knows our frame, He remembers we are dust.' Sometimes maybe we just have to do what seems best and pray God will change things if that isn't right."

"But to vow?"

He wished he could find words to comfort her, but his conscience stung as much as hers.

"I would expect God to turn His back on us," he said, "but I don't think He has."

She grabbed his hand and pulled his attention to her. "When that man pulled me from the stagecoach, I could have been badly hurt. The baby—" She shuddered and couldn't continue.

He wrapped an arm around her shoulders hoping she felt his strength but not an echo of the fear that had shot through him with more force than the bullet that had torn through his arm.

"God helped me land in a way that didn't hurt either of us," she managed to say.

He nodded, unable to speak past the tightness in his throat. If something had happened to her or the baby, or Missy...

She gave him a curious look. "Don't you agree?"

He swallowed hard and forced the words from his throat. "Thank You, God," he said, looking upward, then he turned to her. "You're okay. You are, aren't you? You're not just pretending?"

"I'm fine. And you know the first thought that ran through my head was the same. I thanked God, too."

Her look went on and on, touching chords deep within his heart, awakening memories of shared times, filling him with a desire for something he couldn't put a name to.

But it felt strangely like the moment he had stood in the barn with his pa watching the mare eat, being promised the new foal. A feeling of joy and promise.

Someone walked past then and greeted them, a stranger bidding them a good evening, but the interruption jerked him from his fanciful thoughts.

There had been no fulfillment of the promise back then, either.

But he had a future. He had only to get back in time to meet the owner of the land he wanted to buy. Why did he let himself see how empty the cabin would be without Louise and the baby?

Chapter Six

Louise was tired. Too tired to move. Besides, it was nice to sit on a bench that didn't rock and bounce.

She and Nate had talked about things. Especially the marriage vows they'd made with no intention of keeping. Did God understand? It comforted her to think Nate thought so.

She felt the baby move and rubbed her belly. Earlier today, when she'd landed safely on the ground outside the coach, her trust in God had built. She could have been seriously hurt. The baby might have been killed. But He had protected them.

The door to the store behind them opened and closed, and a man stood beside them. A French Canadian according to his red sash.

She smiled at the way he stood, legs wide, arms akimbo, as if he ruled the world.

He turned, saw them there and indicated the spot next to Nate.

Nate moved over to make room.

"She is a wonderful night for love," the red-sashed man said.

Amused, Louise nudged Nate in the ribs.

"I miss my lady." The man gave a long-drawn-out sigh. "But I has things to do to keep me mind and hands busy while I am away." He opened a leather sack and pulled out a piece of wood with the rough shape of a bear.

"You're a carver," Nate said.

"It passes me time. You like to see more?" He didn't wait for either of them to answer, which was fine. Louise was eager to see his work.

He pulled out a moose with intricately carved antlers. Then he pulled out a cat sitting on its haunches with a benign expression. *"Le chat."* He held it toward Louise. "You like?"

"It's beautiful."

"Is yours." He pushed it closer to her.

She pulled back. "I didn't mean for you to give it to me."

"Is yours for *bébé.*"

"For baby." She took it. "Thank you. It's beautiful."

He put away his things and got up.

"Wait," she called. "We don't even know your name."

"I am Pierre." He said it with so much pride she couldn't help chuckling. "I pray for your *bébé* every day now." He touched his forehead with his fingertips and marched away.

"He said he'll pray." She knew her words were filled with surprise. "I feel like God sent him to answer the questions we voiced a moment ago. Or am I grasping for straws to convince myself that what we've done is okay?"

"Maybe sometimes God sends people and events to show us His presence, and we dismiss them as ordinary."

She rubbed her fingers along the textured fur of the wooden cat. "That was a little out of the ordinary." She handed him the carving. "Look at the fine handiwork. He should sell his things."

"Perhaps he does. Or maybe he does it for his pleasure alone. Who knows?"

Who knows? Didn't that describe her feelings about God? Who knows if unusual things were indications of His interest in her or if they were random? On the other hand, who was she to dismiss such things as ordinary?

She rested her hands on her tummy again.

She always did her best to trust God. It wasn't as if she could count on anyone else.

If she could truly believe God cared for her, she would not fear the future.

Nate shifted his weight and stiffened when his arm bumped hers, reminding her of his injury.

"How's your arm?"

"Louise, Louise, Louise. When will you believe it's barely worth a moment's notice?"

"I'll believe it when I see your arm without blood and raw flesh. When you can bump it without flinching. Did you at least clean it and cover it?"

"Yes, to both." He took her hand and squeezed it. "I am okay. I will see you safely to the ranch."

And then what? She knew the answer. The marriage would be annulled and he would move on. She would have her baby and as soon as she was able, she would find a position to support herself. A nanny, perhaps, or a housekeeper? She tried not to worry about what she'd do. It was a problem she'd deal with after she succeeded in getting to the ranch and had safely delivered this child.

She took in a long, satisfying breath. She would not fear the future. God was with her. Yet she couldn't quite stop worry from wrapping around her thoughts.

"By the way," she said. "You're a hero."

"Me?" He stared at her. "I'm no hero."

"You rescued me, putting your own life at risk."

He chuckled. "Seems to me you were the one who kicked the gun from the man. All I did was object to the way he manhandled you."

She patted his arm. "I'm grateful for it."

He smiled down at her, making her feel as if she mattered in a special way.

Why was she always looking for someone to care about her? Such a childish thing. She'd soon be a mother and her baby would need her to be strong and self-sufficient.

"It's getting late and cold." He rose, then pulled her to her feet. Keeping her hand tucked around his arm and pressed close to his side, he led them back to the hotel. At the door he said goodbye and waited until she lumbered up the stairs before he left.

Missy was in their room, reading by lamplight. She closed the book as Louise entered. "I was beginning to worry about you."

"Nate showed me a bit of Fort Benton and we met a French Canadian named Pierre. Look what he gave me for the baby." She handed Missy the wooden cat.

Missy exclaimed over it, then put it on the little table. She faced Louise. "I'm happy for you."

"Thanks." She wasn't sure what Missy meant and really didn't care to discuss her situation with her sister-in-law.

"But I'm also worried," Missy added.

"What are you worried about?" Louise knew what she was doing. She had to move on. Stand on her own as soon as she reached Eden Valley Ranch. Maybe sooner if Nate took it in his mind to leave.

"What if you have the baby while we're traveling?"

Oh, she meant the baby. "I won't." *Please, God, don't let it happen.*

"How can you be so sure?"

"It can't happen until we get to our destination." She had no trouble convincing herself. Now, if she could just convince the baby it should wait until Christmas.

She prepared for bed and sank into the mattress with a contented sigh. "It feels mighty good to be on something soft."

Missy turned to consider her. "All that bouncing around might bring the baby on."

Louise sighed. "And what do you propose I do about it? We weren't safe back in Rocky Creek." She hadn't told Missy of Vic's plans to sell the baby. In fact, she'd told no one but Nate. "Nate assures me we'll be safe at Eden Valley Ranch. So I have to make the trip."

Missy nodded. "I know." She shivered. "That horrible Vic ruined everything."

Louise pressed her hands to her tummy. "Not everything."

"I'm glad you and Nate got married. I've always been fond of him. Where are you going to live when we get there?"

"At the ranch." She hadn't told Missy the truth about her marriage, and she couldn't now, not until she had to.

"Does he have his own house?" She sat up on one elbow. "You don't have to worry about me. I'll find someplace else to live."

Louise propped up on one elbow, too. "What? And deprive this baby of his aunt?"

Missy smiled. "I can hardly wait to meet him or her."

Not until they reached the ranch, Louise silently pleaded. "Go to sleep now."

* * *

The next morning, Nate looked at the pair of new passengers headed for Fort Macleod. Sparky was staying in Fort Benton. But still, Nate wouldn't fit inside unless Sam or one of the two new men decided to ride up top. None of them volunteered.

He pulled Missy aside. "I was hoping to ride with Louise so I could keep an eye on her. Can you do it for me? Let me know if she needs anything. I'd ask her myself, but she'd say she's fine."

"I'm prepared to watch her. I'm as concerned about her as you. But like you say, she's determined to make this trip. As am I. Vic hasn't left us much choice but to leave our home behind."

Nate hadn't thought of how difficult this must be for Missy. He patted her shoulder. "You're a brave young woman. Just the sort that does well on the ranch."

She smiled. "I'll do my best." She was the last to climb aboard.

Nate swung to his saddle and followed the departing stage, riding to the side where Louise sat, so he could watch her as they traveled.

They climbed up the steep side of the coulee to level prairie and looked down on the river and town for the last time. From here on, the road grew rougher, the accommodations more primitive. If not for Vic, Nate would never have embarked on this journey with Louise, though he knew she would have gone without his approval. And without his protection.

Four miles later, they crossed the Teton River and continued on the Whoop-Up Trail that would take them to Fort Macleod in Canada.

The wheels rolled on and on, occasionally hitting a rut

and pitching forward, then jerking back. Each time he glanced at Louise, worried how she managed the rough ride.

After the first bump, she looked out the window at him. Their gazes caught and held, hers steady, as if informing him she was doing fine.

But by the third jolt, her gaze was less certain. Her lips grew thinner and her eyelids twitched.

When they stopped for their first change of horses, he rushed to help her down. "This is too difficult for you."

She stood straight, even though the effort caused her to flinch. "I am fine. Besides, what do you suggest I do? Stay here?" She pointed to the crude setup—a run-down cabin and corrals, and a hard-looking man with a cigarette hanging from his mouth.

She patted his arm. "I'm fine," she repeated. "How are you doing?" She touched the hole in his coat sleeve where the bullet had gone through.

He didn't bother to answer. After all, what more could he say than what he'd already said?

"Are you sure it's wise to travel with your injury? Are you warm enough?" she asked, her voice overly sweet and solicitous.

He chuckled. "You're mocking me."

"Maybe a little. How does it feel?"

"A little annoying, if you must know."

"Exactly. So stop fussing at me."

He grinned. It was good to see she still had a hefty dose of fight in her. "Guess you're feeling better than I thought. Good enough to be a little feisty."

She narrowed her eyes. "Best you remember it." And she made her way gingerly toward the coach.

"Yes, ma'am. I'll remember." He rushed after her to

assist her up the steps. Seeing her fall down them once—or more accurately, yanked down them—was enough for him.

But remembering not to fuss was easier promised than done. As they continued, crossing more bumps than he thought possible, his concern for her grew.

It wasn't helped any when Sam said, "I'd sooner sit a bucking horse any day than spend another hour tossed about in that cage."

"Is it that bad?" Nate glanced toward Louise, who used the next break to splash water on her face.

"Say, why don't you ride inside and I'll ride the horse," Sam asked. Then realizing he might have provided a good reason for Nate to refuse him, he quickly added, "I'm just tired of being cooped up when I could be enjoying wide-open spaces." Sam glanced around. Nothing but prairie to see, but he smiled as if it was the best scenery in the world.

Nate could have saved him the effort of trying to convince him. He was only too happy to ride inside where he could be with Louise.

When he helped Louise into the coach and followed her, she said, "What are you doing?"

"Sam begged to trade places."

The three ladies sat on one side. Nate made sure he got the spot directly across from Louise and sat down.

She studied him long and hard.

He grinned and shrugged. "I didn't have the heart to refuse. After all, I know how hard it is for a cowboy to be stuck inside for hours at a time. Isn't that right, boys?" He turned to the pair beside him.

"That's right, ma'am," the older of the two new men said. "Not that I'm a cowboy, of course." He introduced himself as Archie Adams. "This is my son, Gabe. We're planning to open a hardware business in Fort Macleod." He turned to Nate. "I understand you've been there. What's it like?"

Relieved to have Louise's attention shifted to the others, Nate told them about the fort. "It's a bit rough around the edges. It's built on an island." He'd spare them the news that spring floods threatened its very existence every year. "It's the home of the North-West Mounted Police."

Young Adams leaned forward. "Now, there's a noble occupation."

"Indeed." Nate spent the rest of the afternoon being plied with questions. And bouncing over the rutted trail.

Seeing him occupied with conversation, Louise closed her eyes and clung to the strap by the window. At some point she fell asleep, and her hand released the strap, her head tipped back.

He edged forward, worried she'd fall when they hit a nasty bump.

The next rut threw her forward.

Louise's head snapped up as she tumbled toward him. Her eyes flew open, wide with fear as she waved her arms in an attempt to stop her fall.

He steadied his feet and caught her, then pushed her back against the bench. "You're safe. You're okay."

She swallowed audibly, holding to his arms with such strength, he knew he would have five little bruises on each arm.

"Missy, trade places with me." He kept his eyes on Louise as Missy edged past him.

She slowly released her hold on him and he sat down in the middle of the seat, placing one arm around her shoulders. "Put your head here." He patted the spot on his arms where her head would rest. "I'll hold you so you can sleep."

She shook her head. "I'm not tired."

"Then you must be the only one here who isn't."

The others murmured agreement.

"I've a very soft shoulder," he said, hoping to tease her into relaxing.

She eyed the spot, then lifted her gaze to him. "I'm fine." The protest on her lips did not reach her eyes.

He cupped his hand over her cheek and drew her head down to his shoulder. "Now, that's not so bad, is it?"

He held her close with one arm about her shoulders. With the other, he grasped the leather strap so that she was held securely in his arms.

She resisted for a moment or two, then with a sigh that reminded him of a cat purring, she leaned into him and fell asleep.

Nate looked down at her, so peaceful, yet even in sleep, he detected signs of strain. He shifted his gaze to Missy.

"I'm worried about her," Missy whispered, which did nothing to alleviate Nate's concerns.

"I'll take care of her."

Missy nodded. "I know you will." She opened her mouth as if she meant to say more but glanced at the others in the coach and didn't speak.

Nate adjusted his position, getting as comfortable as possible, considering the way he sat. The stage jolted a bit and he held Louise steady. If only the trail would remain smooth for the next hour so she could sleep.

He no sooner thought it than the front wheels lurched

into a rut and unseated them all. He braced his feet and held on tight, keeping both himself and Louise planted.

"Oh," she groaned and pressed a palm to her bulging belly. Her eyes flew open and her gaze hit Nate's, full of surprise and fear. Then she pulled her stubbornness back into place. "I'm fine."

"Yup. Of course you are. No doubt enjoying this rough ride as much as the rest of us."

She had the good grace to look less defensive. "No more, no less than the others." She pushed aside his hand holding her in place.

"Did you have a good sleep?" he asked, keeping his voice so innocent that she frowned at him.

"Don't tease me. It's not kind."

Missy leaned forward, an innocent look on her face. "After all she's huge and uncomfortable. You should show her extra kindness."

"Missy, not you, too!" Louise blurted out.

Missy widened her eyes. "I don't know what you mean."

"You've been fussing at me since we left. Just like Nate."

He and Missy grinned at each other.

"I live for the day she'll see me as an adult," Missy said.

Nate replied, "I live for the day she'll say she appreciates my concern."

Miss Rolfe sighed. "She's fortunate to have you. I'd give anything for a man who looked at me the way you look at her."

Him? How did he look at her? He felt Louise's questioning gaze on him, but he couldn't meet her eyes. Not until he figured out what Miss Rolfe meant and could change it. But surely it was only the wishful thinking of a woman desperate to find a husband.

Slowly he brought his gaze to Louise, his eyes revealing nothing but denial.

She squinted at him long enough to make him want to blink, but he would not. If he looked at her in any fashion, it was only that he didn't want to see something bad happen to her before they reached the ranch. Partly because anything bad would mean a delay and he didn't have time to waste if he meant to buy himself a ranch before Christmas, and partly because, yes, he cared for her, for the sake of their shared past.

It was in his best interests in every way to keep her safe and able to travel every day. That's all it was.

Chapter Seven

Louise wanted to tell Nate she didn't need his tender care—she'd only accepted his help to get her away from Vic—but it had felt so good and safe to rest on his shoulder. What was the harm in relaxing in his arms for a little while?

By the time they stopped for the night, she was weary clear through and only too happy to let him lead her into the way station.

"This is where we spend the night," he said.

She looked around the long room mostly filled with a wooden table, a few cupboards and a stove. Through one door she could see a narrow cot in an equally narrow room. There were no other doors. No other rooms. "Where do we sleep?"

"We sleep on the floor." Nate sounded apologetic.

"I knew that." She'd read about those traveling by stagecoach. But somehow knowing it and being faced with it were two different things. "It will be fine."

"Then maybe you can stop squeezing my arm. My fingers are going numb."

"Okay."

"I still can't feel my fingers."

She looked at her hand. "Really? I told it to let go." But her fingers still gripped him so hard she knew she would leave permanent indents in his flesh.

He slowly pried her fingers open and held her hands, palms down so she couldn't latch on to him again.

"I'm fine," she said.

"I can see that. Do you want to sit?"

"I've been sitting all day."

"I know. Do you want to walk?"

She nodded. Why was she being so silly? To a large degree she had taken care of herself all her life. She'd lived in rough mining camps where accommodations were more primitive than this. She didn't need anyone to hold her hand. If it weren't for Vic's threats she wouldn't even have appealed to Nate in the first place. It had to be pregnancy doing this to her…making her needy and weepy.

No. She would not cry. Deep breaths. She had to take deep breaths to keep the tears at bay.

"Come." He pulled her outside into the cold air and held her by the shoulders. "Are you going to faint?"

"I'm fine." She swallowed twice. Fainting had not entered her mind, but tears were so close to the surface she tasted their salty brine in the back of her throat.

"Yeah, I know."

She chuckled at the droll tone of his voice.

"That's better. Now, if you'd boss me around, I'd feel even better."

She sputtered a protest. "I am not bossy."

"I know."

They both laughed.

"Are you feeling better now?" he asked.

She pretended to be huffy. "There was never anything wrong with me. I'm fi—"

"I know. You're fine. You are enjoying the journey. Just as you'll enjoy the food here and the nonexistent bed."

She turned away from him as her tears threatened to overflow. She'd give anything for a soft bed to rest on, but if everyone else slept on the floor, so would she. She shivered as a cold winter wind blasted around the corner. "Let's go inside."

He led her back, held the door open and followed her inside.

The driver and the man who ran the stopping place came in behind them.

"The temperature is falling tonight." The man hurried to the stove and threw in two chunks of wood. He was short and moved as if his boots were full of springs. "Stew's about ready. And bread fresh from the oven." He opened the door, and the aroma of freshly baked bread wrapped around Louise. How bad could things be when the man made his own bread?

Miss Rolfe sidled up to him. "You make bread? I'd say that makes you a rare gem."

The man blushed clear to his hairline. "Matter of survival, miss, and I ain't never found any of the passengers complained about being served it."

"My name is Rowena Rolfe. Miss Rowena Rolfe. And yours?"

The man turned to face the others who watched Miss Rolfe as if they'd paid for the entertainment. "Sorry, folks. I forgot my manners. I'm your host, Peace Lewis. Everybody just calls me Peace. Ain't that right, Dutch?" he asked of the stagecoach driver.

Dutch? Why had she not heard his name before now?

Dutch shed his big buffalo coat and parked on the bench on one side of the table. "That's right, Peace. And I've been counting the miles since noon hoping you'd have bread in the oven when we got here."

"Everyone, sit," Peace said. He grabbed a stack of tin plates from the cupboard and skirted Miss Rolfe.

When Nate and Louise sat down, she leaned over to whisper in his ear, "Miss Rolfe looks as if she's measuring the poor man for a wedding suit."

He grinned at her and nodded. "I doubt she can run fast enough to catch him."

Peace handed the plates around, then brought over the pot of stew. He placed the hot bread before them along with a big knife for cutting.

Louise glanced around the table. Everyone looked as eager as she felt to dig in.

Peace stood at the end of the table. "Folks, we're civilized out here, even if things might appear crude to your way of thinking. So we say grace before we eat." He bowed his head.

Louise jerked hers down. His reminder made her realize how quickly it was possible to forget her manners. She'd been ready to dig right in. Sometimes it was hard to remember to think about God. No wonder her faith was so small. She didn't have her own Bible, had always used Aunt Bea's or shared with someone else, but right here and now, with Peace Lewis praying over the food, his guests and the weather, one of the first things she decided to do when they reached civilization was purchase her own Bible.

"Amen," Peace intoned. "Now hand me your plates."

After the first taste of his stew, she didn't care what else the place lacked. The food was excellent. His bread would put many a woman's attempts to shame.

Miss Rolfe had chosen the place at the end of the table closest to Peace. She asked him question after question, and he politely answered, though it was evident to everyone that her interest made him twitch. Everyone, it seemed, but Miss Rolfe.

"I'll wash the dishes," she said as soon as the meal was done.

"Oh no, ma'am. You're my guests. You've paid for the meal and that includes the cleaning up." He grabbed a stack of dishes and backed away.

She followed, every eye in the place on her. Would she succeed in getting his interest or drive the poor man out into the cold?

Louise caught Nate's gaze on her and they smiled in shared amusement. But then she couldn't look away. It was as if he held her in his grasp, their thoughts as one, their wants the same. For a moment she could almost think her future was promising, see herself held in a pair of strong hands, feel an unbreakable bond.

Peace grunted and Louise freed herself from Nate's invisible hold and drew her attention back to Miss Rolfe and her determined pursuit.

Peace handed her a towel. "Very well. I'll permit you to dry the dishes, though I normally put them on the towel and let them dry by themselves."

Miss Rolfe almost snatched the towel from him and stood as close to his side as possible. Peace made sure it wasn't too close by putting the basin of water on the corner of the table and parking himself kitty-corner to his pursuer.

Mr. Adams brought a book out of his breast pocket. "I'm anxious to get back to my story."

Young Mr. Adams likewise pulled a book out of his breast pocket. "This is a story about the march of the North-West Mounted Police from Winnipeg to Fort Macleod. They faced and conquered tremendous odds. It's a thrilling story." He opened the book and was soon lost in the retelling of the adventure.

Missy had her book and turned to it.

Even Sam had a book.

Louise had not brought anything to read, not realizing there would be times she wished for something to while away the hours.

Peace noticed her sitting with nothing to do. "Ma'am, I have a supply of books. You're welcome to borrow one. Just send it back with Dutch when you're done." He opened a cupboard to reveal several dozen titles. "Invitation is open to everyone."

Louise eagerly went to select one. Having done so, she turned and plowed into Nate as he reached for a book.

He grunted as the air whooshed from his lungs.

"I'm so sorry. It seems I'm always causing you a problem." For some silly reason, the words caught in her throat and wobbled.

He clasped her shoulders and looked into her face as if searching every corner of her mind. "You are not a problem to me."

She told herself they were only words, perhaps for the benefit of those who couldn't help overhearing. Despite her arguments to the contrary, she believed him.

For the moment, she'd allow herself to be comforted by his admission.

She nodded, the book clutched to her chest.

He reached past her to get the title he'd chosen and they returned to the table to sit side by side.

She read the words and turned the pages, but couldn't have said what the story entailed. Her thoughts wouldn't settle. It was merely worry, she told herself, about getting to Eden Valley Ranch before the baby came. Concern for the safety of the little life she carried. But in a moment of honesty, she admitted that her predominant thought centered on Nate. Why was he being so nice to her? Treating her as if he really cared, when they both knew he was only doing this out of a sense of obligation to the Porters. Or at least that was the explanation she had given herself. He'd given none. Would he if she asked?

She turned another page. She'd soon bring another Porter into the world. She and Missy were this little one's only relatives. She'd do her best to raise the child, but she'd never had two parents and it was something she'd always dreamed of giving her child.

She swiped at her eyes. She would not cry. Hadn't she decided to trust when it was hard? *God, I'm trying to trust, trying to believe You will see me through the many decisions and problems I will encounter.*

She looked around the room, trying to find a diversion from her thoughts and emotions. Peace and Dutch played checkers with Miss Rolfe's avid attention.

"You win again," Dutch said and stretched.

Peace put the game pieces away. "Folks, it's time to bed down. There's bedding in this cupboard." He opened the doors, revealing stacks of woolen blankets but no pillows or mattresses.

I can do this. I'm young and strong and brave.

And heavy with child. And weary to the bone from bouncing and jolting.

"Hey, Dutch," Nate said. "Do you have buffalo robes in the stagecoach?"

"Surely do. You'll be needing them tomorrow if the temperature continues to drop."

"But they aren't being used tonight, are they?"

"Nope."

"Why not bring them in and let Louise—Mrs. Hawkins—sleep on them?"

Even as everyone turned to look at her, Louise hoped she was the only one to notice the way he hesitated over calling her Mrs. Hawkins.

"That's an excellent idea," Missy said as the others murmured agreement.

Louise shook her head. "That's not necessary."

But already Nate and Sam had left and returned with their arms loaded.

As Nate spread the furs on the side of the room where Peace indicated the women would sleep, Louise went to him. "This isn't necessary," she whispered. "I don't expect special treatment."

"It is necessary. I want to get you to Eden Valley safely."

Of course, it was all about him and his promise to get her there. He would take care of her to make sure she wasn't the cause for any delays in the trip.

"I don't plan to be a bother." She managed to keep her voice to a whisper despite the anger coiling inside her. Anger at herself even more than at him. Both of them had understood the terms of their agreement. A pretend marriage. Escape from Vic. Refuge at Eden Valley Ranch. That was all.

She swiped at her eyes, hoping Nate didn't notice her tears.

It was only her stupid emotions being tampered with by the knowledge she would soon be a mama.

And the fear of what lay ahead.

Nate wanted to bang his fist on his forehead. Why had he made that comment? Still, they both understood they'd entered a pretend marriage in order to get her safely to Eden Valley Ranch. Once there, he'd get on with his plans. And she'd get on with hers.

Which were? He didn't know. He had never asked what she meant to do. Not that he needed to. That was her business.

But he shouldn't have reminded her of the future. She'd been weepy all evening, tears so close to the surface he feared they'd spill over.

He looked at her, tempted to reach out and take her in his arms and apologize, but Peace erased any opportunity. "Men," he called out, "let's go outside to give the ladies privacy to prepare for the night."

Nate gladly grabbed his coat and joined the others in leaving. At least with the men and animals he didn't have to worry about saying the wrong thing and triggering tears.

He moseyed over to the barn to check on his horse. Sam had rubbed the animal down well and given him feed.

He stayed there, leaning on a gate. He could sleep in the barn with the animals. It might be more peaceful. But he wouldn't. Someone had to watch over Louise, whether she wanted it or not.

Archie Adams stepped into the barn. "Thinking of bedding down here, are you?"

Was it that obvious? "I guess not."

"Good, because your wife needs you now more than ever."

It felt awkward to have someone say she was his wife. "She's not usually like this."

"What do you mean?" Archie rested his arms on the top of the gate beside Nate.

"She's usually feisty." From what he remembered. "Now she's weepy. Seems the least little thing will bring on tears."

The two of them studied the horses for a moment.

Archie chuckled softly. "I remember when my wife was in the family way. She'd swing from happy to sad in the blink of an eye."

"Is that what it is?"

"I expect so."

"That's a relief." He hadn't acknowledged it but wondered if she somehow blamed him or regretted marrying him even if only temporarily.

"Just be patient with her. She'll be back to her old self soon."

"Soon?" His heart kicked into a gallop. Did the man see something Nate didn't? Not that it would be hard. Nate had no idea what to expect. Would there be signs when the baby was coming? What if it wanted to come before they reached the ranch? Would they have to stop? For how long? He could hardly breathe. Would she want to go on if the baby was born? Or stay in that spot?

Archie chuckled again and clapped him on the back.

"She won't be normal until the baby is born. Be patient," he said.

But Nate wouldn't likely be around by then. She'd be at Eden Valley Ranch and he'd be finding a man to buy himself a little bit of land.

"We can go in now," Peace called, and the men traipsed inside, keeping the lamp turned low. He had no problem distinguishing Louise on the pile of buffalo hides, wrapped to her chin in gray woolen blankets. Two smaller bodies lay on either side, as if the two other women sheltered her.

Archie signaled Nate to take the spot nearest the women. "You'll be able to hear her if she needs you," he whispered.

Before Peace turned out the lamp, Nate unrolled his blankets and stretched out. He was reasonably comfortable, and warm and dry. His muscles relaxed, but his mind refused to follow suit, which was odd. Sleep usually came readily, even when he shared quarters with men who snored, snorted and even a couple who yelled in their sleep.

But none of those sounds disturbed him near as much as the faint sighs coming from Louise's direction. He had no way of knowing for certain if they came from her. But he also had no assurance they didn't.

Missy was at her side. If Louise needed anything, she had only to tell her. Relieved by that thought, he drifted off.

He didn't know how long he slept or what wakened him, but he was wide-awake, his heartbeat pounding. He strained to hear whatever had roused him.

A groan from the other side of the room.

"Louise?" he whispered. "Is that you?"

He heard nothing but silence except for the men's snores.

"Louise, are you okay?" His whisper was a little louder.

"I'm fine." Despite her soft whisper, he heard a large dose of annoyance.

"I heard you groan."

"I'm fine. Go to sleep."

"You're sure?"

"Nate, go to sleep," Missy ordered.

"Go to sleep," Sam said.

"Please, let me sleep," Miss Rolfe murmured.

"Are you satisfied?" Louise almost growled the words.

"Sorry," Nate muttered. "I was only concerned."

No one replied. There was nothing he could do but go back to sleep.

The next morning, Peace rattled about at the stove. As soon as he was sure they were all awake, he shooed the men outside to allow the women to dress.

"Chores to do," he chirped as he hurried to the barn.

It was cold in the predawn morning, and the men, eager for the shelter of the barn, followed Peace and helped feed the animals.

They returned to the house, ate a hurried breakfast of fried potatoes and salt pork. Peace and Dutch went to hitch the animals to the stagecoach.

"It's cold out there," Dutch said when he returned, rubbing his hands together. "You'll be grateful for the buffalo robes today."

Miss Rolfe looked about the room. "Either Nate or Sam will have to ride. Won't they be awfully cold?" Before anyone could answer, she nodded as if she had solved the problem to her satisfaction. "I could stay behind.

Keep Peace company until the next stage." She smiled at him.

Peace's mouth fell open. He sputtered several times before he could get a word out. "Ma'am, that's not possible. It would be highly improper."

Miss Rolfe sighed. "I suppose so, but you can't blame a person for trying."

"If you say so."

Nate reckoned Peace had never been so anxious to see a stagecoach and its passengers depart.

"I'll get my horse." He started for the door, but Sam stopped him.

"I'll ride. You stay with your wife."

Nate grinned at Louise and mouthed the words *my wife*. She glowered at him, but he didn't care. He kind of liked having an excuse to keep an eye on her and she couldn't do a thing about it.

Chapter Eight

Louise had had it clear to the top of her head with Nate calling attention to her condition with his constant worry about her comfort. Like waking everyone last night with his question. Now everyone looked at her with interest or concern. No doubt they wondered if she'd delay their journey.

Nothing she said would ease their minds because they had only to look at her to know she wasn't long from having the baby. And if her size wasn't enough indication, she often pressed her hand to her belly before she could stop herself. But having Nate hover over her made her feel all prickly inside. Pretending he cared because she was his wife was even worse! It defied common decency.

She stepped outside and gasped as the cold air hit her lungs. Dutch helped the three women aboard while Nate and the two Mr. Adamses carried out the buffalo robes.

Miss Rolfe lowered herself to one seat. Louise grabbed Missy and pulled her down next to her on the cold leather seat beside Miss Rolfe.

Mr. Adams and then his son climbed in. Nate came

last. He tipped his head at Missy to signal her to let him sit in her place.

"Missy—" But before Louise could order her to stay where she was, the younger woman hopped over and sat facing her, a pleased smile on her lips.

Louise smiled back but only with her mouth.

Mr. Adams spread the buffalo robe over the three on that bench.

Nate unfolded the one he held and pulled the robe around the three of them. He let Miss Rolfe tuck it in about herself, but he turned to Louise. First, he pulled her shawl over her head and tightened it under her chin.

"Your head is like a chimney. All the heat goes out there unless you keep it covered."

Her gaze drilled his, warning him not to take his pretend-spouse role too literally.

He smiled, his blue eyes dancing.

He was enjoying this far too much.

He tucked the robe around her legs and shoulders. "That will keep you warm and cozy."

She couldn't move beneath the heavy buffalo hide. But he was right. She was warm and cozy, and felt safe and protected.

She was enjoying his attention far too much.

As the stagecoach rolled away, Miss Rolfe glanced back at the way station until it was out of sight, then she turned forward with a breathy sigh. "I wouldn't have really stayed."

No one replied. Louise stifled a laugh. She, for one, thought Rowena would have stayed without a second thought if given the least encouragement from Peace.

They traveled onward, their breath making wisps of fog in the cold air.

Miss Rolfe spoke again. "But he seems like an awfully nice man."

Beside her, Nate couldn't hold back a chuckle. "He did. But I suppose the reason he is so nice is due to the high morals that he lives out in everything he does."

Miss Rolfe nodded. "I think you are right."

Louise stared at Nate. Did he realize he had just condemned her and himself, as well, as immoral people who followed moral values when it suited them and flouted them when it didn't?

She could think of nothing more immoral than vowing before God without the intention of following through on those vows.

He seemed to know she studied him and turned to meet her gaze. Perhaps reading the confusion, shock and challenge in her eyes, his smile faded and he met her look with equal strength.

Finally, he blinked and his expression grew indifferent. "Are you warm enough?"

She shifted her gaze to the window but couldn't see any of the passing scenery, as the curtains had been lowered to keep out the cold. "I'm fine, thank you."

A sense of mischief urged her to turn the tables on him. She looked at him. "Are you warm enough? Comfortable enough? Did you get enough to eat? Did you sleep well?" She eased her arm from out of the warm covering and adjusted the scarf he had wound about his head. "There. You wouldn't want to lose heat out your chimney."

Missy giggled.

Miss Rolfe looked startled.

Mr. Adams grinned widely while his son watched with wide-eyed interest.

Nate looked at the curtained window. He sighed deeply

for several seconds. "You'll all have to excuse my wife. She's a little touchy. I understand it happens to ladies in her condition."

Missy laughed again, but the others sat back, wondering perhaps if Louise would let the comment pass.

She considered their reaction. Did they think she would get all defensive? Perhaps say something shocking or inappropriate? Well, she had no intention of providing them with entertainment. Not today. She extracted her arm from the warmth of the robes and patted Nate's shoulder. "Perhaps I am a little touchy. But I really have no need to be. You take such good care of me, don't you, dear?"

She felt him stiffen, then a grin spread over his face and he laughed.

"You can't blame me for being concerned, can you?" He grinned down at her and again tucked the covers tightly around her, as if to corral her, making it impossible for her to move.

Maybe he was hoping he could make her stop talking, too.

His gaze caught and held hers, and in his deep blue eyes, she read the truth behind his words. He was truly concerned.

She wished it could be because of her and not because of the need to get back to Edendale in time to talk to a man about a ranch.

Rather than face him and the truth in his gaze, she closed her eyes and rested her head on the side of the coach. Today the road seemed less rough. Or had she simply grown used to it? Either way, she was grateful. There'd been only one bump so far this morning and it had been a little one that barely budged her from the bench.

The covers cocooned her in warmth and she let her thoughts drift aimlessly.

Straight to the first time she had seen Nate.

Did he recall the day? Perhaps she'd ask him when they stopped. It would give them something to discuss besides her comfort.

They pulled in at the first way station to change horses. Despite the cold, Louise wanted to get out and stretch her legs. Otherwise, they cramped up something fierce.

It didn't surprise her that Nate clung to her side, his arm around her shoulders. He likely meant to steady her so she wouldn't trip and fall. She allowed it because having him close kept her warm.

She would admit no other reason.

"I remember the first time I saw you," she said.

"Yeah. Guess you were impressed, right?"

She jabbed her elbow in his ribs. "Where's your humility?"

"Don't think I had any at fourteen."

She nodded. "That's true. You and Gordie were daring each other to see who could jump the widest puddle. You made it across and Gordie ended up with his feet in the mud. What I remember the clearest is you standing there laughing at your poor friend."

"Guess you thought I was a braggart and a bully."

What she thought was he was strong and handsome and had the nicest laugh. Not that she'd tell him. "Were you?"

"Sometimes. But only because I envied Gordie having a ma and pa who cared so much for him."

She'd never realized that. "But you had your ma."

"And she did her best. I'm not faulting her. But she worked all day at someone else's house and came home too tired to do anything but sit." He shrugged. "I missed my pa. Guess I still do."

She squeezed his arm. "I miss mine, too."

"But yours is still alive."

"But he doesn't care enough to see me or want me with him." They exchanged infrequent letters. Nothing more.

She and Nate had stopped walking and faced each other. "I begged him to let me come home after Gordie died, but he refused."

"So I'm second choice?"

She wanted to say that it was no choice, that she'd acted out of pure desperation. But something about the look in his eyes and the tremor in his voice at the mention of his father wouldn't allow it. Besides, it would not be totally true. "I knew I could count on you." That was the whole truth. She knew, in the depths of her heart, that once he gave his word, he would keep it, no matter what.

His gaze searched hers, looking for hidden meaning, searching for a revealing clue. She knew the moment he realized she meant what she said. His eyes darkened and held hers like a vise. She wanted to turn away before he saw deeper, saw the things she didn't want anyone to know, wouldn't even admit to herself. How afraid she was of the future, how she'd care for a baby on her own. Where they would live. Whether anyone would ever care for her the way she longed to be cared for—in a way that would make them stick through thick and thin, and not walk away when something more convenient came up.

He cupped his leather-clad hand to her cheek. "You honor me with your trust."

Trust? She hadn't said she trusted him, only that she knew she could count on him. Of course, she understood how he would see it as the same thing. But in her mind it wasn't.

She knew she could count on him because he had an obligation to Gordie, to Gordie's parents and because he'd given his word.

But she didn't trust him to provide the kind of caring she wanted. He left when things got hard. Not only had she seen it when Gordie's parents had died, she'd seen it before when he'd walked away from challenges he considered beneath his interest. Like the time Jean Black had told a bothersome boy she was Nate's girlfriend. It wasn't true, but she had only wanted someone to make the boy leave her alone. Nate had simply looked at her, told her to stand on her own and then walked away.

Louise had been angry at the time. But now she wondered if she had been unfair in her assessment. Perhaps Jean did need to learn to stand up for herself.

But that wasn't the only time Nate had expected people to stand on their own and not expect help from him. He had not come for Gordie's funeral. Had not even sent a message of condolence. Louise figured it was because he couldn't face another loss in his life. It had been easier for him to stay away than face something difficult.

"Why didn't you come for Gordie's funeral?" she asked him now.

His hand remained on her cheek, soft and gentle and warm, but his shoulders sank almost imperceptibly. "I had been sent to move cattle and was gone until fall. That's when I learned the news. Seemed a little late to do anything. Besides, I planned to visit my ma in a few weeks."

"Would you have come and spoken to me if I hadn't run into you at the cemetery?"

It was her turn to look deep into his eyes and see the truth. And his uncertainty.

"I don't know." He spoke softly. "I tried so hard to get Gordie to break away from Vic, but I failed over and over."

Seeing his hurt, she slipped her mittened hand up to his face and cupped his cheek just as he did hers. "He would not listen to anyone when it came to Vic, so don't blame yourself."

"Maybe if I'd stayed."

"You left so you wouldn't have to witness Gordie's involvement with Vic?"

"Of course. Why else would I leave?"

She shrugged. She tried to break from his gaze, lest he read her thoughts. "I don't know. I never did."

He dropped his hand to his side. "You thought I went because it was easier than staying."

"Wasn't it?"

"I couldn't stand by and watch Gordie getting in deeper and deeper with Vic. I only wish I could have talked you into leaving, too, but when you married Gordie, I understood why you wouldn't. I hadn't realized you loved him."

"He was all I had left."

"What does that mean?"

But she never got a chance to answer his question. Dutch called them back to the coach. "Let's go, folks."

Truthfully, she'd never before been so glad to get back into the stagecoach. It saved her from answering the question. What did her words mean? Her mother was gone. Her father had sent her away. The Porters had died. Nate had left. The words meant she hadn't loved Gordie as more than a friend, but he was all she'd had left and she hadn't wanted to lose him.

There was no reason for Nate to know that.

Nate settled back with Louise at his side. She closed her eyes and slept. Or maybe only pretended to. What had she meant about marrying Gordie because he was all she had left? She made it sound as if she didn't love him, but he couldn't believe that. He'd seen them together and they were the best of friends.

But was that the same as love?

He didn't know. He was nothing but a cowboy who pretty much stayed to himself. Not that he was unfriendly or that he didn't enjoy the social gatherings at the ranch. But since Gordie, he'd never been close to anyone else. He knew too well that nothing lasted—not family, not friends, nothing. Not even marriage.

The miles passed. No one seemed inclined to make conversation, which suited him fine. Except it gave him far too much time to think. By the time they stopped for the night, he had made up his mind to talk to Louise about what she'd meant.

It was easier to plan to talk than to find a place and time for it to happen. The way station was small and not half as inviting as Peace's had been. The owner had whiskers down to his chest, soiled with chewing tobacco and other things.

Louise drew back as they entered the building, dark and dank with unpleasant odors.

"It's warm," Nate said.

She turned to him, her eyes wide. "It's...awful." She barely whispered the word.

He couldn't argue the point, but it was all they had for the night.

The whiskered man went to help Dutch with the horses while Archie and Gabe brought in the buffalo robes.

"For Mrs. Hawkins," Archie said.

Miss Rolfe looked ready to cry. "I wish I'd stayed with Peace."

No one corrected her. Likely they all wished the same thing.

None of them sat on the benches beside the greasy-looking table.

Dutch returned with the whiskered man at his heels. "Folks, this is Moses. He's our host for the night."

Dutch seemed comfortable with the accommodations, but clearly Louise was not. When Nate led her toward the table, she balked.

"I'd like to go for a walk, if that's okay."

Nate didn't know who she meant to ask permission from.

Dutch poured a cup of coffee from the blackened pot. The liquid was so thick it glugged from the spout.

Nate decided then and there he would not be drinking coffee.

Dutch sucked back some of the coffee and grimaced. "It's cold out there, but if you don't mind, I see no reason not to stretch your legs."

Louise didn't even wait for Nate; she walked out. He hurried after her.

She didn't stop until she reached the corral fence and leaned over it, gasping for air.

"Are you okay?" he asked, even though he knew what her answer would be. Maybe someday she'd change her answer.

"I'll be fine."

He smiled to himself. She'd varied her reply slightly.

His smile disappeared. "You aren't going to be sick, are you?"

She spun on him. "Of course not. What do you take me for? I can handle whatever this journey requires."

"Yes, ma'am. Of course you can."

"I just hope there aren't fleas." She made no indication that she might want to walk and he was content to stand near the barn, sheltered from the wind.

He reasoned that this was the opportunity he'd been waiting for and returned to their earlier conversation. "You didn't get a chance to answer my question before."

"Really? What question was that?"

He laughed, knowing she knew full well. "I wanted to know what you meant when you said Gordie was all you had left. Seems you gave it as the reason for marrying him."

She looked past him. "I always thought my mother had died. But Aunt Bea told me the truth. She'd left Pa and me. Only later did she die."

"I'm sorry." He lifted his hand, intending to pull her close, but the brittleness in her expression made him reconsider.

"Like I said, my pa didn't have time for me. Taking care of me interfered with looking for gold."

Nate thought the man might have something to answer for in putting his own pursuits ahead of his daughter's needs. Besides, if he'd but looked, he would have found the gold right before him—a daughter who longed for love and had so much of it to give. He couldn't say how he knew that but he did.

Louise continued, still staring into the distance. Slowly

her gaze came to his. "Like you, I found a family who cared when I discovered the Porters. And then they were killed."

Knowing they shared the same sorrowful loss, he pressed his hand to her shoulder.

"Then you left. There was only Gordie, Missy and I. I did what I thought would keep us together." Again her gaze drifted away. "Then Gordie died. What does a person do when there's nothing left?" The final words were harsh.

He placed both hands on her shoulders, his fingers clasped behind her neck. He wanted to point out she had him, the baby and Missy, but he understood the depths of her despair. He'd felt it, too, and decided to leave it behind. "You move on. That's all you can do. Make new plans. Seek a better future."

Her gaze bored into his. "That's what *you* do. I only want something to stay the same. No, that's not even what I want. I wish people could care enough to stay."

It was a pointed accusation. But he hadn't promised to stay. Only to get her safely to Eden Valley Ranch. That's all she'd asked. Surely it was all she wanted from him.

If she asked for more, would you agree?

He wanted to ignore the niggling voice in his head that asked that question but he couldn't.

He thought of the land he meant to buy, the work that would require him to be busy every daylight hour and more for more days than he cared to consider. He'd be gone from home much of the time. And as he'd told her, the cabin was far from adequate for a woman and baby.

He couldn't offer her what she wanted, even if she asked.

"Someday, Louise, you will find that kind of love."

She jerked from his grasp. "There's no way you can promise that."

There was one way...if he was the one to love her and be at her side. Just as he'd vowed before the preacher.

But was that something he could promise?

Chapter Nine

Louise had had enough of fresh air and exercise, even though she'd walked no farther than the corrals. Why had she told Nate she wanted someone to stay? And why had he said she'd find that kind of love? What a cruel promise. Yet it was one she wished would come true.

With someone like Nate?

She knew it wasn't possible. He meant to move on, make a fresh start, plan a new future. As he'd said, he put the past behind him and looked to the future. She wished she could do the same. It sounded so easy when he said it. But she seemed chained by the past—unfulfilled wishes and dreams, lost relationships and a deep ache that would not let her go.

Even though she hated to step inside the tiny cabin, rank with a thousand unpleasant odors, she had little choice and sucked in her last breath of fresh air before she crossed the threshold.

Missy and Rowena both wore pinched expressions. The two Adams men looked uncomfortable. Even Sam looked as if he'd prefer to be somewhere else. It wouldn't have surprised Louise if he insisted on sleeping in the barn, with some excuse about watching the animals.

Louise crossed the narrow space from door to table and sat beside Missy. Nate crowded in beside her.

Moses placed a big pot in the middle of the table and handed around tin bowls. "Supper time. Help yerselves."

Louise wasn't about to be the first to test the contents.

Dutch seemed to have no problem with the food and dished himself up a generous helping.

The smell was enticing despite the dirty surroundings.

"What is it?" Mr. Adams asked.

"Potage," Dutch said, then seeing the confusion on Mr. Adams's face, added, "French-Canadian habitant pea soup. Try some." He reached for Mr. Adams's bowl and filled it to the brim. One by one, he filled the other bowls. "Dig in."

Louise noticed there was no praying for the food here, though Moses crossed himself before he ate.

Louise drew in a deep breath to still her stomach and gingerly tested the soup. The second taste was much more generous. "This is extremely good."

Moses smiled. At least she thought he did. It was hard to tell through all the whiskers.

The others added their approval. After that, the group relaxed. A man who made food like that couldn't possibly be too bad.

That night, they slept on the floor again, the women in one corner, the men in the opposite one. Under a scratchy blanket, Louise curled up on the buffalo hides the men had brought in for her. She'd spread the furs enough to allow Missy and Rowena to share them, and the three women huddled together for warmth. She waited until the lamp was out and quiet settled over the room to look for

Nate. He was barely six feet away, close enough that if she needed anything, she had only to whisper his name. The thought comforted her. She sighed and slept.

The next morning, the men slipped outside to allow the women privacy. They hurried back inside shivering.

"It's awfully cold," the elder Mr. Adams said.

"Dutch is hitching up the horses," Nate explained when he saw Louise watching for the man to enter. "We better eat as quickly as we can."

"I have biscuits and syrup," Moses said, and he set the food before them.

Louise had barely swallowed the last of her food when Dutch returned. "I don't like the looks of the weather. Best we get moving."

He waited at the door.

Louise got to her feet, as did the others. They grabbed up their belongings and hurried outside.

Today, Louise welcomed Nate's attention as he tucked the robe around her, pulling the top over her shoulders.

"Are you warm enough?"

She smiled into his eyes. "I'll be fine." There wasn't anything to be done about the cold but stay under the covers and pray it didn't get worse. She lowered her voice to a whisper. "What if—" She couldn't voice the many what-ifs troubling her thoughts. What if it snowed? What if an axle broke and they were stranded without shelter? What if the baby decided to make this the day?

He brushed his gloved hand along her jaw. "Don't worry. Dutch is a good driver."

She nodded. If it wouldn't make her sound weak and needy, she would confess her other fears, knowing Nate would say something to ease them.

He tucked the robe around her again, though it hadn't

shifted, and sat with his shoulder pressed against her, sharing his body heat.

She wasn't about to complain.

The travelers were quiet as the stagecoach rattled along the trail.

When they rode over a bump, Louise felt a cramp clutch her stomach. She breathed against it and fought the urge to bend over. The spasm ended and she relaxed. But midmorning, another one squeezed her muscles. She feared it was more than just being jostled, more than just her body revolting against the ordeal she'd put it through. Was it the baby? But again it passed after a moment and she leaned back against Nate.

Hours later, when they stopped to change horses, Dutch did not allow more than enough time to hitch up the fresh team before he said they must be on their way. She'd barely got out to stretch her legs.

At the first stop in the afternoon, Nate turned to Louise. "You should stay inside this time."

"I can't."

"It's cold and the wind has come up."

"I can't. Really can't."

He finally understood her meaning and nodded. "Very well. But make it quick." He helped her down and escorted her across the yard, where he gave her some privacy.

"You weren't wrong," she said when she rejoined him. "The wind has a real bite to it." It also carried hard pellets of snow.

Nate rushed her back to the stagecoach and she didn't object, welcoming the protection of the thin walls. "Sit in the middle this time. I'll sit next to the window." Even with the heavy curtains down, a draft came through the opening and she gladly relinquished the spot.

But if she thought Nate meant to give her extra attention, she soon discovered he had other things on his mind. He lifted a corner of the curtain and watched outside.

"What's wrong?" she asked after several miles of this.

"Nothing. Just watching the weather."

She leaned closer and peered over his shoulder. Snow came down, thick and wind driven.

He glanced at her and shook his head.

She nodded, understanding he didn't want her to say anything and alarm the others. Her own concern was enough to deal with. She faced straight ahead, avoiding Missy's questioning stare, and pressed her palms to her round belly. She'd had no more cramps. That was good. But if they got stranded out in the open…

Now would be a good time to trust God. *Please get us safely to shelter.*

They stopped once more to change horses. The passengers took one look outside, saw the wind-driven snow and remained huddled inside, except for Louise. She had to exit the coach despite the cold. Again, she clung to Nate's hand as he sheltered her against his side across the yard.

When they returned to the coach, Sam tied the horse to the back of the wagon and climbed up beside Dutch.

Louise had been in the West all her life. She had experienced raging snowstorms. She knew Sam rode up there to help watch for the trail.

They had not gone far when the coach stopped and tipped as the men climbed down.

"No need for worry," Dutch called. "I'm only checking on the horses."

But when they didn't return to the seat, Louise knew

they were on the ground leading the animals through the snow. Her lungs grew so tight it made breathing difficult. She wished she could blame it on the cold but it was fear.

She again peered over Nate's shoulders into a solid white wall. She grabbed Nate's hand under the robe and squeezed hard.

He tried to smile but didn't succeed in hiding his worry.

She prayed as she had never prayed before, because never before had she been worried about so many others besides herself and her baby. She had no desire to freeze to death in the white fury. She meant to get to Eden Valley Ranch in time for Christmas and the safe arrival of her baby. After that, as Nate said, she would move on with her life. And stop trying to hold on to the past.

Please, God, guide us through this storm.

Nate wished he could be in two places at once—at the front helping guide the horses and in the stagecoach, making sure Louise was safe.

His fingers grew numb from the way she squeezed his hand. She had seen the storm, felt its fury when she left the stage. She had more reason than the others to fear being stranded.

Out of nowhere he remembered something he'd heard, that too much anxiety could bring on birth. Seemed being in a snowstorm might qualify as a source of anxiety, and if the grip of her hand meant anything, he figured she was plenty worried.

He tried to recall what he knew about the birth of babies. Very little. Ask him about a horse or cow about to give birth and he knew every warning sign. Such knowledge proved of little value under the present circumstances.

There was little he could do except pray.

Since working at Eden Valley Ranch, he had learned the value of prayer and turned his thoughts to asking God for help. *Our Father who art in Heaven, guide us safely to the way station. Keep Louise and the baby safe. And the others, too.*

The stage stopped moving. Were they stuck? Lost? He ached to join Dutch and Sam but couldn't bring himself to leave Louise's side. If they were lost or stuck, he wanted to be right there, helping her, protecting her.

Slowly the stage continued on. He tried not to imagine the men peering into the blinding snow, eyes crusted with frost, having to wipe ice from the horses' nostrils so they could breathe.

There was nothing he could do but continue to pray and hold Louise's hand, providing as much strength and comfort as he could.

The interior, already dim because the heavy curtains were down, grew even darker as the storm clouds shut out the sky.

Nate quit looking out the window. No need to see what he already knew—there was nothing to see but white. Looking only let in a cold draft.

Missy's eyes, about all that showed above the buffalo robe, were wide.

He wanted to assure her they were going to be okay, but apart from God's hand leading them to safety, he could not give such assurances.

Both Adams men had their eyes closed. Nate guessed they were praying.

He didn't have to look at Miss Rolfe. He knew she'd

We'd like to send you two free books from the series you are enjoying now. Your two books have a combined cover price of over $10, but are yours to keep absolutely FREE! We'll even send you two wonderful surprise gifts. You can't lose!

Each of your FREE books is filled with joy, faith and traditional values and women open their hearts to each other and join together on a spiri journey.

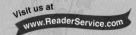

GET 2 FREE BOOKS!

HURRY!
Return this card today to get 2 FREE Books and 2 FREE Bonus Gifts!

◄ **DETACH AND MAIL CARD TODAY!** ▶

YES! Please send me the **2 FREE books** and **2 FREE gifts** for which I qualify. I understand that I am under no obligation to purchase anything further, as explained on the back of this card.

PLACE FREE GIFTS SEAL HERE

102/302 IDL GHQJ

FIRST NAME

LAST NAME

ADDRESS

APT.#

CITY

STATE/PROV.

ZIP/POSTAL CODE

be wishing she'd stayed with Peace despite the man's protests.

Aside from praying and observing his fellow travelers, Nate wondered about the cattle of the Eden Valley Ranch and the nearby ranches. Chances were, this storm would not go that far north, but then again, it might. Snowstorms could be deadly on cattle if they drifted too far or ran out of pasture.

Good thing Eddie Gardiner had the foresight to bring his animals down to lower pastures, which were less burdened by snow and, even more, Eddie put up hay to see the cattle through times when the snow was too deep for them to find grazing.

The afternoon passed slowly. Without being able to see sun or sky, he couldn't tell how late it was.

Louise's head dipped, then settled on his shoulder. Good, she'd finally fallen asleep. What better way to pass the uncertain hours until they reached shelter?

It took him a moment to realize the coach had stopped moving. He was instantly alert but managed not to move a muscle so he wouldn't disturb Louise.

Dutch opened the door. "You folks follow me."

Nate glanced past the driver. He could see nothing but white, swirling snow. The whine of the wind filled his ears.

Nate held Louise back as Dutch helped the others down, then he dropped to the ground and reached up to help her. He wrapped her heavy shawl about her and pulled her into the protection of his arms. She was his wife. He would not let her go until they found shelter. It might only be a pretend marriage, but at the moment, his responsibility felt very real.

His concern felt like more than responsibility—a

thought he didn't have the time or desire to analyze at the moment.

"Stay close," Dutch said, leading them into the snowstorm.

"Where are we going?" Miss Rolfe asked, her voice quivering.

Dutch, his head bent into the wind, didn't answer.

Nate continued to pray. *Could You please see us to safety?*

Through the snow a dark shape appeared before them. After another ten feet he made out a cabin. A door opened to reveal warmth and soft light, and one by one they hurried inside.

"Thank You, God," Nate said, still holding Louise in the shelter of his arms, close enough he felt her relieved sigh. He wanted to tell her that this was surely a sign God had not forgotten them.

He looked around. "Where's Sam?"

"He's still with the horses," Dutch said. "I'll help him and then be back. By the way, meet Dusty. He's an old cowpoke." He introduced the leather-faced older man who lived there. His eyes were faded blue as if a hot sun had soaked away the color, and his thinning blond hair hung raggedly to his shoulders. Still, for Dutch and the rest of them he was a welcome sight, and so was his home. "Dusty, my man, I have never been so glad to recognize the tree at the side of the road in all my life. I knew where I was when I saw it. Almost ran into it." He left them in Dusty's care and went out to tend to the horses.

"I expect you're all cold to the gills," Dusty said. "Why don't you step up to my stove and warm yourselves while I make some fresh tea."

"Tea has never sounded more welcome," Archie said. He introduced himself and the others.

They needed no second invitation to stand by the stove. Soon they began to shed their mittens and scarves, and then their heavier outerwear.

Except for Louise, who huddled by the fire, her shawl drawn close.

"Louise, is something wrong?" Nate asked.

She didn't even look at him, but worse, she didn't object to what she called his fussing.

He glanced toward Missy, seeing his concern reflected in her eyes.

Louise sucked in a deep breath and shook her shawl from her shoulders, holding it in the crook of her arms. "I'm quite fine, thank you. But that cup of tea will be most welcome."

He'd never been so glad to hear her say she was fine.

Nor so uncertain it was true.

Dusty served tea in a big blue enamel pot that Nate discovered, at first taste, had recently been use to boil coffee in, giving the tea a most unusual taste.

Sam and Dutch returned, shaking snow from their clothes.

"We won't be going anywhere until this lets up," Dutch announced. "Sure hope it doesn't turn into a three-dayer."

Nate stared out the window at the darkening sky. Out here, he knew snowstorms often lasted three days. He hoped this one didn't. Taking the stagecoach had already slowed his journey a good two days. Add three days due to the storm and he'd be in danger of missing the mountain man.

He had no intention of losing his chance to buy that land. Surely they were far enough away from Rocky

Creek that Vic wouldn't follow them. Besides, would the man even want to leave the comfort of home to venture into the trials of winter travel?

So that left Nate with the option of leaving Louise and Missy to complete the trip on their own while he made up for lost time on his fast horse.

He stayed at the window even though there was nothing to see. For some odd reason, he didn't want Louise to see the expression on his face and perhaps read his determination.

Chapter Ten

Louise watched Nate, tension in the set of his shoulders. There was nothing to see out the window. What was he thinking? Whatever it was, how would it affect her? Dutch had suggested they might be stranded three days. No doubt that weighed heavily on Nate's mind. Would he leave them at the first opportunity?

She shivered at the thought. At least if anyone noticed, they wouldn't think it odd. They had all been chilled to the bone before they reached this stopping house.

She'd meant to pray through the hours of their afternoon travel in the blinding snow. After all, she had much reason to call upon God, to seek His help and trust He'd answer. Not the least of which was the baby kicking at her ribs.

But to her surprise and annoyance, she'd fallen asleep. If her position when she'd wakened meant anything, she'd spent the afternoon practically curled in Nate's lap.

No reason she should be embarrassed. He was, after all, her husband.

She almost laughed at the presumption of her thoughts. Still half asleep and completely confused by her feelings of safety and security in his arms, she'd stood by the stove unfocused and distant until Nate's concern had jerked her to attention.

Then she'd been foolish enough to agree to a cup of tea.

She forced herself not to grimace as she swallowed another mouthful. It was wet and warm. That was the best she could say about it.

With a barely audible sigh, Nate turned from the window and sat at Louise's side, his hands around the cup of tea Dusty had handed him before he joined them at the table.

Dusty perched beside Missy, crowding to her side, though perhaps it was unintentional as the bench was not wide. He turned to Missy. "You're a pretty little thing. Did you know that?"

Missy gave the man a look that would have discouraged anyone with half a brain. "So I've been told." Ice dripped from every word.

"Can I get you sugar for your tea?" He'd offered none to the others.

"I don't care for sugar, thanks."

Dusty edged closer, though there was wasn't enough room to insert a knife between them to start with.

Louise scowled at the man. His face looked like weathered leather, full of deep wrinkles. And he was old enough to be Missy's father twice over.

If he wanted to pay attention to a lady, he should bother Rowena. She wanted a man.

Dusty leaned against Missy.

She scowled at the man, but he paid her no mind.

"Let me out," Louise said, forcing Nate to stand so she could slip from the bench. She marched to the other side of the table and jammed her fists on her hips. "I'd like to sit beside my sister-in-law," she announced, not caring that everyone stared at her.

Miss Rolfe nodded.

Louise accepted it as encouragement and tapped her foot.

Dusty ignored her.

Louise poked him on the shoulder. "Would you please move?"

He merely spared her a brief glance full of stubborn denial.

Nate took a step that brought him to Dusty's side. "The lady asked you to move." There was no mistaking the challenge in his words.

Slowly Dusty swiveled his head toward Nate. "Don't seem like it's any of your business."

Nate gave him a feral smile. "Considering she's my wife, I think it's completely my business."

The two men stared at each other, the moment crackling with tension.

Then Dusty jerked to his feet. "Have it your way. After all, you're guests of the company that pays my wages." Each word dripped with resentment. He stomped to the stove and began banging pots and pans, making it impossible for the others to carry on a conversation.

Louise settled in beside Missy, and Nate sat back down.

"You don't have to take care of me," Missy said.

"I know." Louise realized she hadn't been giving Missy much thought for the past couple of days, occupied, as she was with her own concerns. From now on, though, she'd pay her more attention.

She lifted her gaze to Nate's. He grinned widely. She couldn't think what he found so amusing. Unless…

Did he think she'd sprung to Missy's defense too readily?

Well, little he knew.

His smile fled and his eyebrows went up as if he'd read her thoughts. "It's nice to see your concern for Missy," he murmured, then got up and returned to the window.

She'd judged him wrongly. He wasn't mocking her; he was complimenting her. What was the matter with her? He'd been nothing but kind and helpful on this journey. But something about the way he looked out the window put her nerves on edge. Somehow she knew—or thought she did—that he regretted having agreed to marry and accompany her. It had slowed him down.

She went to his side. "You're worried about the storm, aren't you?"

"We're warm and safe for the night."

"You don't have to stay with us any longer. Missy and I can make the rest of the trip on our own." She kept her voice low, though she doubted anyone could overhear her with Dusty's racket.

"I hope you're not suggesting I go out in this." Nate didn't take his eyes from the darkened window.

"Of course not, but when it's safe to leave, don't worry about me…us."

"We might not be leaving anytime soon if this storm doesn't let up." His voice had deepened with what she took as disappointment or worry.

"I'm sorry."

He shrugged. "You're not responsible for the weather."

Maybe not for the weather but the delay.

Short of apologizing again, there seemed nothing more to say and she returned to the bench.

Dusty set a pot in the middle of the table and added a stack of plates and spoons. "Dig in if you're hungry."

She was, but the stew had an unpleasant odor. The others ate as if it was okay, but after one mouthful, she couldn't eat more.

The evening stretched before them. Louise took out her book and started to read, grateful Peace had lent both her and Nate a book. She sat at one side of Missy, Rowena on the other, making it impossible for Dusty to get close to her.

Nate sat at Louise's other side, also reading, as were the others, except for Dusty, who prowled from one side of the narrow room to the other, muttering under his breath, making it hard to relax. Nate, she noticed, would turn one page and then watch Dusty go back and forth.

Louise inched closer to Nate, though they were already crowded on the narrow bench. If Dusty grew violent or even just belligerent, she wanted to be where she knew she would be protected—next to her husband.

She almost laughed at the thought.

Nate must have heard or felt her capping her humor as he looked at her, a question in his eyes.

She shook her head. He'd never understand even if she could explain without sounding like an absolute idiot.

He tipped his head toward Dusty and raised his eyebrows. She knew he had the same concern she did as to the man's mental condition.

With a sound of half growl, half exasperation, Dusty opened the door, letting cold and snow race across the room.

Dutch looked up from his book. "What are you doing? Close the door before we freeze."

Dusty ignored the order and bellowed, "Weasel, where are ya?"

Louise and Nate stared at the man, then turned to Dutch for explanation.

"That's his dog," Dutch said, then spoke again to Dusty. "Do you think the dog isn't smart enough to find shelter? He won't come running to you in this weather if he has a lick of sense."

Dusty bellowed again, "Weasel, get in here." Then he slammed the door. "Confounded dog. Who needs him anyway?" He threw his bedding on the floor and lay down, pulling the covers to his nose. "I'm going to sleep." Within seconds he was snoring.

The others looked about in confusion. The room was too small to provide the women any privacy and no one suggested the men should go out into the storm.

Nate made the first move. "I'll turn the lamp down low and we'll turn our backs so you women can prepare for bed."

There didn't seem to be any other option. Louise had never shed a few layers and crawled between the covers so fast in her life.

"We're in bed," Louise said when both Missy and Rowena had finished their preparations.

Missy giggled, the sound muted by the blanket she pulled to her face. "That was mighty fast."

"I didn't trust someone not to look," Rowena answered.

"If I ever run a stagecoach business," Louise said with utmost conviction, though it wasn't something she'd ever consider doing, "I will provide separate sleeping quarters for the ladies, and some better-quality blankets."

"Amen to that," Rowena said.

Nate spread his blanket close to Louise. "I'll sleep nearest the women in case my wife needs me," he said to the whole group, but looked at Louise as he spoke.

She thanked him with a grateful smile. With Nate so close, Dusty would not be able to bother Missy, who crowded to her side.

"Time for you three to turn your backs," Nate ordered, and turned out the lamp to ensure further privacy. The thud of boots and rustle of covers signaled the men retiring.

In the tiny room, the women were crowded into one corner and the men were equally crowded and but a few feet away. But Louise felt safe and warm knowing Nate was within reach. Even the whine and wail of the wind and the rattle of the snow against the walls did not keep her awake.

It felt like the middle of the night when a noise startled her from her sleep.

She made out the dark shape of a man bent over the table and then the lamp glowed yellow and harsh in the darkness. Dusty. What was he doing?

She reached out and found Nate's blankets. He took her hand and held it.

Dutch sat up, rubbing his eyes. "Dusty, you old coot. What are you doing?"

"Gotta find Weasel."

"I tell you that dog is safe and sound. He won't stir in the middle of the night no matter how loudly you call or how many threats you holler."

"It's almost morning."

"Too dark to be morning." The argument continued between the two men.

"It's dark because it's still storming."

Dutch groaned. "I don't care for delays."

Nate's grip grew firmer and Louise squeezed back. He didn't care for delays, either, but at least this one was weather related and, as he said, she couldn't blame herself. Nor could he blame her.

"Please, God, bring an end to the storm." She hadn't planned to pray aloud, but it seemed like the right thing to do at the moment.

"Amen," came from several directions.

"You could pray for my dog while you're at it," Dusty said, then slammed out of the cabin before anyone could stop him.

He'd taken the lamp with him, plunging them back into darkness.

"Go back to sleep," Dutch said with a yawn. "No point in getting up until it's light out unless Dusty returns with the lamp."

Nate still held Louise's hand and she wasn't going to be the one to pull away. It felt strangely good to be held, secure and reassuring, as well as a feeling she couldn't quite describe. If he didn't want the touch to continue, he had only to release her hand and she'd tuck it back under the covers.

But he didn't and she fell asleep wishing she could hold things this way forever.

Some time later the sound of stove lids rattling woke Louise. She opened her eyes. Dutch was putting wood in the stove and shaking the blue enamel pot. The aroma of coffee pushed away the remnants of sleep.

"I see you're awake." Nate sat on his rolled-up bedding. The Adams men and Sam held similar positions.

At Nate's words, all the men turned to look at her.

From the heat racing up her cheeks, she guessed they grew bright red.

Nate turned away. "We'll give you ladies some privacy." The five men lined up facing the wall.

The women hurriedly adjusted petticoats, stockings and dresses.

When they were done, the men returned to their activities.

"Dusty hasn't returned?" she asked.

Dutch grunted. "He's crazy to go out in a storm looking for a dog. My guess is the dog has more sense than old Dusty." He poured coffee for each of them.

Dutch was on his third cup and there was still no sign of Dusty. Or breakfast.

Louise's stomach growled loudly. She'd eaten nothing the night before and she was hungry. "Does anyone object to me finding something for our breakfast?"

She turned to Dutch. Seemed he was the only one who could give permission.

"You go right ahead."

"Dusty won't mind?"

Dutch shrugged. "He's not here to mind."

She rummaged through the cupboards and found a store of flour, cornmeal and oatmeal, as well as a few vegetables and a stack of canned goods. Surprisingly little for a man facing a Montana winter.

With an ease born of preparing meals most of her life, she mixed together a large batch of biscuits and after they were baked golden, served them with a jar of preserves that were so out of place with the rest of Dusty's supplies that she wondered if some woman friend had given it to him. The idea of Dusty with a woman friend gave her the shudders.

"That was wonderful," Rowena said. "Maybe you *should* run a stopping house."

Nate's eyebrows jerked toward his hairline.

Louise explained her comment.

Dutch considered her. "I believe there will come a time when accommodations such as you describe will be the norm. Though I wonder if the stages will continue to run. The Canadian Pacific Railway will soon bring passengers and freight across Canada from the East. And lines are coming from the East in the States, too." He sounded so morose, Louise wished she could assure him the railway wouldn't change anything. Trouble was, she knew it would.

Missy and Rowena helped clean the kitchen, then there was nothing more to do but wait for the storm to end.

Dutch reached for his heavy outerwear. "I'm going to look for that crazy Dusty."

"I'll help you." Nate slipped into his coat.

"Me, too." Sam followed suit.

Louise gripped her hands together in front of her. She wanted to beg Nate to stay inside. The storm had not abated one bit. It was impossible to see more than a foot ahead.

But she sat quietly as the three stepped outside and the door closed behind them.

"What if they don't come back?" Missy croaked.

"Think any of us can drive a stagecoach?" Louise looked about, hoping the others would know she spoke in jest.

But both Missy and Rowena looked worried and the Adams men shook their heads.

Louise turned to the door, a spasm clenching her stomach muscles.

Nate better come back. He'd promised to see her and the baby to Eden Valley Ranch.

Nate, Sam and Dutch went to the barn and stepped inside.

"Dusty," Dutch bellowed. The horses neighed but no human voice answered.

The three of them searched each stall but didn't find Dusty.

"Are there other outbuildings?" Nate asked.

"An old soddy," Dutch said. "But not much left of it."

"Should we look there?"

"I don't know that I could find my way to it in a storm and I don't fancy getting lost in this." The wind battered the walls of the barn.

"My sentiments exactly," Nate said, and Sam echoed agreement.

Nate perhaps had more reason than the other two to avoid foolish decisions. Louise and her baby depended on him. He'd given his word.

Last night, he'd held her hand until her fingers relaxed and her breathing deepened, signaling she'd fallen asleep again. Only then did he let go of her and reach over to tuck her arm under the covers. He'd been happy to offer her comfort and the promise of protection should Dusty do something strange—stranger than going out into a storm to look for a dog that, as Dutch said, likely had enough sense to find shelter and stay put until the storm ended.

Too bad his owner didn't have the same healthy sense of self-preservation.

But Nate did. "Let's return to the house."

They tromped through the snow, squinting into the

swirling powder. Nate knew how easy it was to grow disorientated in such a storm. He only hoped Dusty had found shelter someplace.

Louise rushed to him as he stepped inside the house. "You're back. I was afraid—" She didn't finish but helped him out of his snow-covered coat and scarf, and draped them next to the stove to dry.

"Any sign of Dusty?" Archie asked.

"No, but we only went as far as the barn. We decided we couldn't risk getting lost out there." Nate watched Louise. Her hands fluttered as if she wanted something but couldn't remember what.

He caught her hands and pulled her close. "We'll stay here until it's safe to move on."

She nodded and edged closer.

He touched her chin. "I'll make sure you're safe." It seemed to be what she wanted to hear, because she nodded and the worry fled from her eyes.

He led her to the table and they sat down. Soon the others gathered around. Rowena poured them coffee.

Dutch chuckled, bringing all eyes toward him. "I know we're stranded here until this storm passes and maybe to some of you, it seems primitive. But I gotta tell you, I've endured far worse. Worse surroundings. Worse company. One time I was holed up for three days with an old miner who only opened his mouth to spit 'baccy juice." He shuddered, as did Louise, who was still sitting close enough to Nate that he felt her every breath.

He kind of liked knowing she wanted to be so close, even if it might only be because she feared the storm.

Dutch nodded sagely. "I've hated chewing tobacco ever since."

That brought a chuckle from everyone.

Sam leaned forward on his elbows. "That reminds me of the time I got stranded in a storm. I might have been willing to trade places with you, Dutch."

Dutch snorted. "I doubt it."

"I got stuck in a house with a preacher and his maiden sister. The preacher wasn't too bad, but the sister—" He shuddered. "Any of you ever hear of a woman who was a man hater?" He didn't wait for an answer. "This one was. I was only there one day and overnight, but I have never been so happy to ride out in breath-freezing cold in my life." He rolled his head back and forth as if trying to erase the memory.

Miss Rolfe wasn't about to let him stop there. "What did she do?"

Sam made a great show of drawing back. He held up his hands. "Please, I'd rather forget."

"Well, I want to know," Miss Rolfe insisted.

"Me, too," Missy said.

Beside Nate, Louise laughed softly. "He's making it up. Stringing us all along."

Sam shook his head. "I'm not. It was awful, I tell you. She kept ordering me to sit up straight." He jerked to rigid attention to illustrate. "Square my shoulders." He did. "Mind my manners. 'Please, ma'am' and 'Thank you so much.'"

"That's not so bad," Miss Rolfe said. "No reason to complain."

"You weren't there. If I stood up, she told me to sit down. If I opened a book, she pointed out I held it wrong. Shoot, she even complained that I closed it wrong. Too loudly." He illustrated the right way to close a book by slowly bringing his palms together.

As he continued, he soon had them all laughing at the fussiness of his hostess.

A lull followed his story. Louise turned her face toward Nate. "You must have had some exciting experiences while out cowboying. Tell us about them."

Nate thought of a storm he'd been in a couple years ago. "Me and three other cowboys got stranded in the open for two days and a night. In a storm that sounded like it came from the depths and felt like it came right off the North Pole."

Louise's eyes widened and she reached for his hand. Was it as natural to her as it felt, he wondered, or did she do it on purpose to convince the others they were truly married? But why would she care what they thought? Except for Missy, they would likely never see any of them again after this trip.

"What happened?" Louise asked.

"One by one we perished."

She blinked, gave a mirthless laugh, then flicked her hand against his shoulder. "You did not."

The others laughed.

Missy leaned forward. "Tell us how you survived."

He brought his gaze from Louise back to those around the table. "We were smart enough to pull down a bunch of willow branches to form a canopy. Then we banked up snow until we had a snug little cave. We weren't exactly warm, but we survived with all our fingers and toes."

"It sounds so exciting," Gabe said. "Like the North-West Mounted Police crossing the country. They encountered snowstorms, thunderstorms that stampeded their horses. They ran out of supplies, couldn't find water and yet they persevered and set up the fort where we are headed. I can't wait to see Fort Macleod."

Nate decided he wouldn't inform the young Adams that the fort was not as glamorous as he might expect.

Gabe proved to be a good storyteller and continued with tales of the Mounties' trek west and then turned to stories about the railway that was meant to unite the eastern colonies with the West.

"Seeing as Dusty isn't back, should I make some dinner?" Louise asked during a break in the conversation.

The door rattled and they all turned toward the sound. But no one came in.

"It was only the wind," Dutch said. "I surely wouldn't mind something to eat."

Louise bustled about the kitchen and soon a savory smell filled the room. The group continued to share tales as Louise served up the vegetable soup she'd managed to concoct.

"You're an excellent cook, Mrs. Hawkins," Archie said after he'd cleaned his bowl. "Nate here is a privileged fellow."

"Thank you. I hope he remembers it." She nudged Nate in the ribs.

He grinned at her. "I will."

She tore her gaze away and grabbed up the used dishes.

Missy and Miss Rolfe hurried to help wash them, and in a few minutes returned to the table.

"What about you, Miss Rolfe?" Sam said, bringing their attention back to storytelling. "Tell us about yourself."

She sighed softly. "This is the biggest adventure I've ever been on. My mother passed on when I was fourteen and I stayed home and ran my father's house." She worried a fingertip. "He began to forget things about five years ago. It got worse and worse so he couldn't remember ordinary things. Like whether to put sugar or flour in his tea. I couldn't leave him alone for the final two years of his life. He passed on last winter. It's taken me that long to decide to do something different with my life."

Archie smiled. "Good for you—both for caring for your father in difficult circumstances and being brave enough to take hold of life with such courage."

"Why, thank you. But you and your son are moving on, too, it seems."

Mr. Adams nodded, his expression sober. "My wife died of consumption a year ago."

"I'm sorry," Miss Rolfe said.

The others murmured sympathy.

Archie looked around the table. "This is about as much adventure as I care for, though I'm excited about starting a new business and a new life."

Nate thought of how many of them were hoping for a new life. "My wife's father raised her in a mining camp. Louise, you must have seen some strange things there."

She laughed. "There were plenty of odd characters." Her gaze went to the door as if the thought of odd characters made her think of Dusty. "Guess the one that impressed me most as a child was the man who slept beside his donkey."

Nate didn't find that unusual; he knew plenty of cowboys who spread their bedroll close to their horse at night.

"Maybe it would be more accurate to say the donkey slept beside him," she said.

"What does that mean?" Missy asked.

Louise lifted her hand as if to indicate it was nothing. "Just that the donkey went inside the man's house and slept on the bed with him."

Stunned disbelief turned her listeners silent for a moment, then Miss Rolfe said, "*Eww*, that's awful."

Nate wondered if it was true or just a good story.

"I think the man was a little touched." Louise tapped her forehead to indicate what she meant. "Last I recall hearing of him, he'd taken his donkey and an ax into the woods."

"Louise, what a dreadful story."

She shrugged. "People do strange things when they lose their minds, sometimes without any warning."

A scratching came from the outer side of the door, along with a sound—half growl, have moan.

Missy's eyes were so wide, the whites were visible. She grabbed Louise's hand. "Dusty's come back. Maybe with an ax."

All eight people sat motionless at the table, staring at the door where the noise continued.

Chapter Eleven

Louise grabbed Nate's hand and squeezed it so hard she knew she had to be hurting him, but no amount of telling herself to ease up on her grip persuaded her to do so.

Dusty was not a man to mess with. She'd seen the wild look in his eyes last night when he went out into the storm.

In fact, holding Nate's hand did not provide near as much comfort as she needed and she edged closer until he had little choice but to put his arm around her shoulders.

All of them stared at the door. No one made any sign of answering the continued thumping and scratching. Dusty must surely have lost his mind to stand out there making such strange noises.

Louise forgot how to breathe. She tried to disappear into Nate's side but was far too large to hide behind anyone.

Dutch was the first to move. "Best see who it is. Or what."

"Don't open the door," Rowena begged, giving voice to the fear Louise shared. "You might regret it."

Dutch detoured to the stove and grabbed a hunk of firewood, then reached for the door handle.

Sam and Gabe likewise grabbed pieces of wood and stood at his back, ready to defend the place. Archie stood behind the other three, holding the poker.

When Nate tried to join them, Louise held on to him so tightly he couldn't get to his feet.

"Guess I'll stay here," he said, settling back down, but she felt his muscles coiled and knew he would spring up at the first sign of crisis.

Slowly Dutch reached for the door.

Louise sucked in air and held it. Her eyes were riveted to the door.

Dutch turned the knob and cracked the door open, but it flung from his hands and a huge, shaggy dog with an overly large head burst in. He half dragged, half led Dusty behind him. Both were snow covered.

"Weasel." Dutch dropped his piece of wood. "And Dusty. Where have you two been?"

Dutch and Sam grabbed Dusty and helped him to his feet and half carried him to the stove. As if relieved of his duty, the dog shook himself, spraying snow across the room.

Archie continued to stand guard with the poker.

Louise, too, maintained her alertness. She continued to stare at the man as they took off his snow-covered coat. He certainly didn't appear to be any threat. No ax dangled from his trembling hands. But she couldn't relax. No normal man went out in a storm. But then, she'd known from the beginning that Dusty wasn't normal. She tried to stop squeezing Nate's hand so hard, but contact with him was the only thing that helped her stay halfway calm.

Dutch seemed to be the only one who knew what to do.

"Let me see your hands." Dutch didn't wait for Dusty to obey but eased off the man's mittens and examined his fingers. "Looks like they're okay. How about your feet?"

With no chair to sit on, Dutch pulled a log close to the stove and had Dusty sit. He unlaced the boots and eased them off the man's feet, along with the dirtiest socks she'd ever seen.

Dutch sat back on his heels. "Dusty, I think the layers of dirt on your feet saved them."

"No," Dusty croaked. "'Twas Weasel."

Dutch filled a cup with coffee and handed it to the near-frozen man. "Now take it easy."

Dusty cradled his hands about the cup and leaned over it, as if he'd been longing for the aroma. Then he lifted the cup to his lips and drank back several swallows. "Ah, that hits the spot."

Dutch stood over him. "You gonna tell us what happened?"

Dusty sighed. His expression calmed and he looked less likely to turn into a raving madman.

Louise's nerves stopped twanging and she relaxed her grip on Nate's hand. He pulled away from her grasp and curled and uncurled his fingers as if restoring circulation.

She quirked one eyebrow at him. "Did I hurt you?" She couldn't keep the teasing tone from her voice.

"The feeling is starting to return. Lady, you could maim someone with that grip of yours."

She chuckled. "I'll keep that in mind should I ever need to do so."

He laughed, too, and pulled her a little closer. "Let's hope you never have such an occasion." Both of them were teasing, yet his gaze was not one of amusement. He looked deep into her eyes, saying things she could only dream of hearing and likely only imagined now. *I'm glad you're safe. I want to take care of you.*

She forced herself to turn from his look. They knew this was a temporary arrangement. He had plans. He didn't have time for a wife and child.

That was okay. She had plans, too. Plans that involved making a life for herself, her child and Missy, and staying as far away from Vic Hector as was humanly possible.

Dusty grunted. "Weasel, you crazy dog."

Louise's attention returned to their host, though he really didn't fill the bill of host. She could see him more readily in the role of dungeon keeper. The thought made her shiver.

"I found him in that old soddy. Kind of figured I would. He likes to hunt vermin in there." He drained his cup and held it out for Dutch to refill. He savored several more mouthfuls, then held it to the dog who lapped the liquid eagerly.

When it appeared he'd forgotten his story, Dutch prodded him. "Did you stay there till now?"

Dusty scowled at his dog who lay before the stove, his eyes never leaving Dusty's face. "Do you think I could persuade that crazy dog to come back with me to the house? No sirree. He blocked the door and growled at me. I have a good mind to teach him to obey me."

Louise gasped before she could think better of it.

Nate pressed his hand to her shoulder and whispered in her ear, "I don't think he'd ever lay a finger on the dog and would likely not look kindly on anyone else doing so." His breath warmed her cheek. "That's poor old Dusty's way of showing affection."

She turned to put her mouth to Nate's ear. "Then small wonder he's not married."

Their gazes caught and held. What she saw in his blue eyes made her heart swoop and soar in a way she'd never felt before. She tried to pull away but couldn't find the strength, as if she'd exerted the last of her store in squeezing his hand so hard.

"Then all of a sudden—" Dusty's voice ended the moment between them, making her jerk her attention in his direction.

It had only been her vivid imagination that made her so foolish. Nate was kind and thoughtful and everything she might want in a husband, but that wasn't part of their agreement.

She had to admit, however, she was finding it harder and harder to remember the specifics of their pretend-marriage agreement.

"Weasel barked to get out of the soddy. I said, 'I'm not going,' but he wouldn't shut up. Only way I could get any peace was to follow him." Dusty lowered his head and his voice fell. "Guess I was in worse shape than I realized. Couldn't hardly stand up. Weasel guided me here." He nudged the dog with his bare foot. "I suppose I should thank him for taking care of me before I froze to death."

Louise understood the rough tone hid his true feelings.

Dusty reached for his socks and worn boots. "Guess I'll see what I can build for supper."

Louise vowed she would not eat a thing that man prepared. She suspected a person could die from contact with those dirty socks. Even indirect contact.

"Listen." Dutch held up his hand to signal quiet.

Louise strained for a sound at the door but didn't hear a thing.

Not even the wind?

Nate dropped his arm from around her shoulders and

rushed to the window. He scraped away enough frost to see outside. "The storm has stopped. The road is about blown bare. The snow is heaped up around the buildings."

Louise hurried over to his side. "It's so white and beautiful."

The others crowded around, and she stepped back to give them space, as did Nate. She smiled at him. "Now we can resume our journey." Hopefully, the delay had not been long enough to make him miss his meeting.

Dutch turned to face his passengers. "If this is the end of the storm, we'll leave at dawn tomorrow and try and make up some time."

The baby kicked in happy delight and Louise's stomach muscles responded with a squeeze.

The next morning, she wakened to Dutch calling, "Let's get ready, folks."

The men were already up and dressed.

"We'll give you some privacy." Nate smiled down at Louise. "So you can make yourselves presentable."

She pulled the covers to her chin until he strode from the door, then sat up and turned to Missy. "Am I a mess?"

Missy grinned. "Your hair is all tangled up. Didn't you braid it before you went to bed?"

Louise reached over her shoulder and found no braid. "It must have come loose." She fixed her clothes, then searched her bag for a brush.

"Let me." Missy took the brush and Louise turned around to let her tackle her hair. The brush caught on one tangle and then another.

"I think I'm grateful old Dusty doesn't have a mirror in his house."

"I'll soon have you looking your best for Nate."

Louise opened her mouth to protest. But what could

she say? Missy believed the marriage to be real. For both their sakes and the baby's, it seemed best to keep up the pretense until they reached Eden Valley Ranch where Vic, if he should follow her, would not be allowed to bother either of them.

Besides, for some silly reason, she wanted Nate to see her looking her best. Considering she was as huge as a circus tent and awkward, to boot, about all she could do to improve her looks was fashion her hair attractively.

She sat as Missy brushed and braided, then wrapped the braid into a coronet.

"That's beautiful." Rowena admired the hairdo.

Louise touched the braid. "It's a little fancy for stage-coach travel, don't you think?"

"Not at all," Missy assured her. "It looks nice and will keep your hair out of the way."

A secret part of Louise wondered if Nate would notice at all.

Again, a cramp gripped her stomach. It seemed to come every time she got excited. Good reason to remain calm, she told herself. She did not want to have this baby before they reached their destination.

The men waited outside what they deemed a suitable length before Nate headed for the house. Time to get on the road. They'd encounter some drifts that would slow them down, so the sooner they started, the better. He had almost reached the door when he saw the ladies through the window and stopped. His mouth went dry. His heart beat erratically. It was dusky out yet and the lamp glowed within the cabin, giving him a view of the occupants. Louise sat the table, her back to Missy as the young girl brushed Louise's long, light brown hair.

The brush rippled Louise's hair, filling it with static so it fanned about her head.

It wasn't as if he hadn't seen her hair many times before, especially when they were younger. He'd seen it streaming out behind her as she rode a horse, seen it tumbled about her head as she hung upside down from a tree branch, saw it curled up fancy at a church social. He'd even felt it blowing against his face as they rode double...before his ma forbid him to be so careless of her reputation. Ma should be proud of how he had done everything he could to protect her reputation as they made this journey north.

But seeing her hair now had been different. Being her husband made it so.

"Are they decent?" Archie called.

Nate jerked as if he'd been stabbed. He scrambled to think what the man meant. Slowly his brain began to function and he realized Archie wanted to know if the men could return inside.

"Yup." He wondered if anyone would notice his hoarseness.

He waited for the others to enter, needing the extra time to regain his composure. But when he entered, he saw Louise's braid coiled about her head, catching the lamplight at various angles so her hair was shades of golden brown and coffee color.

He had to force himself not to stare and fisted his hands at his sides to keep from reaching out to touch it.

He was grateful for the distraction provided by Dusty banging about at the stove.

Dutch shifted from one foot to the other. "This meal going to take long, Dusty?"

In reply, Dusty slammed a steaming pot on the table. "Eat."

Nate's wobbly legs took him to the table. Louise smiled up at him as he sat beside her. "Everything okay? You look a little strange."

"Everything is fine." But it wasn't. And he couldn't figure out why. Nothing had changed.

Yet everything was different.

He filled his bowl with whatever the gruel was Dusty served and ate every bit. He didn't taste a thing.

He might not be able to concentrate on his own actions but knew every movement Louise made. She took only a mouthful of the food and seemed to have trouble eating even that.

He'd ask if she was ill, but he knew what her response would be. He would simply keep a close eye on her throughout the day. Sam had already arranged to ride the horse again, so Nate would be in the coach beside her the whole time.

After the meal, they departed, settling into the stagecoach with sighs of relief.

"It's good to be on the road again," Archie said. "I wouldn't want to be stuck there for the winter."

"None of us would," Miss Rolfe said with such conviction, the others laughed. "He has to be the worst cook in the world."

"Certainly the worst I've ever encountered," Archie agreed.

Nate leaned back, content to have Louise at his side. But as the others compared bad-food stories, he felt her tense. She pressed her hands to her stomach. He was about to ask them to change the subject, when Miss Rolfe leaped to her feet and pushed aside the curtain on the window, just in time for her to be sick.

"So sorry." She wiped her mouth on her hankie.

A few minutes later, Missy did the same.

Nate's own stomach rolled and twisted. "What did that man serve us?"

Louise groaned. "Whatever it was, I don't like it."

He gripped her hand and tried not to think how such an upset would affect her in her condition.

Nate took slow, deep breaths, trying to settle his stomach as both Gabe and Archie got sick.

By the time they reached the first stop to change horses, the passengers tumbled from the coach and raced for the well. They each rinsed their mouths and drank deeply.

Louise had not been sick, but Nate could tell she was fighting it.

"Are you okay?" he asked, daring her ire.

"A little uncomfortable, but I doubt I'll be sick. I didn't eat a lot of Dusty's food."

"You were wise."

She caught his arm as he prepared to return to the coach. "How about you? You feeling ill?"

It would likely be more heroic to deny it, but his stomach continued to protest. He nodded.

"Perhaps it would be best to rid yourself of the spoiled food."

"Maybe." He hung back as she made her way to the stage. Then he made for the corrals and did as she suggested. She was right. It did help, as did the cold water.

Everyone was on board by the time he climbed inside.

"Better?" Louise whispered as he settled in beside her.

"Better."

Under the buffalo robe she found his hand and squeezed it.

He turned his palm to hers and intertwined his fingers with hers. Now he felt lots better.

The others soon leaned back and slept. He, too, felt exhausted from the stomach upset. But Louise was not comfortable. Several times she moaned, the sound captured inside her mouth, yet he heard it. Felt it. Her hand squeezed his. He knew from experience she had the strength to numb his fingers. Just as he knew she tried to hide the cramps in her stomach that made her lean forward.

"Maybe you should take your own advice." He rubbed the back of her neck.

"Maybe," was all she said.

By the time they stopped for the noon meal, he was really concerned.

"I'll be all right," she insisted. "Just give me a little time alone. I'll walk a bit."

He nodded and watched her walk around the barn out of sight. Missy started to follow her, but Nate called her back. "She needs her privacy."

"You're sure she's okay?"

"I hope so." They had a long way to go yet and being sick and uncomfortable would make the journey intolerable.

Chapter Twelve

Louise hurried out of sight around the barn, then bent over her knees and moaned. This could not be labor. Not now. Not here. She wanted the baby born on Christmas Day when it was due, and born at Eden Valley Ranch where they'd be safe and welcome. Not where his or her birth would cause a delay.

Besides, it seemed significant that the baby be born where she meant to start anew.

She would walk it out. It was the only thing she could think to do and she trod back and forth on the snowy trail. When no more cramps came, she let out a huge sigh. Maybe the pain was from the food, after all, and because she'd barely touched what Dusty served, she had not been as affected as the others.

She stopped walking and waited. Nothing. She smiled skyward. "Thank You, God."

Feeling as if she could face whatever the rest of the day handed her, she went to the stopping house. Missy and Nate waited at the door.

"Are you okay?" they asked in unison.

"I'm quite fine."

They joined the others around the table where biscuits and syrup waited for them. She glanced around for their host, not sure she could eat if he was anything like Dusty, but he was a tall, thin man, neatly groomed.

Dutch introduced him as John. "John used to be a lawyer."

"Indeed. Until I got weary of looking at criminals all day long. Out here I can enjoy my own company and a good book."

Louise decided the food was safe and took a biscuit. But she could barely get a mouthful down and, not wanting to start the cramps again, she wrapped the biscuit in her hankie and put it in her pocket to eat later.

Dutch was in a hurry to be on the road again. "We've a long afternoon before us," he said as he urged them to finish up and return to the stagecoach.

Louise was as anxious as Dutch to get going. Two more days to get to Fort Macleod, then the trip to the ranch—two more days, as far as she could tell. Nate had been a little vague on the details. Four days and she'd be able to relax.

When they had only gone a few miles, swaying back and forth in the stagecoach, the pains returned. But they were not regular, not close together. They couldn't be labor pains. It was only something she'd eaten. Except she felt no nausea. Only a deep, intense pain accompanied by an inner twisting. As if the baby wanted out.

Well, she thought with some annoyance. She wanted him or her out, too. Just not here and now. *You'll just have to wait, young one.*

The pain disappeared and she leaned her head back and eased air into her lungs in slow, steady breaths as she tried to remember everything she'd been told about birthing—which was surprisingly little. At Rocky Creek, she would have called the midwife. After she left home, she'd been counting on Mrs. Gardiner's help at the ranch.

She drifted into a troubled sleep filled with floating images of rolling wagon wheels, a barking dog named Weasel and Nate drifting in the distance, his hand stretched out to her, calling her name though the sound of it never quite reached her.

She jerked from her sleep with a pain that brought a cry from her lips. She arched her back against the pain, then, realizing everyone watched her, she sucked in air and forced herself to sink back into the seat. She tried to smile, but it felt more like a grimace. "Guess the food is still bothering me."

Mr. Adams gave her a steady look. "Ma'am, I don't believe it's from something you ate."

She looked hard at him, silently begging him to keep his opinion to himself.

Nate shot forward and peered into her face. "You're going to have a baby?"

She patted her bulging stomach. "What does this look like?" Ugh. Her belly tightened with another pain. She would not give in to it. She would not let the others see.

"You're going to have it now?" His voice had gone up several notes.

Missy leaned closer. "Louise, is that what's the matter?"

Louise closed her eyes. She just wanted all of them to go away and leave her alone to ride out the pain. Slowly it receded and she looked into Nate's cloudy blue eyes. "I am not going to have a baby now. Not until I get to Eden Valley Ranch." She tried another smile. It felt more natural. *No more contractions. Please. No more. Not for four days. Please, God.*

Nate studied her hard enough to make her want to look away from his gaze, which would no doubt give him more reason to wonder if she spoke the truth.

"Please, everyone, stop staring at me. I'm fine."

Mr. Adams shifted his gaze. Gabe turned back to his book. Rowena peeked out the curtain at the outdoors. But Missy and Nate continued to study her.

Then Missy slid her gaze to Nate. "Do you think she'd admit it if the baby is coming?"

Nate gave Missy his attention, which made it possible for Louise to relax.

"Nope. She's far too stubborn."

She poked a finger into his side. "I am not stubborn."

Missy and Nate continued to look at each other. "Yes, she is," they said together and smiled.

Louise snorted. "Aren't my husband and sister-in-law supposed to be on my side?"

"Oh, we are," Nate said. "As much as you'll let us." A challenge blared at her from his eyes.

"I'll let you know when I need help."

"Promise!" His eyes demanded so much from her. And right now she had nothing to give. All she wanted was to be left alone to wait for the next pain and to ride it to its conclusion.

"I promise." She closed her eyes and leaned back. After several minutes and no more contractions, she relaxed and let sleep claim her.

She had no idea how long it was till once more the pain yanked her awake with a gasp. She realized the coach no longer moved. They'd reached the way station where Dutch traded horses.

"I want to walk," she said, and Nate helped her down.

"Nate, can I talk to you?" Mr. Adams said.

"Missy, stay with her." Nate handed her off to Missy as if she needed a keeper and went over to speak to Mr. Adams.

The two of them walked away so she wasn't able to overhear what was said. Then the pair went to Dutch.

The way all three looked at her, she knew she was the topic of conversation. If they thought to leave her here at this desolate place with only a grumpy old man and a tiny wooden shack, they would have to reconsider.

"Let's go back," she said to Missy and they hurried over to climb in to the stagecoach. They'd have to drag her out if they figured to leave her behind.

The men returned and settled themselves. Dutch climbed to the driver's seat and hollered, *"Giddyap!"* They galloped along at a furious pace that had her clinging to Nate for stability.

"Was this your idea?" she managed to say through clenched teeth.

"I suggested he should hurry. He seems to have taken my words seriously."

"Why would you tell him that?" She guessed, but she wanted him to have to confess it was a mistake.

"Seems you might be glad to be at a stopping house before the baby is born."

"I'd be glad to be at Eden Valley Ranch."

She scowled at him and he scowled right back.

Then he chuckled. "Let's hope and pray one of us is right."

The stagecoach raced around a corner and she was thrown against him. He wrapped his arm about her shoulders and held her tight.

It felt good to be able to lean into his steady grasp and not be thrown from side to side. So good that she made no effort to pull away when the stage straightened. Another contraction came and she squeezed the life from his hand.

To his credit, he didn't mention it.

And then sleep, blessed sleep claimed her for a time.

She jerked awake to the most powerful contraction she'd had yet. As if someone had grabbed her insides and proceeded to wring them out like a wet dishrag. This one lasted longer than the previous ones.

She hoped it was false labor, but if it was, she did not want to think what the real thing felt like.

Nate seemed to know when the pain had passed. Maybe because she stopped squeezing his hand so hard.

"Okay?"

She nodded, even though there was nothing okay about any of this. The baby was supposed to wait until they reached Eden Valley Ranch. Now she'd be grateful to be at a stopping house. *Oh God, please let it be clean and warm.*

Nate had long since given up the hope Louise only suffered a digestive upset. Archie had made it clear that he recognized the symptoms.

"It might stop. Sometimes it does. But you best be prepared for your baby to be born soon."

His baby. Louise had made it crystal clear this was Gordie's baby. But Gordie wasn't here and Nate was. What's more, Nate was her legal husband, so, for now, it was best if everyone saw the baby as his.

He longed to flex his cramped fingers, but Louise held on to them like a lifeline. He wasn't about to take that from her. The latest pain had lasted a long time, though he supposed it was less than thirty seconds.

How long before they reached the next stopping house?

If Dutch had his way, it would be in record time. They rumbled along at a furious rate that half frightened him. An axle could snap on the rough ground. The stage could tip over on one of the corners.

But none of them fancied seeing a baby born in the cold, cramped quarters of the stagecoach. So no one complained about the fast pace.

Except for Louise, and even she had stopped saying anything.

He looked into her face, expecting she would be sleeping again, but her eyes were open and she regarded him with such desperation that he pressed a kiss to her forehead. "You'll be fine. I promise."

She nodded. "I know," she whispered, and turned her face into his chest, where she remained.

He held her close and rubbed her back as she was gripped by another pain. He didn't know what else he could do and felt so powerless it twisted his insides.

She slowly relaxed and he knew the pain had passed. Minutes later, he guessed by the way her head rolled that she'd fallen asleep, and he closed his eyes, resting his cheek on the top of her head.

Funny how all day he'd wanted to touch the braid in her hair and now he could. Her arms were under the robes, but her head was open to the cold and he pulled her shawl up from her shoulders and tucked it about her head, letting his fingers linger over her silky brown hair.

From outside he heard Dutch command the horses. "Whoa," he called.

The stage swayed back and forth, then grew motionless.

Dutch yanked the door open. "We're here."

Louise jerked awake and sat up.

No one moved. Nate realized they waited for Louise to exit first.

He slipped his arm from around her, pushed back the heavy robe and edged toward the door. He jumped down and reached up to help her.

Before her feet hit the ground, he swept her into his arms.

"Put me down," she ordered.

"When we get inside."

"I'm not a cripple."

He continued toward the stopping house.

She struggled, but he wouldn't release her. "I'm fine."

"No, you're not. You're about to have a baby."

"I'm sure it's just from bouncing around. This will settle down now we've stopped moving. You'll see."

They reached the door and he opened it and set her down. "I hope you're right, but Archie is the only one among us who seems to have any experience in this matter and he seemed quite certain your discomfort means the baby is coming."

She straightened her clothes. "I guess I'm the one to know."

The others trooped in, followed by their current host.

Dutch stepped forward to make the introductions. "This is Phil."

"Short for Philomena. Welcome."

Every eye turned toward the speaker.

"A woman," Missy squeaked.

"That's right." Phil laughed as if their surprise amused her.

"Consider yourselves smiled upon," Dutch said with a chuckle. "Phil runs the best stopping house anywhere."

"Thanks, Dutch." Phil talked as if laughter was just

below the surface. She was as tall as most men. Her hands were darkened from work, but she had the sweetest smile Nate had seen in some time. She removed her hat and thick black hair tumbled loose to the middle of her back. If Nate hadn't been so concerned for Louise, he might have stared at her like the others.

"You folks make yourself comfortable while I finish supper." She waved them toward the table, covered with a blue-flowered oilcloth, and opened the oven door to release the aroma of roasting meat.

No one seemed inclined to sit.

Nate wanted to ease Louise toward a bench, but she walked back and forth behind the table as if feeling the need to stretch her legs.

She turned, saw him regarding her and gave a wide smile, meant, no doubt, to reassure him.

He smiled back, hoping he hid his worry.

She stretched her arms overhead and sighed. "It's good to be out of the stagecoach for a few hours. Something about the swaying and jerking doesn't agree with me."

The words were for his sake, but there was a general sense of relief.

Missy hung up her coat and scarf, and did the same for Louise.

Miss Rolfe joined Phil at the stove. "Can I help you with anything?"

"Can you make gravy?"

Miss Rolfe chuckled. "I can do most anything."

Dutch headed for the door. "Anyone want to help with the animals?"

"I'll be right along," Phil said.

Dutch waved aside her offer. "No need. These men are all good at helping."

Gabe and Archie trotted after the man. After a moment's hesitation, Nate turned to follow, but Sam sat watching Phil.

Nate nudged him. "You coming?"

Sam jolted. "Huh?"

"We're going to feed and bed the animals."

"Right." Sam followed, paused at the door to look back.

Nate chuckled. "Phil's a good-looking woman."

"Yeah."

"Strong and independent, too, to run a stopping house by herself."

"Yeah."

Nate chuckled. Sam seemed to have lost the ability to talk.

When they reached the barn, Sam unsaddled Nate's horse. He hung it over the rack provided and stared at the wall before him, seeming to be wrapped in a daydream.

Nate grinned as he found a curry brush and tended the horse while the Adamses helped Dutch with the bigger horses.

"Sure glad we got here in good time," Archie said, pausing between tossing forkfuls of hay to the animals. "Your wife is mighty close."

Nate continued brushing. "She says it's only from bouncing around."

"Could be. But things like that tend to speed up the process."

"How long do you think it will take?"

Archie shrugged. "That's impossible to guess. Each woman, each baby, is different. It takes however long it takes."

That was hardly reassuring, especially for Louise's

sake. The few pains he'd been aware of made him want to stop the process entirely. He didn't want to see her in pain, hear her gasping.

They finished the chores and hurried back to the house. Funny, it was the first time he'd thought of one of the way stations as a real house. Guess that's what a woman's touch did to a place.

His thoughts went to the little cabin on the piece of land he hoped to acquire. He hadn't given the dwelling much thought. Mostly his plans had focused on growing a herd of cows and horses. But wouldn't it be nice to come home to a place more like this stopping house and less like Dusty's? Maybe he could clean up the cabin he was about to purchase and even add a room.

Whoa. He put an instant stop to the direction of his thoughts. There was no need for adding more space. What he had would be good enough for just him.

Indoors, the women all bustled about the kitchen. Miss Rolfe stirred something on the stove. Missy set the table. Louise sliced a golden loaf of bread while Phil took care of the roast.

Louise looked up as the men entered. Her gaze searched for Nate and latched on to his eyes when she found him, seeking something from him. He couldn't say what she sought, but he met her look for look, offering strength, encouragement and promises he didn't have the right to give.

He understood the terms of their marriage as well as she. But he had to admit he was growing to like the idea of having her as his wife.

"It's all ready, thanks to help from these ladies," Phil said as the women carried platters and bowls to the table. "Please sit down. I'm sorry I only have benches for you. Someday I hope to have regular chairs."

There was a rocking chair and a footstool near a little bookshelf. Phil had certainly added some homey touches to the place.

Nate waited until Louise sat, then slid in beside her.

Phil looked around the table. Her gaze stopped at Archie. "Sir, would you object to asking the blessing on our food?"

"My honor." He bowed his head and prayed.

Nate thought his words of gratitude for a fine meal were entirely heartfelt, echoing how all of them felt. Good food, beautifully served. What a pleasure.

His pleasure grew as they passed around roast venison, mashed potatoes, rich gravy, bright orange carrots.

"This is a feast fit for a king," Sam said, color racing up his neck.

"Thank you. I love to cook." Phil laughed. "I love hunting and riding, too. I love watching birds sing and flowers grow. I guess I love most everything about life out here."

Sam just stared at her.

"Tell the others how you got to be here," Miss Rolfe said, drawing attention from poor Sam, who seemed completely besotted by the lovely Philomena.

"Wasn't anything special about how I came here. My pa brought me with him. He set up this way station. Many bull trains come by in the summer and we had a nice little business." Her smile faded momentarily. "Pa got sick last winter and died this spring. I buried him out back with the help of some bullwhackers." She grew solemn for a moment, then smiled again. "I planted bluebells over his grave. He loved those flowers. And no one has complained about me running the station for him."

"Everyone is grateful," Dutch said.

"That's for sure," Sam said, and color raced up his neck again.

Nate turned to Louise, to share amusement over Sam's state.

She grinned back at him and he felt a connection that excluded the others.

Relief eased through him that she ate a decent meal and seemed to have no more pains. He could think of nothing he'd like more than for her to complete the journey and have the baby at Eden Valley Ranch as she hoped.

Phil gathered up the food when they were finished and brought a plate of cookies for dessert. "I've made tea if anyone cares for it."

Nate hesitated. The last tea he tasted had left a metallic taste in his mouth. But this wasn't Dusty's place. "I'd appreciate some," he said, and the others echoed him.

The cookies were fine, the tea even finer and they sat around visiting.

"Tell me where you are all going," Phil said.

One by one, they told of their destination.

Nate's turn came. "I'm going to meet a man and hopefully buy me a small ranch." He glanced at the calendar hanging by the stove. According to Rufus, the mountain man usually visited the week before Christmas in order to send gifts to his daughter, and stayed a few days, often celebrating Christmas with Rufus before he returned to his cabin up the mountain. Nate still had time to get back to Edendale and meet him.

Phil rested her elbows on the table and leaned her chin on her hands. "A little ranch. That sounds lovely." She chuckled. "Not that I mind running this stopping house, but maybe I'll buy some cows and operate a ranch, as well."

Sam's eyes flashed admiration.

Nate thought the man saw where he could fit in.

Eventually, Phil moved to wash dishes. Miss Rolfe, Louise and Missy joined her.

"Looks like you need more wood." Sam hurried outside and they heard the *whack* of an ax applied to logs. He returned with his arms full, and stacked enough wood to last her a day or two. "Anything else you need done?" he asked.

Phil chuckled. "I pretty well can do anything that needs doing." She grew thoughtful. "But if you hear of someone nearby with cows they'd be willing to part with, you could let me know."

"I'll do better," Sam said. "I'll find you some. I'll bring them in the spring."

"You do that and I'll be forever grateful."

The pair looked at each other, unmindful of their audience. Nate turned away, feeling as if the moment should be private.

He slid his attention toward Louise and was caught in her dark, probing gaze. He couldn't look away. All this talk about plans and the future had him thinking differently, wishing for things that were out of his reach. Wishing his cabin could be a real home.

She closed her eyes and sucked her lips back. Then she grabbed the edge of the cupboard.

Another pain. He'd hoped they had ended.

Missy noticed it, too, and reached for her elbow to guide her to the bench. Louise sank down beside Nate and rocked back and forth.

He rubbed her back until the pain passed.

Phil watched Louise, her face sober. "The baby?"

Louise shook her head. "I hope not. Maybe I just ate

too heartily." She gave a sound that was half chuckle, half groan. "It's been days since we ate so well."

"It's something more than the food." Phil sounded concerned.

"We'll see." Louise sat upright and waved away Phil's comments. "You were telling us about starting a ranch."

Phil shrugged. "You'll know if it's real soon enough." She sat down. Somehow she managed to be at Sam's side. As the pair talked about cows and horses, Phil's gaze came often to Louise.

After a bit, Louise began to rock back and forth again. Another pain.

Nate rubbed her back and she grabbed his free hand and squeezed so hard his fingers were mashed together.

When the pain passed, Phil pushed to her feet. "You are going to sleep in my bedroom tonight." She pushed open the door to reveal a bed covered in a quilt, a rag rug on the floor and another table with a stool beside it.

"Oh, I couldn't," Louise protested.

"Yes, you can," Nate said.

"Now who's bossy?"

He chuckled. "I learned it from the best."

But already another pain grabbed her middle.

Phil waited for it to pass, then shooed the men outside. "We'll call you when the women are ready."

Nate held back. "Louise, are you okay? If you need me…"

"I'm okay." Her mouth said one thing, her eyes another. Only Phil making shooing signs persuaded him to leave.

Louise needed him. Maybe just for the evening. Maybe for the night. Might even be a bit longer. He knew it wasn't permanent, but as long as she needed him, he meant to be available. She could count on him.

He left with the other men, but when they went to the barn, Nate hung around outside the way-station door just in case Louise needed him. In a few minutes, Phil called out for them to come back. Sam must have been waiting for the call even more anxiously than Nate, for he was the first through the door, practically running over Nate in his rush to get back inside. Nate grinned. Seemed Sam and Phil were interested in more than cows and ranching. They just might be interested in starting a home together.

Nate thought of the cabin on the ranch he hoped to buy. If he put a little work into it, could it be a home? Only a woman and a baby would turn it from a house to a home. He shook off the notion as he stepped inside.

Missy and Miss Rolfe were gone, presumably behind the curtain drawn across the far end of the room.

"Your wife is in my bedroom," Phil said.

"I'd like to say good-night to her."

"Go right on in."

He tapped on the door. "Louise, it's me." He waited a moment, then went inside, closing the door behind him.

Her eyes were big.

He knelt beside the bed and cradled his arms about her. "Are you scared?"

A flash of denial crossed her eyes and then they grew teary. She reached for his free hand. "I've never done this before."

He stroked her hair. "I know. I'm right on the other side of the door. If you need me, just call."

"Thank you," she whispered.

They clung together. "I can stay here if you want. There's plenty of room on the floor for me to sleep."

Her eyes devoured him. He would stay at her side as long as she needed him. Then she drew in a breath and found a source of inner strength. "There's no need for that. I'll be fine."

Yet, the way she held his hand said otherwise.

He pulled her closer, resting his forehead against hers. She smelled sweet.

"Did Phil wash you in rosewater?" he asked.

Louise chuckled, a sound that eased through his heart like honey. "She insisted I would feel better after a good wash and she did it for me. She's a wonderful person."

"I think Sam would agree."

Louise smiled at him with a twinkle in her eyes. "They both deserve someone nice."

He stroked her forehead. "So do you."

She caught his hand and pulled it to her cheek. Tears clouded her eyes. She was about to say something, when another contraction gripped her.

He rubbed her back until it passed.

"Are you sure you don't want me to stay?"

"I'll sleep now," she whispered. "You should, too."

He got to his feet. "Good night, then." He leaned over and kissed her forehead. He didn't want to leave, but he could hear the men shuffling around as they prepared for bed. "I'm here if you need me." He stepped from the room before he could change his mind.

Phil waited at the curtain. "Everything okay?"

He shrugged, not knowing what to say.

She seemed to understand. "I'll listen for her."

He unrolled the clean-smelling bedroll and lay on top of it. He'd never be able to sleep knowing what she had to face.

Yet at some point he drifted off.

A sound jerked him awake and he sat up in a sweat. Louise! He was on his feet instantly.

Phil held up her hand. She had lit a lamp and was heading for the bedroom door. "I'll tend her."

He wanted to argue. Louise needed him. He needed to do something to help her, even if it was only to rub her back and speak words of encouragement. But Phil closed the door firmly behind her. It was no place for a man, not even a man posing as the husband. Though at the moment, he didn't want to pretend. He wanted the right to be there with Louise and assist.

"Go back to sleep," Archie whispered. "It could take a while."

Hours later, the sky turned to gunmetal grey. Dutch got up, stretched and yawned, then said, "I'll see to the horses." He left the room.

Nate had been pacing in his stocking feet for an hour, listening to the muted sounds of pain. "How much longer can this go on?" Louise was brave and made little noise, but, alert to every sound from the bedroom, Nate had heard her groan time after time. Every sound of pain had ripped at his innards until he felt weak and battered.

The others rose and put away the bedding.

Missy hurried over and paused at the door. "I'll see how she's doing." She disappeared inside.

Nate stared at the door as the minutes ticked by. Why wasn't she coming out? There must be something wrong. He was her husband. He had a right to know. He took a step toward the door, intending to forgo convention and go to Louise's side, when Missy stepped back out.

"Phil says it will be a while. I said we'd manage breakfast on our own. Meanwhile, there's a trunk on the coach that has the baby things in it. Someone could bring it."

Dutch, who had entered at that moment, heard Missy and swung about. "I'll get it." He was back in moments. Miss Rolfe helped Missy push the trunk into the bedroom, then they stepped out and began meal preparations.

"Why don't you men go outside and help with the chores?" Missy suggested.

Sam took Nate by one arm, Archie took the other, and they guided him outside and over to the barn.

"Boys," Dutch said, "it's almost dawn. We need to move on."

Nate stared at him. "We're not going anyplace until that baby comes."

Dutch shrugged. "You couldn't ask for a better place to hole up than here."

"Hole up?" The meaning hit him. "While you and the others go on?"

Dutch nodded. "There's no need for the others to stay here. They paid for timely passage. It's my job to get them to Fort Macleod as soon as possible. We're already one day behind schedule because of the storm."

"We're not in that big a hurry," Archie said.

"I don't mind staying here a bit," Sam added, grinning widely.

Dutch shrugged. "It's your decision, but it has to be unanimous."

"I'll ask Miss Rolfe," Sam said as if he couldn't wait to get back in the house. He trotted away and returned in a few minutes with the news that Miss Rolfe indeed would delay her journey until the baby came. Missy was also in agreement.

"That's it, then," Dutch said. "Let's hope that little one doesn't take too long. I've heard it can take days."

Nate felt the blood rush from his face and he grabbed the nearest gate. "Days? You're joshing."

Dutch nodded. "Yup, and it gets worse before it gets better."

Archie took Nate by the arm and led him away until they were by themselves. "Your wife is young and strong. She'll be fine. Sometimes I think it's harder to be the man and not able to do anything but watch and wait."

Nate shuddered. "I would take the pain if I could. It's not fair for her to endure so much."

Chapter Thirteen

Searing pain ripped through Louise. Phil rubbed her back and encouraged her.

The pain passed, but she knew it would come again. Wave after wave.

"How much longer?" she asked.

"Not long. Soon you'll have a little one to hold."

"Can't you make it stop?"

Phil shook her head. "'Fraid not."

Another contraction gripped Louise. "Where's Nate?" She wanted to squeeze his hand, have him rub her back.

"I sent them outside. Men aren't good with this sort of thing."

When another contraction hit, Phil tried to soothe her. "Don't fight it," she said in a soft tone.

Louise wondered how Phil knew about birthing, but it didn't matter. All that counted was getting through the next contraction and the next one until this ended.

Phil turned out the lamp and drew back the heavy curtains on the window at the end of the room. Dazzling light flooded the room.

Louise sat up. "It's dawn. Have they gone?" Had she been left behind?

"They've decided to delay for the day."

"Delay? Oh, no." Nate might miss his meeting and it would be her fault. He would never forgive her. She had to tell him to go. But she didn't want him to. It wasn't a rational thought, but how could she be rational when this pain took over her body.

She lost track of time and every other thought except making it through the next contraction.

Through the pain, she heard Phil's voice. "Tell me when you feel like pushing."

"Now." She grunted.

Phil went to the foot of the bed. "It will be soon now."

A bit later, Louise decided Phil's idea of soon was vastly different than hers. She fell back on the mattress, soaked in sweat and exhausted.

Phil patted her shoulder. "Rest a minute. I'll be right back."

Louise closed her eyes. *Please let Nate come. I need him.*

The door reopened and Louise looked up into Missy's worried smile.

"She's going to help you," Phil said. "She's going to sit behind you and hold you up so you can push better."

Missy climbed into bed and held Louise.

Drenched in pain and in sweat from the strain of pushing, Louise lost track of time. She had no idea how long it was until Phil called, "It's a girl. A perfect little girl." A thin cry announced her daughter's entrance into the world.

Louise managed a smile. "A girl. Let me see her."

Missy eased from the bed to look at the baby. "Oh, she's beautiful."

Phil wrapped the baby in a square of flannel and laid her on Louise's chest. Louise smiled at her daughter. "You are the prettiest baby ever." Dark blue eyes considered her solemnly as if to demand who was responsible for bringing her into this bright world.

Louise traced the rosebud ears, checked for the correct number of toes and fingers. "She's perfect."

Phil and Missy chuckled. "She certainly is."

Phil opened the door and called, "It's a girl."

"I want to see her." Nate's voice brooked no more delay, but Phil pushed him away. "Give us time to clean them up." She closed the door.

Louise lay back exhausted and content, her baby on her chest.

"I'll bathe her." Phil took the baby and sponged her clean, then put one of the handmade nightgowns from the trunk on her. "Did you make these?" she asked, admiring the delicate embroidered flowers along the neckline and hem.

"I sewed them. My aunt embellished them." *Oh, Aunt Bea, if you could only see your grandniece.* As soon as she got a chance, she would send a letter to Aunt Bea and another to Pa.

Missy helped Louise wash and put on a fresh gown.

"It seems strange to have you taking care of me."

"I know," Missy replied. "You've always thought you should take care of me. It's about time the roles were reversed."

Missy brushed Louise's hair and braided it as before, then Phil put the baby in Louise's arms. "Ready for your husband?"

Louise nodded. She wanted him to see the baby.

Nate came in and the ladies slipped out, closing the door behind them.

Nate knelt at the side of the bed. "Are you okay?"

"I am now." She laughed with pure joy. "Isn't she a beauty?"

Nate touched the baby's head, put his finger in her hand, and the baby curled her fingers about his. His eyes grew watery.

"I think she likes me."

She'd learn there was much to like about Nate—except their journey would soon be over. But all she said was, "Of course she does."

"Have you picked out a name?"

She met his eyes. "I thought you could help me."

He looked surprised and then pleased and then thoughtful. "Wasn't Mrs. Porter's name Chloe? I like that."

"I do, too. How fitting to name her after her grandmother and a woman that was special to us both."

"So Chloe it is?"

She nodded, almost overcome with emotion. Tears stung her eyes and she couldn't talk.

Nate cupped her cheek with his hand and waited for her to calm herself. "The others are anxious to meet her."

"Let them in."

He opened the door and the group crowded into the room.

"Did you choose a name?" Missy asked.

"Chloe."

Missy's eyes clouded with tears. "After my ma?"

"Yes."

"Chloe Hawkins. I like it."

She had no wish to correct Missy, and Nate didn't seem to notice. Of course, everyone else assumed the baby would have his name. She would not ruin the moment by thinking of the future.

One by one, the others slipped out. When she and Nate were finally alone, there was something she had to say. "Nate, you didn't have to stay back on my account. I didn't expect you to. Guess it surprised me that you did."

He stared down at her, his expression unreadable, his blue eyes as dark as an evening sky. "Why didn't you tell me you were so close to having the baby before we left?"

"Would you have taken us if you knew?"

"Probably not."

"Then that's your answer. But we'll be okay now. Phil is a good sort."

He crossed his arms. Standing above her like that, he looked formidable. Angry, even. "Do you really think I'd abandon you?"

"You wouldn't be the first."

He studied her for a moment. "Do you mean your mother?"

She nodded, shifting her gaze to the wee one in her arms. "Do you have any idea how it feels to have your mother leave you? I simply can't imagine leaving my baby."

He sat on the edge of the bed. "I suppose a woman would have to have some pretty major problems to leave her child."

"I suppose so."

"Problems that had nothing to do with the child."

She considered his words as he waited, giving her time and space. Finally, she sighed. "I expect you're right."

"You know I am. Now, look, I promised to get you to

the ranch and I will do so." He patted her arm. "Think you can remember that?"

"I'll try." She wanted to ask if he would miss his meeting but couldn't bear to risk this feeling of harmony between them. "We can leave yet today. I'm ready to travel."

He chuckled. "It's almost time for supper. Don't think Dutch will want to set out now. So you relax and enjoy one more night in a comfortable bed." He pushed to his feet. "Now I'll let you rest before Phil chases me out."

She didn't need to sleep. She needed to get up and prove to them all she was ready to travel. But first she must tend the baby.

After she fed her newborn, Phil came in. "I'll put her down and you sleep while you can."

Louise wanted to protest but was too drowsy. As soon as Phil left the room, she fell asleep.

"Congratulations. She's pretty as can be." Archie was the first to offer his best wishes, but the other men clapped him on the back, too. Nate grinned, feeling as if he deserved the praise. Chloe was so cute. He could spend the day looking at the way she puckered her mouth. And the way her fingers curled around his made him want to hold her. Only, he was a little afraid he might drop her or break her. She was such a tiny little thing.

But Louise! She really thought he might have gone on without her. Of course, she might have cause. Her mother had left her. Her father had sent her away. The Porters had died, effectively leaving them all.

Then he'd left three years ago. Did she see his leaving as more of the same?

How was he to convince her it hadn't been the same at all?

Or was he misunderstanding her? Perhaps she wanted him to leave so she could be alone, so she could depend on no one.

No, he couldn't believe it. She'd clung to him many times since they'd left Rocky Creek. Not in a needy, weak way but in a way that said he could help her be strong. He liked that. A strong woman willing to accept help when she needed it.

He was so deep in his thoughts that he didn't notice Phil and the others had made a meal until she called him to the table.

"I'll take something in to Louise," he said.

Phil pointed to his plate. "Eat first. She's tired. They don't call it labor for nothing."

He tried not to rush through the fine meal but wanted nothing more than to check on Louise and Chloe again. Chloe! A sweet name for a sweet baby.

What was to become of her once they reached Eden Valley Ranch and ended the pretend marriage? Didn't she need a papa?

He wanted to be in Chloe's life. In Louise's, too. He wanted them in his home where he could take care of them every day.

Could he convince Louise to make their marriage real?

Unable to wait any longer, he took her plate of food to the bedroom.

Louise wakened at his entry and sat up when she saw what he carried. "I'm famished."

He sat on the foot of the bed, where, as Louise ate, he could watch Chloe sleeping in a basket.

The baby jerked as if surprised by an imaginary noise. "She's making sucking sounds." He chuckled. "Now she's pressing her fist to her cheek. It's so cute and innocent."

Louise had finished eating and shifted so she sat beside him where she could also watch the baby. "Do you think Mrs. Porter would be pleased we named the baby after her?"

He took her hand. "She'd be thrilled."

Louise's expression grew worried.

He caught her chin and lifted her head so their eyes met. "What's the matter?"

Her forehead wrinkled as if her thoughts were troublesome. "I was thinking of Gordie. He never got a chance to see his little girl."

No doubt she meant to remind him he had no part in Chloe's life. A few days ago he would have said it didn't matter. But now it mattered more than almost anything. His powerlessness to change the facts sent razor-sharp regret up and down his spine.

"Gordie would have been very proud," he said, relieved that his voice sounded normal.

"Sometimes—" She broke off and shifted her attention to something past his shoulder.

"What?"

"I shouldn't say it."

He might regret pressing her, but better to hear than to have secrets and misunderstandings between them. "Tell me."

She shuddered. "You'll be angry."

So it was something she knew would upset him. Perhaps another reminder that Chloe would never be his daughter. Or that their marriage was a farce. "I promise I won't." At least he'd not let her know.

"Sometimes I am so angry at Gordie, I can hardly stand it. It was his bad choices that caused so many problems and so much trouble for us all."

"So you understand why I had to leave rather than be drawn into it? I hoped my leaving would make him see the error of his ways."

Her eyes found his again, full of wonder. "I do." She ducked her head again. "But he never changed. And then he got greedy and tried to trick Vic. I'm sure it's what got him killed."

Nate's thoughts slammed into his brain with a viciousness that was reminiscent of Vic's behavior. "What do you mean? Are you suggesting what I think you are?"

She nodded. "I believe Vic killed him. I told the marshal my suspicions, but he could find no proof."

Nate bolted to his feet, so full of anger and frustration he couldn't stand still. "Why didn't you tell me sooner when I could have done something about it? I should go back and bring Vic to justice."

She tried to stand, but her face grew as white as the sheets on the bed.

He grabbed her and edged her back to the mattress. "What are you doing?"

"Trying to stop you." She grabbed his arms. "Promise me you won't go after Vic. He has absolutely no scruples. Let it go. Please. Remember what you said to me? Forget the past. Look to the future. Promise you won't go back."

He couldn't stand to see her so worked up, even though he experienced a little thrill that she cared so much. "Okay. I promise. I won't go back to Rocky Creek except to visit my ma."

"And you'll stay away from Vic?"

"Yes, I'll stay away from Vic."

She let out a gust of air. "Thank you. If anything happens to you—" She broke off. "Never mind. So long as you get us to the ranch as you said."

"I always do my best to keep my word." He sat beside her again and they watched baby Chloe sleep.

"Nate, don't be mad at me at what I'm about to say."

"I think I can handle it." He'd been exposed to surprise after surprise and he had maintained his self-control.

Her voice dropped to a whisper. "Sometimes I am angry at God."

He nodded, not knowing what he could say to that.

She clutched the hem of the sheet and twisted it round and round.

He thought about telling her to have a care for the fabric. Phil wouldn't appreciate having her linens ripped, but he sensed the action would distract Louise from her troublesome thoughts.

"I tell myself I will trust God no matter what, but sometimes I can't. Why does He allow men such as Vic to get away with their evil deeds? Why does He allow Vic to even live?"

Nate wrapped his arm about her shoulders and drew her close. "Louise, I simply don't know. The only thing I can say is…" He thought of some of the talks Bertie had delivered at Sunday services at the ranch. "God loves Vic and is giving him a chance to turn around."

Louise made a dismissive noise. "That's impossible."

"Lots of impossible things have become possible with God." It was a truth he meant to cling to. So many things looked impossible at the moment—getting back to Edendale in time to meet the mountain man, persuading Louise to let him be a part of Chloe's life. Convincing Louise to help him start up a ranch. Doubts clouded his mind. Why would she want to share a run-down cabin with him?

"You know what I'd like?" Her words broke into his thoughts.

"Nope."

"I'd like a Bible of my own. Do you think I could purchase one in Fort Macleod?"

"I would expect you can."

"If I could learn to trust God more, I could face the future without worry. Me and Chloe and Missy together."

She'd left him out of the picture.

Seemed he needed to restrict his impossible hopes to getting back in time to buy the bit of land he wanted. Yet it no longer seemed enough to satisfy his heart.

Chapter Fourteen

After Nate left, Louise lay back staring at the ceiling. Had she really said, "If anything happens to you…"? At least she hadn't finished the thought. *I don't know what I would do.*

Being responsible for a baby made her realize how small and weak she was. She turned her face to the pillow and let a tear or two fall to the sweet-smelling cotton.

She'd get a Bible and read it every day, finding her strength in God alone.

She would not heed the silly need crying out in her heart for someone to share her life with. Someone good and noble and strong like Nate.

Stop it, she ordered herself. Hadn't she learned her lesson about needing people, depending on them? She'd start a new life without depending on anyone.

Phil came in. She must have noticed Louise's damp cheek, because she said, "You're feeling vulnerable right now and that's normal. It won't take long for you to get your strength back and more."

"That's good to hear. How did you get to be such an expert on birthing and babies?"

Phil chuckled. "My mama was a midwife. A very good one, if I do say so myself. Before she died, I helped her on many occasions."

"Seems God prepared you to be here when I needed you. Or me to be here when I needed you. I'm not sure which."

"And it doesn't matter. We both know God brought us together at the right time just as He always does."

Louise clung to the idea of God bringing her to the right person at the right time. Maybe He'd done the same thing many times and she simply hadn't noticed.

Like bringing Nate home when she and Missy needed to escape Vic?

Like having Nate agree to marry her? No, she couldn't believe God had a hand in that or even approved of it.

"Does God really care about people even when they do bad things?" she asked Philomena.

Phil sat on the edge of the bed. "You don't have to read much in the Bible to know He does. Just think of the children of Israel. God rescued them with many miraculous signs. You'd think they'd never forget that, but they did time and time and time again. But He never forgot them. Sometimes He let them suffer for their sins but only in order to turn them back to Him. Our God is a great and loving God." She patted Louise's hands. "Now I'll get little miss Chloe who is fussing for her mama, then you need to get some sleep. Are you planning to resume your journey tomorrow?"

Louise nodded.

"You will need to get plenty of rest and make sure the baby is kept warm," Phil advised her.

"I wish you could come with us."

"I belong here for now. But you are most welcome to stay with me if you want."

"I have to go on."

"I know. Follow your heart. God will be with you each step of the way."

Phil left Louise with the baby and plenty to think about. Her words strengthened Louise.

The next morning came far too early. Louise had been up several times in the night with the baby and wished she could sleep another four hours. But she had no intention of being the cause of another delay or being left behind. She might be safe here for now, maybe for the winter, but if Vic showed up, she had little defense and no desire to pull Phil into her situation.

She slipped from the covers, moving quietly, lest she disturb the sleeping baby.

She put on her dress and ran her hand down the tummy. It was not quite flat, but she could see her feet. Feet that felt farther away than they should because of her slightly wobbly legs.

The next few days until they reached the ranch would be challenging, but she could handle it.

The noise and voices beyond the bedroom door informed her that the others were up, and she straightened and stepped out to face them.

Missy rushed to her side. "Are you ready to be up?"

"Ready as I'll ever be." No one would ever know how much effort it took to stand tall and steady.

Nate stood by the stove. He looked at her, his eyes filled with concern, and then he smiled as if glad to see her. Her heart fluttered at the thought, then she settled it down with the facts of her situation. Likely he had been concerned she might cost them another delay.

Phil insisted Louise sit down and brought her a cup of coffee. "Strong and fresh. Just what you need. And lots of oatmeal." She filled Louise's bowl and signaled the others to join them at the table.

Louise dug in as soon as the blessing had been asked and cleaned up the porridge in record time. She was hungry enough to eat two bowlfuls but would never have asked.

Phil looked at her empty bowl and laughed as she filled it again. "My mama said a woman feeding a baby eats for two. She needs lots and lots of good food." She turned to Nate. "You be sure she gets it."

He laughed. "Yes, ma'am. I'll do my best."

As they prepared to leave, Phil filled a syrup pail with cookies and biscuits, and handed it to Louise. "In case you don't get enough north of here."

"Thank you." She'd packed a bag with essentials for traveling with the baby. Chloe, cradled in one arm, wore a knit bonnet and sweater on top of a clean nightgown. Louise had wrapped her in several blankets. One Aunt Bea had knitted for the baby and one Louise had knitted. The third was one Aunt Bea had pulled from her big trunk. "I made it for you as a baby. Your pa gave it to me when you no longer had need of it. I hoped I would someday be able to give it back to you for your own baby." There were times Aunt Bea's kindness surprised her. Louise had decided her aunt simply didn't like a young girl upsetting her routine.

Louise had fingered the soft yarn of the blanket, missing a mother she couldn't remember. She pushed aside the lonesome thought and vowed Chloe would always know how much she was loved.

"I'll take her." Nate held his hands out to hold Chloe so Louise could climb into the stagecoach.

She hesitated. Had he ever held a newborn?

"Show me what to do." He sounded eager.

Louise welcomed the help and what better person to turn to than her husband—pretend though their relationship was?

"Support her head at all times." She shifted Chloe into the crook of his arm. Tears clogged the back of her throat at the way he smiled at Chloe and touched her cheek with his fingertip.

He looked up at Louise, his eyes glowing with enjoyment and perhaps a touch of pride.

She turned away quickly, lest he notice her emotional state, and climbed aboard. Nate handed up the baby, holding her head in one hand and her bottom in the other. She had to smile at how naturally he did it.

He'd make a good papa.

She dismissed the idea before it could take root and flourish into impossible wishes.

She settled beside one window next to Missy.

Missy peeked under the covers at the baby. "Hello, Chloe, I'm your aunt Missy. You and I are going to be best friends."

Nate climbed inside and sat across from Louise. She saw concern and something more in his eyes as he looked at her.

But she wasn't about to try to guess what the something more might be. Likely only another part of her silly, impossible dreams and wishes. Seemed having a baby had triggered a deep nesting instinct that made her want to build a home with a man who would care for them both.

Dutch hollered giddyap and they were on their way.

Louise looked about at her fellow travelers. "I know I caused you all to lose a day of travel and I apologize."

"Nonsense," Rowena said. "We voted on it and not one of us wanted to move on until you had the baby."

The others agreed.

"She's special to all of us," Archie said. "Consider each of us a guardian for her. If she needs anything or you do, all you have to do is ask."

Her throat threatened to close off, but she managed to get out a couple of words. "Thank you." Could they give her a home where she could always stay? A husband who would never leave?

She pushed her shoulders back. She would manage on her own. In the process, she'd learn to trust God more.

The rocking seemed to calm Chloe and she didn't fuss until they stopped. Missy held her while Louise took advantage of the break to take care of her personal needs, then she resumed her seat and pulled the baby close. Phil had shown her how to nurse while maintaining her modesty but she was grateful Missy—not Nate—sat beside her.

The day seemed interminable. She was weary clear through but couldn't sleep because of the need to hold the baby. The rolling motion made it impossible to stay awake and, despite her best intentions, she drifted off, jerking to full attention, her heart pounding at a furious rate. What if she dropped the baby? Yes, the buffalo robes swaddled Chloe, but only a secure pair of arms ensured her safety.

Chloe fussed again. Had it really been several hours since she last ate? She nursed the infant again and the baby fell asleep.

Louise vowed she would not do so, as well.

"Can I hold her?" Nate asked, leaning forward and taking the baby gingerly before she could find any reason to object.

Truth was, she appreciated a break.

"You rest until she needs you again."

"Thank you." She tipped her head back and slept, though she remained faintly aware of the activity around her, as if being a mama had given her a new ability.

It took her a moment to realize the stage had stopped moving, and the occupants had begun to shuffle about.

"We're here," Nate said.

Louise didn't have the heart to look out the window and see where "here" was. Was it too much to hope for a place like Phil's? She could never have imagined it possible to miss someone she had known for less than two days.

Nate stepped down with Chloe cradled safely in one arm, and helped Louise down with the other hand as naturally and competently as if he'd been doing it for years.

She thanked him, then gave him a long, hard stare.

"What?" he asked.

"I was thinking how natural you are with all this—the baby, helping me down and all. You're sure you haven't done this before?"

To her amazement, his cheeks turned a ruddy color. "I'm just a good observer."

"Of course." Why would it make him uncomfortable to confess so? Unless he'd watched other men with their wives and babies, and wished he could enjoy the same. Was it possible?

Or was she putting her own wishes on his shoulders? She'd had a husband, but not an attentive one. She'd had a home, but it had never been hers. It belonged to Gordie and he never let her forget it. Not that she minded. To her, it was the Porter home and reminded her of better times.

Now it was too late for such dreams and wishes. Dreams were for the young and innocent, not for widows and mamas raising a child on their own.

Nate felt the heat creep up his neck and pool in his cheeks. He was blushing like a schoolgirl. Louise must think him strange, especially when she'd asked a perfectly innocent question. But one that sneaked right past his defenses. He had tried for years to deny that he had once thought Louise might care for him in a special way. After he'd left, he hoped she'd follow, or contact him to come and get her. During that time, he used to watch young men with their girls or husbands with their wives and think what it would be like to be able to help Louise from a wagon. Or hold a door for her. Or feel a baby sleeping in his arms.

Her marriage to Gordie had made those silly thoughts wrong and he'd put an end to them. Until now. It seemed as if everything he'd once hoped for was his. Except it wasn't. It was only pretend. And as she was so fond of reminding him, they would forget the past and follow a new path into the future.

But for now, he was living his dream…taking care of Louise and little Chloe.

He led Louise toward the stopping house, Chloe still in his arms. The baby was content, so Nate did not hand her back to Louise.

The stopping house wasn't much from the outside, but he was pleasantly surprised when they stepped inside a warm, clean room with a delicious smell coming from the pot on the stove.

"Thank You, God," he murmured.

"Amen to that," Louise said.

Their host was out helping Dutch, so they didn't meet him until he, Dutch and Sam tromped inside, stomping snow and straw from their boots.

"Folks, this here is Oxley. He's a fine host."

Oxley was tall and lean as a whip with trimmed brown hair, though it looked as if the man cut his own hair without consulting a mirror. He had dark brown eyes that were warm and welcoming, and he was clean shaven except for a handlebar moustache that quivered as he smiled. "Welcome, make yourselves at home." His voice rumbled as though it came from a spot far below his feet.

Everything about the man made Nate relax. Here he knew Louise and the baby were not in danger of food poisoning, vermin or some kind of dreadful disease.

They gathered around the table as Oxley served up thick, delicious stew. When the meal was over, Miss Rolfe and Missy offered to wash the dishes. At first, Oxley refused.

"You all paid for the meal. That means you don't have to clean up. That's my job."

Miss Rolfe ignored his protest. "It's our way of showing our gratitude for a good meal."

Louise tried to join the other women, but they waved her aside.

"Rest while you can," Missy said.

Archie nodded agreement. "My wife always said a new mother should sleep whenever she could. Of course, if she has half a dozen little ones that meant never."

So Louise sat down beside Nate.

Pleased she had chosen to do so, he put an arm around her shoulders and cooed over the baby, who opened her eyes and waved her little pink fists.

There was no separate bedroom for Louise that night. But Nate again brought in the buffalo robes and made a bed for her and the baby. No one objected.

"Here, this blanket is softer than yours." Gabe traded blankets with her.

Sam moved the benches to give her more room.

"She'll need a lamp in the night for feeding the baby," Archie said.

"She can keep it turned low if that doesn't bother the rest of you," Oxley said.

Louise looked about the room, her eyes awash. "You are all so good to me when you have every right to resent me for causing you delay, and now you'll have to listen to Chloe cry in the night."

"A baby's crying won't bother me," Archie said. The others agreed.

"Sweetest music a man could ever hear," Oxley added.

Nate grinned at him. "I couldn't have said it better myself."

Louise's smile was half teasing, half regretful. "You might all change your minds before we get to our destination."

"No, we won't," Sam said.

Nate didn't say anything, but he knew he wouldn't.

But during the night, he wondered if the others might change their minds, for Chloe cried a good deal.

Nate could see Louise feeding her, but it didn't seem to satisfy the baby. He edged closer. "Can I help?"

"I don't know what to do," she whispered. "I've fed

her and changed her. She seems warm enough. What else is there?"

"I don't know." He kept his voice low so as not to disturb the others.

But Archie murmured, "Maybe she's missing the rocking motion of the stagecoach. After all, she'd probably grown used to it the last few days."

"Give her to me." Nate took the baby and did a swaying walk back and forth across the narrow space between the door and the table.

Chloe sobbed twice more, then stopped. Archie was right.

He walked and swung her a few more minutes, then eased her down into Louise's arms. He crawled back into bed.

Chloe slept off and on through the night. The only thing that would settle her when she fussed was to be walked and rocked. Louise and Nate took turns till he saw how exhausted she was. "You rest while I walk her," he said to Louise.

It seemed he had barely put his head down when Dutch pushed from his bedroll. "Time to move out, folks. We got a long ways to go today."

Nate wondered how much sleep Louise had gotten. He sure hadn't had much. But he wasn't about to complain, not after all Louise had been through. He vowed to do all he could to help her for the next few days. Perhaps once they reached the ranch, Chloe would realize the world didn't have to rock constantly.

After a hurried breakfast, they were on their way again.

At least Chloe slept while they traveled. Nate rested

his head on the window frame. He wakened when the baby fussed and waited for Louise to nurse Chloe.

"I'll hold her while you get some sleep," he said, and took the baby. Louise considered him somberly for several minutes before she closed her eyes.

When Nate realized Louise was asleep, he took the opportunity to study her. She was a strong woman, but how was she going to do this on her own? How could she take care of a baby while providing for herself and Chloe? And Missy until she found a way to take care of herself? The more he considered it, the more convinced he grew that he could offer her what they needed—a home on his ranch. A place where he would be around to help her take care of Chloe.

All he had to do was get back in time to buy a bit of land from the mountain man, and according to his reckoning, he would do so.

Of course, he'd need to do a bit of work on the cabin.

Oh, and persuade Louise that it made sense for them to remain man and wife and raise Chloe together.

Would she agree?

Chapter Fifteen

Louise slept and woke according to Chloe's demands. She could barely remember stopping at noon, though she was almost certain they had.

They arrived at another stopping house run by a dapper little man. She couldn't even say what his name was, though she surely must have heard.

That night was a repeat of the previous one. Chloe slept as long as she was jostled or swayed or walked. All of which required enormous amounts of Louise's waning energy.

If Nate hadn't helped, she wondered how she would have managed. She was so grateful when he took Chloe that she almost kissed him. Even so, she felt as if she walked and talked and ate in her sleep.

She even dozed off while nursing the baby and jerked awake in a sweat, fearing she would suffocate her.

Being a mother was a lot more work than she could have imagined. In a few days she'd have to do it alone, though she supposed Missy would be with her. Somehow Missy had the ability to sleep through Chloe's crying, so she wouldn't likely be a lot of help during the night hours.

Morning came all too soon and with it a sense of failure and incompetence that she carried with her through the hurried breakfast. It grew stronger, more pervasive, when she sat in the stage, bouncing and swaying along.

They reached the first way station to change horses and she didn't have the energy or interest to step from the stage.

Nate took Chloe from her arms and got out. He turned and held out a hand to her. "Come on. You need to stretch your legs."

She wanted to deny it. The last thing she needed was exercise. Even with him spelling her off, she'd had plenty of it during the night. But it took too much effort to argue, so she alighted.

He draped an arm over her shoulder and pulled her close, then led her away from the others. They stopped on a snow-covered hill with a gentle, cold breeze drifting across the surface. It was momentarily invigorating.

"Now, tell me what's wrong."

"I don't know what you mean." The words came hurriedly as she hovered at the edge of her pit of misery. One wrong word would send her spiraling downward.

"You look ready to cry and have all morning. I know you must be tired, what with Chloe not wanting to sleep during the night, but I'm concerned it might be more."

The dam broke and her words poured forth. "What am I doing wrong that she won't sleep? How do I know if she's getting enough to eat?" It seemed to her the baby didn't know how to feed and Louise sure didn't know how to show her. "What if she's hungry and I'm too inexperienced to know? Maybe there's something wrong with her. How can you tell if a baby hurts? She cries for every reason but can't tell me what it is."

To her utter helpless embarrassment, she sobbed, tears flowing down her face like a river.

Nate, to his credit, didn't seem to mind. He pressed her head to his shoulder. "Shh. Shh. I worry about Chloe, too. She's so tiny and fragile. But Archie says she's just like every newborn. He says she'll let us know what she wants and needs."

"Maybe she's trying and we don't understand." Each word came out accompanied with a sob. "How do I know?"

He rubbed her shoulder. "I can't answer that, but you're not doing this on your own. I'm right here to help."

Her sobs subsided. It was a comforting thought, even though they both knew it was temporary. But for now, it was all she had and she meant to take advantage of it. Just as she meant to lean on him a few more minutes before they had to return to the stagecoach.

"You've got one thing to look forward to," he said.

Her nerves tensed. Was he about to remind her she would soon be on her own? It was what they'd agreed on. What she wanted. But not right now. Right now she needed help, needed strength from outside herself.

Trust God, she reminded herself.

But at the moment, she needed strong arms and encouraging words. The last thing she wanted was to be reminded that her relationship with Nate was temporary.

"We'll be at Fort Macleod tonight. There's sure to be a midwife or an experienced mother you can consult with."

The words filled her with fresh courage. "Today? I lost track of the time."

Dutch called them back and Louise returned with more energy than she'd felt for several days. Sometime today they would arrive at Fort Macleod. It truly was something to look forward to.

Two days after that and they should reach Eden Valley Ranch. The beginning of a new life.

The end of what she and Nate presently shared.

She would not think of that for now. Perhaps something would change, though she couldn't think how or what it could be.

It was late afternoon when Dutch called, "Fort Macleod ahead."

The passengers crowded to the windows for a glimpse. All Louise saw were the stockade walls with a Union Jack flag flying from a tall pole. At some point, they had crossed into Canada.

She sat back, eagerness mixing with a dozen other nameless emotions in her heart although one had a name she refused to acknowledge. Dread...dread of Nate's imminent goodbye.

She forced herself to focus on all that the fort offered and clutched Chloe to her chest as, a few miles later, they drove through the open gates. A wide lane ran the length of the fort with wooden shanties on either side. "It's not much to look at," she ventured.

Rowena peered out the opposite window. "I trust there is more behind the surface than we see."

Eight red-coated Mounties marched past in perfect formation, paused to salute the arrivals, then marched on.

Rowena pressed a hand to her throat. "Oh, my. If that's what hides within these walls, I'm more than ready to settle here."

Gabe sighed expansively. "Don't they make an impressive sight?"

"Indeed they do."

Louise giggled at the enthusiasm of the pair and slid her gaze toward Nate. Her amusement fled at the serious look on his face. She wanted to ask him what was wrong but not in front of the others. Then he smiled and her worries fled.

He chuckled. "You'll find it a busy place with lots of unexpected offerings." They pulled up before what the sign said was the Macleod Hotel. "Not the least of which is this hotel."

Dutch threw open the doors before anyone could demand explanation.

Nate took Chloe and helped Louise to the boardwalk. She breathed deeply. "Finally, civilization."

"Or the nearest thing to it," Nate said half apologetically.

"Compared to some of the mining camps I lived in with Pa, it's downright inviting."

Louise looked up at the sign—a large silhouette of the back of a man's head and the words *No Jawbone*. She shivered at the sinister sign. "What does that mean?"

Nate chuckled. He seemed to be enjoying her reaction. "It means Kamoose accepts no credit."

"Kamoose? Who or what is that?"

The others hung back, as curious as Louise about Nate's comment.

"Kamoose Taylor is the proprietor of this establishment." Nate enjoyed everyone's interest.

"Strange name," Missy said.

Nate grinned widely. "I believe his real name is Harry, but the Indians call him Kamoose, which means wife stealer."

Louise gaped at him. "He stole someone's wife?"

Laughing, Nate explained, "I believe he stole his wife

when her Indian family refused to sell her despite his generous offer of a horse, two pairs of blankets and some tobacco."

Louise couldn't stop staring at the sign. What kind of world had she come to that a man tried to buy a woman and then stole her and everyone seemed okay with it?

She drew in resignation. It really didn't sound much different than what she and Nate did. Well, maybe she'd overreacted.

Nate and Louise followed the others through the door into the hotel lobby.

"That's Kamoose," Nate said, indicating the man behind the wooden counter.

Louise tried not to stare. The man seemed ordinary enough. Tall and rangy.

"Howdy, folks. You looking for a room or two?"

"Yes, sir," Nate said.

"First off, read the rules." Kamoose pointed to a sign on the front of the desk.

Louise read them silently and gasped. She turned to Nate, who seemed constantly amused by the situation, and whispered, "Surely these aren't to be taken seriously."

Nate shrugged. "I don't think anyone's ever tried to challenge them. Kamoose has been a whiskey runner and likely a number of other things outside the law. I, for one, don't want to see if he means it." He kept his voice very low, but still Kamoose watched him keenly.

"You got a problem with my rules?"

"Nope. They sound fair to me," Nate readily announced.

Louise pressed her lips together to keep from sputtering. There were ten rules. All but one—*Spiked boots and spurs must be removed at night*—were ridiculous, especially the last. *Guests are requested to rise before 6:00 a.m. This is imperative as the sheets are needed for tablecloths.*

But Nate had arranged a room for Louise, Missy and the baby before Louise could think of an alternative.

He escorted her to the room. It was decent enough. Not as nice as Phil's bedroom, but she reckoned not many would be.

He handed Chloe to Louise. "Rest and clean up. I'll be back in a bit to take you to supper." And then he was gone.

Missy and Louise looked at each other, then flipped the covers back on the bed. The sheets appeared clean. They took turns bouncing on the mattress and laughed at the squeaking springs, then lay back, putting Chloe between them.

"It's nice to feel a bed under my bones," Missy said.

"We're almost at our destination," Louise said.

"You'll be glad, won't you?" Missy sounded uncertain.

"I'll be glad to not have to travel all day. What about you?"

Missy didn't answer at first.

Louise turned to regard her. "What's bothering you?"

"I'm trying to imagine what the ranch will be like. I hope it's not too isolated. You see, I want to—" She met Louise's eyes, revealing a deep longing.

"Missy, whatever you want, I won't stand in your way."

"I won't leave you to manage on your own, though of course you have Nate, so—"

"I'll be fine." Louise hoped her smile portrayed assurance. No reason for Missy to know Louise worried how she'd manage once Nate left. "What is it you want to do?"

"Something important. Something that gives me independence." She stared at the ceiling. "I don't want to depend on anyone ever again."

"Have I disappointed you?"

"No. Never. But don't you find it hard to trust people after Vic?"

Vic, Pa, Mama, even Nate. But all she said was, "A little." But rather than make her want to run from her past, as it seemed to do for Missy, it made Louise want to pull things tight and hold on to them. She'd never let go of what she had if she had a choice. She didn't. People, events, things forced her to move on to something new. Usually without allowing her any say in the matter.

They lay there for a while, talking about their past, their hopes and dreams, and mostly about Chloe, who still lay between them.

Someone rapped on the door.

Louise sprang from the bed. "Nate is back and I haven't even tidied up." She reached for her bag, intending to brush her hair, but the knocking came again.

"Answer the door," Missy said, a smile in her voice.

Louise drew in a steadying breath. She was acting like a love-struck girl anticipating an outing with her beau. Ironic that she was a wife, and the man coming for her did not represent love and sweet dreams.

She veered toward the door and opened it to reveal a woman. Her heart stuttered a protest. Just as quickly, she silently insisted she wasn't disappointed.

"Mrs. Hawkins?"

Louise nodded, her ribs so taut they hurt. "What's wrong?" Had Nate been hurt?

"Oh, nothing's wrong, my dear. My name is Mrs. Noble. My husband is a doctor. I am often his assistant, especially with the ladies. Your husband asked if I would have a look at the baby and make sure she is as she should be."

Louise stepped aside to let the woman enter the room.

Missy got off the bed. "I'm going out to look around."

Louise nodded distractedly.

"You have a very handsome husband," Mrs. Noble said. "Also a very thoughtful one. Not too many men would seek someone out to check on their wife and baby."

Louise took the words into her heart. Was his concern only to make sure she got to Eden Valley Ranch and didn't delay his travels? Or did his caring go deeper than responsibility? Then, as Mrs. Noble looked at Chloe, she forgot everything but the baby.

Would the woman find something wrong?

Nate paced back and forth in the hotel lobby, ignoring Kamoose's scowl.

"You're wearing out my floor," Kamoose said when he couldn't stop Nate with his looks.

"You'd pace, too, if the doctor's wife was upstairs with your wife and baby."

Kamoose laughed loudly. "In that case, go right ahead and wear a trench in the floor."

"Thanks," he said, though it wasn't gratitude he felt at the man's sense of humor, which did nothing to ease his concern.

There was nothing wrong with either Louise or Chloe, he told himself over and over. But he wouldn't know that for certain until Mrs. Noble said so.

He slowed his steps to look at the clock on the wall

behind Kamoose. She'd been up there almost thirty minutes. That couldn't be good. He headed for the stairs but stopped at the bottom. Even if Louise was his wife in name, he couldn't go barging in while she was with Mrs. Noble, so he turned around and crossed the room again, his heels striking loudly on the wooden floor.

"Mr. Hawkins?"

He spun around. "Mrs. Noble. Is she okay?"

"The baby is fine. So is your wife. I gave her some tips on feeding the infant and maybe getting Chloe's days and nights turned around, though that might be difficult so long as you are traveling."

"But the baby isn't in pain?" He'd worried about it since Louise had shared her fears.

"Not that I can tell. She's only three days old, so she's still adjusting to a whole new world. It takes time."

A wave of weakness swept over his arms and legs. "They're both okay?"

"Well, don't expect your wife to be as energetic as she was before the baby, especially when the child isn't sleeping at night. Be patient with her. Help her as much as you can."

He grabbed Mrs. Noble's hand and shook it. "Thank you. What a relief."

Kamoose watched from his post, grinning widely, as if enjoying the sight of a man reduced to such a quivering state.

"You're welcome. If you need anything, don't hesitate to ask." Mrs. Noble bade him goodbye and left the hotel.

Nate hurried across the room. His foot reached the first step as Louise appeared at the top with Chloe in her arms. He stalled, staring up at her. Had she grown more beautiful in the past hour?

He raced up the stairs and escorted her down. "What would you like to do?"

Her smile was so sweet and confident, he couldn't take his eyes off her until Kamoose laughed.

"I'd like to look around, if I may?"

He glanced about the room, then realized she meant the fort, not the hotel. "Of course." He led her to the door.

"Supper is served in an hour. Be here or miss it." Kamoose's words followed them outside.

"What would you like to see?" Nate asked.

"Everything." She cradled the baby in one arm.

He knew he wasn't mistaken in thinking she looked more peaceful. "Mrs. Noble said the baby is doing fine."

"Yes, she was very reassuring." Louise smiled up at him. "Thank you for arranging for her to visit."

He pulled her close and they proceeded to walk the length of the street. There was a small store, a blacksmith shop and, of course, the long barracks for the men.

"It's laid out neatly," she commented.

"The Mounties are efficient and orderly." Having been through the fort several times, he was able to point out the parade grounds, the various barracks, the officers' quarters, and other buildings and their use. They reached the end of the street, turned around and made their way back toward the hotel.

A bell rang across the clearing, a man pulling frantically on the rope. "Fire. Fire," he called. "Barracks C." It seemed as if every able-bodied man in the fort raced down the street.

"I need to see if they need my assistance." He was loath to leave her. Not because he thought she needed his assistance, but because he'd been enjoying the few minutes they'd had alone. She'd talked more than she'd done since they'd started this journey.

"You go help. I'll go back to the hotel and wait for you to join us for supper." She slipped from his grasp and gave him a smile that made him even more reluctant to leave her.

Before he could change his mind and stay, he turned and followed the others racing to fight the fire.

Louise watched Nate run to fight the fire. Part of her was proud of his quickness to rush to the aid of others. Part of her worried he might be in danger. *Lord, keep him safe.*

They had been on their way back to the hotel, but she wasn't anxious to return on her own and sit in the little room or stay in the lobby and stare at Kamoose. Neither option offered any pleasure, although she'd been anticipating going to the dining room and sitting across the table from Nate. Not that she hadn't done it for the past nine days, but being in a proper dining room made it seem different.

Though how proper could a dining room be that said it used the sheets off the beds for tablecloths?

Perhaps her restlessness only resulted from her improved mood after Mrs. Noble's visit. The woman had shown her how to make the baby nurse properly, had assured her the infant showed no signs of being in pain and told her what things she needed to watch for.

Louise's life felt good and right at the moment.

Her measured steps had brought her to the store. Some dried apples would taste real fine right about now. She shifted Chloe into one arm and opened the door. The store smelled like old cheese and coal oil and a few things she didn't care to give a label to.

At her request, the storekeeper dug out a handful of dried apples and wrapped them for her. She paid for them and left the store without another thought.

Out in the cold, as she turned her steps toward the hotel, she checked on Chloe, making sure the baby was still well wrapped. She looked up in time to sidestep a man. But she paid him no mind at all. She wanted to get back to the hotel and enjoy her apples.

"Well, well, if it ain't just the person I've been looking for."

That voice. It sent fingers of fear up and down her spine. She'd recognize it anywhere. It belonged to the last person in the world she wanted to ever see again.

Louise lifted her head and gave Vic her fiercest scowl. She should have known he would follow them. "Why aren't you back in Rocky Creek carrying out your nefarious deeds?"

He sneered. "I don't understand those big words and you know it, Miss High and Mighty." He saw the bundle in her arms. "And now ya got yerself a baby. How nice." He rubbed his greedy hands together as if already enjoying the money the child represented to him.

Louise managed not to reveal her loathing and fear. "And a husband, remember?"

"Did you think that would stop me?"

Truth was, she had hoped it would. At least it meant she had the law on her side.

Vic crowded to the side where she held the baby. He pinched her elbow. A passerby might think he was being solicitous and guiding her along, but that was only because they didn't hear his whispered words. "One sound out of you or any attempt to get away and I'll make sure that precious little bundle of yers goes flying."

She had no reason to doubt both his ability and his intention of doing exactly what he said. The best she could do was drag her feet without being obvious, in the hopes someone from the stagecoach who knew her would see her and intervene.

Where was Nate when she needed him?

Gone helping others. Something she'd admired just moments ago but that now put her nerves on edge.

Trust God. Seemed He was the only one whom she could count on.

Her prayer was simple but never more heartfelt. *God, help me get away from this evil man. Protect Chloe.*

Chapter Sixteen

It turned out to be a chimney fire and was soon extinguished.

Nate stopped only long enough to wash the dirt from his hands before he jogged back to the hotel.

Kamoose looked startled at his entrance. "What'd you do with the missus?"

"I went to help with the fire. I'll bring her down now for supper."

"Bring her from where?"

"Why, from her room." He pointed up the stairs.

"I didn't see her come in and I was here the whole time."

"You must have missed her." He took the steps three at a time and banged on the door.

Missy pulled it open. "Is it supper time? I'm ready." She closed the door behind her.

"Where's Louise?"

"She's with you." Her eyes narrowed. "What is this about?"

"She's not with me." He explained about the fire. "She said she was coming straight here." Had she stopped at the store? Perhaps found someone to visit with? "Go ahead. She must have gotten sidetracked. I'll find her."

Missy's eyes widened with fear. She spoke but one word. "Vic?" She swallowed hard and couldn't go on.

"He couldn't have caught us," Nate told her. But even as he said the words, he knew the man could have. They'd been delayed enough for him to have overtaken them. "I'll bring her back." No one—not Vic, not anyone else—would take her, or the baby, away from him.

Outside on the street he stopped in the store. No Louise. He headed for the doctor's office. Perhaps she'd gone to consult with Mrs. Noble again.

"No, I haven't seen her," Mrs. Noble said. "Does she often wander off?"

"No." Maybe he hadn't seen much of Louise over the past few years, but he knew she wouldn't simply walk away. His Louise would stay and fight. Which, he realized with a jolt of understanding, was why she'd stayed in Rocky Creek. She'd hoped she could change things by staying, just as he'd hoped to change things by leaving.

"Thanks." He hurried up and down the broad, rutted street and ended up in front of the Mounties' headquarters. Colonel Macleod exited as Nate was about to enter the building.

"Can I help you?"

"I don't know." He quickly explained Louise's disappearance.

"Have you looked in all the buildings?"

Nate told him the places he'd been to.

"She's just had a baby, you say? Could she have fainted somewhere?"

"Wouldn't I have come upon her?" He scrubbed at his neck. Where had Louise and Chloe disappeared to?

"Come along." Colonel Macleod signaled Nate to follow.

Nate struggled not to rush past the man and dash up and down the street calling Louise. His brain screamed her name. *Louise, where are you and Chloe?*

Vic led Louise behind the buildings, down a narrow passage and into another building. A storage shed of some sort. What did the man have in mind?

He looked about, then pushed her deeper into the dim interior.

She wondered if he had a plan or if he was making it up as he went. He seemed to be thinking hard. While he thought of what he meant to do, she tried to come up with her own plan.

If she called out, would help come before he could escape or harm either of them?

She wasn't about to test the idea.

She had to find a way to escape without putting herself or Chloe at risk. She looked at the items in the storeroom and her eyes lit on an array of axes. Quickly she shifted her gaze, lest he notice her interest. But how was she to get at them and how could she swing one while holding Chloe?

"What do you plan to do with us?" Every word was a challenge.

"I'm going to take you someplace where no one will ever find you."

"You'll be a hunted man and you know what they say…the Mounties always get their man."

"Not this time." He grabbed her arm. "Come on. We're going to my horse."

He didn't say the barn, which gave her cause to think he'd left his horse elsewhere.

"You planning to make us ride double?" She almost gagged at the thought.

He sneered. "One way to make sure you won't get away."

She considered her options quickly. "The baby is going to get in the way." Much as her heart broke to say the words, she told him, "Let me leave the baby here."

He leaned close and lifted the blanket covering Chloe. "Ugly little thing."

Her fists curled, but she knew the only way she could hope to save Chloe's life was to remain calm. She had to make Vic see the wisdom in leaving the infant behind. Chloe would cry when she wakened, which would be soon after Louise stopped rocking her. Someone would hear and save the baby's life.

"Hadn't you better get moving? Nate will be looking for me by now."

Vic squeezed her arm so hard, tears came to her eyes. She blinked them away. She would not show any weakness in front of him.

"Okay, let's get going."

She tried to put Chloe down.

"We're taking the baby. I haven't come all this way in the cold snow to lose out on my sale."

"You'll have a hard time hiding with a baby. They cry a lot, you know."

"So muffle it."

She snorted. "You don't know much about babies, do you? You muffle one and it could well suffocate." Her throat was so dry she could barely get out the words.

"Think about it. We leave the baby here, recognizing it's going to cause you problems, and I go with you."

"I want Missy, too." He shook his head as he grunted. "This isn't going the way I planned."

Which pleased her no end. However, it wasn't exactly going the way she wanted, either. But whatever happened, she must get him to let her leave Chloe.

"Nate expected to meet me for supper. He'll be turning the place upside down looking for me by now."

"Put it down and let's get out of here."

Thank You, God. She set Chloe on a table and tucked some packages around her to keep her from falling. She'd be safe until someone found her. Tears filled her eyes and clogged the back of her throat as she let Vic drag her out the door.

He glanced to the right and the left, then hurried her toward the open gate.

"Did you leave your horse outside the fort?"

"Never you mind." His grasp on her arms hurt like fury, but she welcomed the pain. It helped divert her from the horror of leaving her baby. Had her mother felt the same tearing inside when she left? Vic paused at the last corner before the open gate.

A guard stood in the watchtower, but his attention was on those approaching the fort, not on those leaving it.

If only the guard would look in her direction, she could mouth the word *help*.

But he didn't.

"Now." Vic rushed for the gate, pushing her along. He clung close to the wall as he rushed toward a horse tied nearby.

God, she cried silently, her heart about to burst, *save*

Chloe but save me, too. I want to be her mama. I want to be Nate's wife.

Where had that come from? Likely from her fear. Without Nate at her side, she felt vulnerable. He had taken care of her on every step of this journey. If only he had stayed with her, Vic would not have been able to capture her.

Where was Nate now? For all she knew, he was still fighting a fire. Maybe he'd even been hurt doing so.

She added one more desperate prayer.

Keep Nate safe. Help him be the one to find Chloe.

Then Vic pushed her up on the horse, her legs to one side. "Now we ride. And you best not be a problem if you know what's good for you."

She knew what was good for her and it wasn't riding away with Vic's arms about her.

All she needed was one chance to escape. But the frozen ground pounded under the horse's hooves, taking her away from the fort, from Nate, from Chloe. And she saw no means of escape.

One chance of escape is all I need. Please, God, provide it.

Two mounted men rode toward them. Vic muttered under his breath. He would have reined away, but deep snow lay on either side of the trail and it would bog the horse down. Ahead, another trail veered to the left and he kicked the horse into a faster gallop, aiming for the fork in the road.

If only she could get the attention of the patrol returning to the fort.

She could think of only one way to do that and she shivered at the risk it involved. But she'd prayed for a chance and here it was.

She sucked in three deep breaths, then sneezed as hard as she could, swinging her head back until it connected with Vic's face.

He let out a ragged breath and loosened his grasp on her. At the same time she threw herself from the back of the horse.

The ground rushed up with alarming speed. She fell on her knees and elbows, sending a jolt clear through her body, then her head smacked the ground.

"You little fool," Vic spat out as he reined about and faced her.

Run, her brain said. But her body wouldn't obey.

Nate and Colonel Macleod marched over to the dining hall, now full of men in and out of uniform. The men in the dining hall scrambled to their feet and snapped to attention at the colonel's entrance.

"At ease, men."

After a slight shifting, the men remained standing.

"Nate Hawkins here is missing a wife and baby."

Nate expected the barely contained grins from a couple of men who were brave enough to risk the colonel's reprimand, which came swiftly, then the colonel explained how Nate had gone to assist with the fire and Louise had disappeared. "Has anyone seen a woman and child? Anything suspicious?"

When no man spoke up, the colonel pointed at three men. "You, you and you. Start looking." The three men saluted and hurried from the building.

Nate followed Colonel Macleod as his men fanned out to search the fort. He stood in the middle of the windswept yard and shivered. The temperatures were falling as night descended. Where were Louise and the baby?

He looked about. "Louise," he bellowed. "Louise, where are you?"

"Be calm," Colonel Macleod said.

Calm? Nate had abandoned that emotion about the time he met the colonel outside his headquarters. It wasn't possible to be as cool as the man at his side with Louise and the baby missing. Colonel Macleod stood with his arms at his sides, unruffled as he watched his men search every nook and cranny.

One of the constables signaled for them to come. "Over here."

Nate rushed so fast he would have passed the colonel, but Macleod put out a hand to restrain him. "I'd better see what he's found before you go rushing in."

Nate had no intention of waiting, but the young Mountie barred his way.

"Listen," the man said. "Do you hear that?"

A baby crying. "Chloe! Where is she?"

"I can't say. I called as soon as I heard it."

They followed the sound into a storage shed and he saw the bundle on the table.

"Chloe!" He dashed to her perch and opened the blankets to reveal a squalling, red-faced baby. He picked her up and rocked her until she settled.

"Louise must be nearby. She'd never leave the baby."

The men searched every inch of the building, but there was no sign of her. Nate even looked for himself. His heart pushed hot blood through his veins. "Where is she?"

Colonel Macleod drew him aside. "Has she been acting at all strangely?"

"No, of course not. How could you suggest such a thing?"

"I mean no offense, but occasionally women, after they give birth, aren't quite right for a time."

Nate narrowed his eyes and studied the man with a huge dose of dislike. "You're suggesting she left the baby here and did what? Disappeared into the air? Flew the coop? Even if she did wander off, surely your men can find her." He was angry enough to take on the whole force.

A young constable trotted in. "Colonel, you better come. We have a situation at the gate."

Colonel Macleod left.

Nate curled his fists and gave a feral growl. Surely the situation could wait until Louise had been found.

Unless it was Louise!

Chloe in his arms, he raced after Colonel Macleod, practically tromping on his heels.

Two mounted men were at the gate. One held a body. He recognized the coat and shawl.

Louise! A spasm gripped his body so hard that he couldn't move. Couldn't breathe. Couldn't think.

Couldn't imagine life without her.

"Sir, this woman is injured."

Louise squirmed. "Put me down. I can walk."

Life came back to Nate's limbs. He leaped across the remaining six feet. "I'll take her." He didn't give the man a chance to say yes or no. He shifted the baby into one arm and lifted his free arm as Louise slid from the horse and landed at his feet, her hands resting on his shoulders.

She looked into his face, her eyes dark and full of both fear and relief. Blood ran down her forehead.

"You're hurt."

"You have Chloe. I knew you'd find her." Sobbing,

she fell against his chest, one arm around the baby, the other clutching the front of his coat.

Colonel Macleod stepped forward, "She needs to go to the hospital. Ma'am, perhaps you should let someone carry you."

"No, thank you." At least that's what Nate thought she said. Her words were muffled by her sobs against his chest. She shook as if battered by a fierce wind.

"One of you take the baby," he said.

Sure hands came out and lifted Chloe from his grasp. Nate scooped Louise into his arms despite her protests and followed the colonel to the hospital.

Mrs. Noble and a man, whom Nate took to be her husband, met them at the door.

"Bring her in." Mrs. Noble showed the way. "Put her there."

Nate set Louise on the bed indicated, but he did not leave her side. Not that he could have. She had his hand in a grip he didn't mean to test. He smoothed her hair. There were so many things he wanted to say. But this was not the time or the place. Nor could he force a word from his tight throat.

"You men wait outside while I examine her," Doc Noble said.

Nate didn't move. After all, this was his wife.

"Sir, if you please." The doctor indicated the door.

Louise's hand slowly uncurled. "I'm okay. Go see to Chloe."

Mention of the baby enabled him to step back. But only Colonel Macleod's hand on his back made him step toward the door.

Once the door closed behind him, someone put the

baby in his arms and he kissed her tiny face. What would he do if anything took her or Louise from him?

"Let's hear what happened," Colonel Macleod said to the two Mounties who stood nearby.

"Sir, we were returning from our patrol and as we approached the gate, a man rode out. He had a woman on the horse in front of him. We noted it but didn't give it much consideration." The pair looked at each other. "We figured it was a homesteader come for mail or some supplies and on his way home. But then the woman—Mrs. Hawkins—seemed to leap from the horse."

Nate gasped. "She might have been killed." Would his heart ever stop stabbing him with every beat?

Not until he was certain Louise was okay and not going to disappear again.

The Mounties continued, "We, of course, turned aside to see if they needed assistance. The man saw us approach and rode away. That's when we got suspicious that all was not right." Colonel Macleod waited for the spokesman to continue.

"We went immediately to Mrs. Hawkins. She was struggling to get to her feet. Blood ran down her forehead. We offered assistance, which she accepted reluctantly. She was breathless, barely able to speak. When she could get her words out, she informed us the man who rode away had tried to kidnap her. Constable Brown rode after him, fired off two shots. He abandoned the chase because his horse was already spent."

"Did the bullets meet their target?"

"I can't say, sir."

Colonel Macleod thanked the man and signaled to a Mountie standing at attention nearby. "Stewart, mount up and go after the man. Brown, give him a description. Be sure you take a sturdy horse. The trails will be clogged with snow."

"Sir." The men saluted and then trotted away to do their superior's bidding.

"We'll get him," the colonel assured Nate.

"Very good." But what was taking the doctor so long? Nate shuddered as he thought of Louise falling from a running horse.

She said she was okay, but Louise would say that if every bone in her body was broken and blood poured from each limb.

Nate looked at Chloe, sleeping in his arms.

If something happens to your mama, he silently promised, *I will take care of you.*

Chapter Seventeen

"You are a blessed young woman," Dr. Noble said after checking Louise. "You could have been seriously hurt by that fall. As it is, you are going to be very sore for a few days. I'd like you to stay here overnight so I can keep an eye on you."

"Thank you, Doctor, but I'm sure that's not necessary. I must get to my baby. She'll want to eat soon." She tried to slip from the examining table gracefully, but as the doctor warned, she hurt all over. She managed to straighten without groaning, but when she took a step, her insides twisted and she bent over with a moan.

Mrs. Noble rushed forward. "You're in no condition to be moving about."

"I'm fine."

The older woman tsked. "You know you aren't." She gently guided Louise toward a bed.

Louise wished she had the strength to resist, but it took every ounce of her willpower just to remain upright. *Oh, please don't let there be anything wrong.* She couldn't be responsible for another delay in their trip, though there was no reason she couldn't let Nate go on ahead and make the rest of the journey on her own. No reason but her own reluctance.

Somehow she could not imagine carrying on without him.

"My baby," she managed to protest before Mrs. Noble eased her down on the bed and lifted her legs to the covers where she casually removed Louise's shoes.

"I'll get your husband to bring in the baby." She spread a quilt over Louise and strode away with firm, purposeful steps, leaving Louise alone with the doctor.

"My advice is for you to take it very easy. Get as much rest as possible." Dr. Noble proceeded to itemize all the things that could happen if she didn't.

"I'll be fine." Louise saw no reason to tell him she hoped to continue her journey as soon as Nate could arrange it.

A few minutes later, Nate followed Mrs. Noble into the room.

Louise tried to smile, but at the worry in Nate's face she found it impossible. "Is Chloe okay?"

With one foot, Nate dragged a chair to the side of the bed and sat. "She wasn't happy about being left on a surface that didn't move, but as soon as I rocked her, she settled down." He lowered the baby into Louise's arms and folded back the blanket to reveal Chloe's face. The baby blinked at the light and puckered her mouth.

Louise laughed though it choked off with a sob. "I thought I might never see her again."

Nate touched the dressing the doctor had put over the cut on Louise's forehead. His fingers trailed along her hairline as he examined her for any further sign of damage. His eyes met hers, full of so many things she couldn't be sure what she saw. Relief and worry? Surprise and regret? Though she could think of no reason for either of the latter two.

"You gave me an awful fright, Louise. When I couldn't find you—" He swallowed hard and seemed unable to continue. "Then I found Chloe. I knew you would never leave her. Not unless something awful had happened." Again he choked off.

He bent closer and kissed her forehead. "Louise Hawkins, what am I going to do with you?"

I like what you're doing just fine. But she couldn't make the words leave her mouth.

He lifted his head enough to look into her face, searching deep into her thoughts. He trailed his thumb along her cheek and smiled. "I might never again let you out of my sight. That way I can make sure you're safe."

The smile she gave him came from an unfamiliar place in the depths of her heart, a place where her dreams and wishes resided in secrecy. "I might like that," she whispered.

His gaze went on and on, then shifted to her lips.

Her mouth dried as if she'd been lost on the barren prairie in the heat of summer as she realized he wanted to kiss her.

And she wanted him to.

She closed her eyes and tipped her face to welcome his kiss.

"Louise, don't ever scare me like that again." His words whispered across her skin and then his lips met hers as he claimed her promise.

Then he withdrew, a bemused smile upon his mouth.

One, she imagined, that matched her own.

Chloe fussed, drawing their attention to her.

"It's time to feed her." Louise's voice sounded husky in her own ears.

"Poor baby has been more than patient." Nate grabbed pillows from the nearby bed and propped Louise up. He turned his back as she arranged Chloe in her arms. As soon as she was covered, Louise told him, "You can sit down again."

Nate swung the chair around and straddled it, leaning on the back as he studied Louise.

His intensity made her look away. "What are you thinking?" she asked, not really wanting to know. Before he could answer, she rushed on, "I know you're in a hurry to get to Edendale. You can leave us here—Missy and me and the baby. No need to let us delay you."

He chuckled, pulling her gaze back to his. "Didn't you hear me say I don't intend to let you out of my sight? Especially with Vic out there somewhere?"

"The Mounties will soon capture him." She forced confidence into her voice even though terror forged a cruel trail through her insides. What if Vic circled around and came back?

"Until they do, I don't intend to leave you alone." Every word was a firm promise.

She wanted to believe him, wanted it to be true. Oh, how she wanted it to be real. "But what about your ranch? The man you need to see?"

His jaw clenched. "It's not Christmas yet. We're only two days away."

She nodded. "Did you find the driver for the stage to Edendale?"

"Petey. Yes, I did."

"Is he ready to leave tomorrow?"

Nate sat back and stared at her as the meaning of her words registered. "You won't be up to travel."

"I'm fine. Just a few bruises."

"The doctor warned me you need to take it easy or there could be complications."

He'd warned her, too. "I had a baby and traveled the next day. I fell off a horse and only bruised a few muscles. I think I can ride a stagecoach." Finished defending herself, she pressed her lips into a firm line. She would finish this journey. And she would not be responsible for delaying Nate any longer. How could she live with herself if she cost him his dream?

"You're tough as shoe leather, that's for sure." His smile didn't reach his eyes.

"You can tell Petey we'll leave in the morning." She would be ready for travel one way or another. Two more days until they reached Eden Valley Ranch and she could rest. Her body cried out for that day.

But her heart cried out for it to never arrive because once it did, the agreement between her and Nate would end.

How could she face the future without the man who meant so much to her and had since she was thirteen years old? She remembered one day in particular back then, him challenging Gordie to jump over mud puddles, then later playing ball with his friend, Missy sitting in the grass nearby while Mr. and Mrs. Porter watched them from the back porch.

She'd been welcomed by the Porters, but it wasn't only them, she realized with a deep sense of acknowledgment, that had filled a spot in her empty, hurting heart. It was Nate.

"Do you remember when I walked up to you and Gordie playing ball?" She hadn't meant to speak of the occasion, but the words came without forethought. It was the first time she had made herself known to him. "You missed a catch and the ball tumbled to my feet. I picked it up and tossed it to you." A smile rounded her words as she recalled those sweeter, more innocent times.

"I remember." Did his grin seem a little self-conscious?

"You didn't even try and catch it. Why?"

His grin grew lopsided. "I had never seen such a pretty girl and I guess I stared like the silly boy I was."

It was her turn to stare, unable to move a muscle. "All this time I thought you were angry because a girl threw you a ball."

He shook his head back and forth, reached out his hand and pressed his fingers to her cheek. "You were never just a girl."

She tried to think beyond his fingers on her skin. Tried to think what he meant. Finally she forced words to her mind. "What was I?"

"You were always Louise. A friend. Almost family. I guess I thought you, Gordie and I would always be friends." He lifted one shoulder in resignation. Or perhaps confusion. "But things changed."

She nodded. "The Porters died."

"Vic showed up," he added.

"You left."

"You stayed and married Gordie." Their gazes locked, full of regrets and accusations.

"I wanted to keep the Porter home together and that was the only way I knew how," she said by way of explanation. "It didn't change things."

"When I left, I'd hoped Gordie would decide to leave,

too. Leave Vic and the life that he'd fallen into." He drew in a deep breath. "It didn't make a difference."

They reached for each other at the same time. She held his hand and he held hers as a thousand regrets filled her heart.

"I wish things hadn't changed so much," she whispered.

"But change is inevitable. Time moves on and we must move with it." He grew thoughtful. "God has given us a chance to start over. We don't need to be held back by our regrets and failures. Perhaps we can now build the very thing we wanted all along."

Her heart hammered with anticipation. She could see the future and it looked bright and welcoming. She couldn't help being dazzled by it. But first she had to be sure. What exactly did he mean by *we*? "What is it we've wanted all along?"

"Home. Family. Security. Getting the ranch will enable me to have that."

He'd gone from *we* to *me*. So he'd never intended to include her in his vision of the future. Silly her. Holding back the tears that stung her eyes, she kept any trace of emotion from her voice and pasted on a dim smile. "I'm glad for you. Chloe is my reason to start over."

The baby finished nursing and Louise raised her to her shoulder to burp her.

Nate cupped the bald little head. "What better reason can there be?"

"None." But having a home, family and security shared with Nate sounded awfully nice, too. If she had to start over, and she had no choice but to do so, she could think of no other way that would satisfy her more than to start over with the one person with whom she'd shared her past.

Unfortunately, the past was dead and gone. Nate meant to move on. Louise would have to start over on her own. Only not alone. She had Chloe and would do her utmost to give her child the love and security Louise had so desperately longed for all her life.

Nate now understood Louise had stayed in an attempt to hold on to the home and love she'd found with the Porter family. He understood her need for security and stability.

It was all he could do not to blurt out a request for Louise to consider making the marriage permanent. They could build a future together. Raise Chloe together. Nate could give Louise the home she wanted. And he already loved Chloe.

But he couldn't take advantage of her fragile state at the moment. The doctor had made it clear that Louise was both physically and mentally exhausted. No, he'd do the right thing and wait until they reached the ranch and she'd had time to rest and regain her strength before he suggested they join forces.

In the meantime, he meant to take care of her and the baby. He rose to his feet. "I have a couple of errands to run. I'll be back in a moment."

Alarm flared through her eyes before she could stop it and then she quenched it and smiled. "You go tend to your matters. I don't need a caregiver."

He squeezed her shoulder gently. "I won't go more than a few steps outside the door. Like I said, I don't intend to take my eyes off you until I have you safely at Eden Valley Ranch."

Again her emotions filled her eyes before she could control them. This time gratitude, then she nodded. "I'm fine."

Two words he had come to despise. *I'm fine*. When she was not. What he wouldn't give for her to just once turn to him and ask for his help.

He strode from the room before he could give voice to his frustration and ask if she ever would.

A Mountie stood outside the outer door.

"Have they found that man yet?" Nate asked.

The corporal understood Nate meant Vic. "No, sir. And I'm to stay here and keep guard until they do."

"That's reassuring."

"Yes, sir."

With a guard at the door, Nate could spare a few minutes away from Louise's bedside, so he trotted to the hotel.

Kamoose looked up at Nate's entrance and grunted. "Supper is over long ago but I heard about the adventure you've had with your wife and saved food for both of you. How is she?"

"A little banged up and bruised but okay, I think. The doctor is keeping her there for now so he can watch her."

"Don't you worry, young man. The Mounties will bring that man to justice. Count on it."

"I am. Is my sister-in-law upstairs?"

Missy must have heard his voice, or perhaps she'd been waiting for him to show up, because she clattered down the stairs. "Where's Louise and the baby? Are they okay?"

He repeated his report. "Could you get her things? And Chloe's?"

Before he finished, Missy was halfway up the stairs. "I'll get mine, too," she called over her shoulder.

"Missy."

She stopped and looked at him.

"I'm staying with her, so you might as well enjoy your bed tonight."

She looked at him a long thirty seconds, then sighed. "I guess that makes sense. But I want to see her."

"Then get her things and come along with me."

"I'll get the plates of food." Kamoose disappeared into the dining room and reappeared with two plates generously rounded up with food and covered with cloths. "Bring the plates back when you're done."

Nate thanked him. "You're a generous host."

"I know it." Kamoose laughed heartily. "But I wouldn't want the word to get out, if you get my meaning."

"I'll be sure and tell everyone how tough you are."

Kamoose laughed again.

Missy hurried down the stairs with Louise's bag, and Nate escorted her out into the dark evening and over to the hospital building.

When he stepped inside, he noticed Louise's eyes grow wide.

"Oh, you came back," she whispered hoarsely.

"I said I would." Would she be so unsure of him? Or was she simply feeling vulnerable? He clung to the hope it was the latter.

Missy flew past him and straight to Louise's arms. "I was so scared and worried especially when I heard some man had taken you. I knew it was Vic." She sobbed as Louise rubbed her back. "I hope they get that evil man soon." She sat up and dried her eyes. "They said you fell off a horse. Is that right?"

Nate snorted. "She jumped off to get away from Vic." He didn't know if he was grateful she'd escaped the man or upset at the risk she took.

Louise gave him a steady look. "I prayed for a chance to get away from him and when I saw it I wasn't about to refuse to take it."

"Where was Chloe?" Missy asked.

Louise gave the full details of the story from the time she'd met Vic on the plank sidewalk to being rescued by the mounted patrol.

She neglected to tell how she got to the hospital—in Nate's arms, with his heart threatening to pound right out of his chest. Had he ever been so frightened in his life?

He handed Louise her plate of food and she ate most of it while he devoured his. Colonel Macleod entered about the time Nate finished.

"How are you, ma'am?" he asked Louise.

Of course, she said she was fine and ready to resume her travels.

"Have you found him?" Louise sounded eager to hear good news from the colonel.

"I'm afraid not, but my men will continue to track him until they do. Is there anything I can do for any of you?"

"I'm spending the night here," Nate said. It was the first Louise had heard of his plans and she blinked in surprise. "If you wouldn't mind seeing Missy back to the hotel, I'd be grateful."

"My pleasure."

Missy kissed Louise on the cheek, took the now-empty plates and left on Colonel Macleod's arm.

Louise looked at Nate without revealing any emotion. "You don't have to stay."

He wouldn't ask if she objected because he didn't

want to hear if she did. Nor would it influence his decision. "You'll need help with Chloe. Besides, until Vic is locked behind bars, I'm not leaving you alone. I'll be here all night."

"Suit yourself." She looked at the baby, depriving him of the chance to gauge her feelings.

The doctor came in to check on Louise, and Nate took the baby and stepped out of the room while he did so. The doctor joined him in a few minutes.

"I can hardly believe it, but she seems okay apart from some soreness. I'm glad you'll be spending the night here, though. Be sure and let me know if you suspect anything amiss."

"You can count on it." He returned to the room. Little Chloe needed to eat again and while she did, Nate arranged a bedroll on the floor close to Louise's bed. He was conscious that she watched his every move, but again, she avoided his look, so he couldn't say if she welcomed his presence or found it uncomfortable.

Mrs. Noble came in. "Do you need help preparing for bed or will your husband take care of your needs?"

Louise's cheeks turned a bright red. "If you don't mind helping me…"

"Not at all."

Again Nate left the room. This time he stepped outside in the night air. A different Mountie stood by the doorway. "They still haven't caught him?"

"No, sir. But we will."

His promise was reassuring, but Nate would feel better when they actually did.

He returned to the room at Mrs. Noble's bidding. A lamp burned low, filling the room with shadows. Louise was tucked under the covers, her eyes closed. Assuming she meant to sleep, he removed his boots and stretched out on the bedroll.

Little Chloe fussed softly. How long would it be before she grew impatient with a world that didn't rock? All of about five minutes. "I'll get her."

"Mrs. Noble put a rocking chair over there. Said it might settle her."

He picked up the baby, settled in the chair with her against his shoulder and rocked. She snuffled and settled. "I think she likes it."

"Can a person rock and sleep, do you suppose?"

He chuckled softly at the hint of despair in Louise's voice. "I'll see." He tipped his head back and closed his eyes.

Soon Louise's breathing deepened. Chloe slept. And Nate stayed awake, keeping vigil over these two people who needed his protection.

Not until they reached the ranch, not until Vic was in custody, would he relax his watchfulness.

And then he would discuss with Louise the notion of him giving a permanent home to her and the baby.

Chapter Eighteen

Dawn hadn't yet lightened the sky, but Louise wakened to the sounds of men and horses moving about. Her muscles protested at every move, reminding her of her fall from the horse. She'd give anything to stay in this bed for several days, but she would not be the cause of more delay. She'd suggested Nate leave without her, but he had refused, which meant she must get up and get ready to travel.

She smiled at the sweet thought that he wouldn't leave her, and tucked it into a special place in her heart where she could pull it out in the future when she was alone or felt afraid. For a time, someone had wanted to stay with her.

How much sleep had he gotten? He'd spent most of the night in the rocking chair with Chloe, stretching out on his bedroll only when Louise fed the baby. For a little while once her stomach was full, Chloe was happy enough, at least until she realized her world didn't move. Then she began to fuss. Each time, Nate got up and took her, rocking her while Louise slept.

"Good morning," he whispered. "How are you feeling?"

"I'm fine." She said it without thinking. For the most part, when people asked that question, they didn't want an honest answer, so the words came automatically. But for some strange reason right now she felt the need to speak honestly with him. Even stranger was the notion that she felt he actually wanted to hear the truth. "I'm a little sore but nothing serious. I think moving around will ease the stiffness."

"Doc wanted to see you again this morning."

"There's really no need." What she meant was no matter what the doctor said, she was planning to leave this morning. "But fine, if that's what he wants."

"I'll fetch him."

"While you're out and about, best let the stagecoach driver know we'll be ready to go within the hour."

He stood, the baby in his arms, and glowered at her. "Isn't that a little premature?"

She faced him squarely. "I'm anxious to get to my destination."

"You aren't ready to travel."

"Give me one good reason why not."

"I can give you a dozen but I doubt you'd listen."

No, she wouldn't. "Why not let the doctor decide. If he says my life is in danger if I travel, then I will quietly stay here. But if not, I will go."

They did battle with their eyes and will.

Finally he relented. "Very well." He gave her the baby and stalked from the room.

Dr. Noble entered the room a few minutes later. He checked her over. "Seems you'll survive without any lasting damage."

"So there's no reason I can't travel today?"

He stroked his chin and hemmed and hawed a moment. "I wouldn't advise it. You've recently given birth and had a fall that would have killed others."

"Then I guess traveling in a stagecoach is rather a tame activity." She hoped to cajole him into saying the words she needed to hear. Or rather that Nate needed. "It's not likely to kill me, is it?" The question was certain, not asking for anything but agreement.

He wagged his head. "I don't suppose it will. You're an incredibly strong woman. Just the sort that belongs in this country. You'll do fine, my dear. Just don't overdo it." He listed several symptoms she should watch for.

"Thank you."

His smile was a little strained. "I hope you don't pay a stiff price for your decision."

"I won't."

"Do you want my wife to help you dress?"

She would have loved help, but if she was to prove she was capable of travel, she'd best start with getting herself dressed. "I'll be just fine."

He studied her a moment, shook his head and left the room.

Ignoring the bruises that hurt when she touched them and muscles that protested being forced to move, Louise dressed quickly. She'd barely finished when a knock came to the door. Her heart fluttered in anticipation of her visitor.

"Come in," she called.

Nate entered. His dark blond hair had been slicked back. He'd shaved. A little nick on his chin suggested he might have hurried. "You're up," he said, surprise and disapproval in his tone.

"And ready to travel."

He opened his mouth, but she held up a hand to silence his objection. "Dr. Noble said I'd be fine." He'd also said she was strong. Just the sort of woman for this country. Perhaps Nate would see it, too.

He scooped up the baby without replying. "Kamoose said breakfast was ready."

They said their goodbyes to Dr. and Mrs. Noble and stepped outside into the gray predawn light. Thankful that Nate chose a moderate pace, Louise walked at his side back to the hotel.

Kamoose stood upright, his eyes gleaming with what Louise took for as approval. Being a strong woman seemed to make people take notice.

Missy squealed with delight as they stepped into the dining room. "I'm so glad you're okay. Sam, Mr. Adams and Gabe said to tell you goodbye. Rowena has joined her brother and sends her regrets that she wouldn't be here to say goodbye."

They sat down to the food brought by a waiter. She ate heartily, knowing it might be the last good food she'd see for a couple more days. Besides, her milk had come in and her appetite had increased as a result.

Nate finished, paid for their meal. "Wait here."

A few minutes later, the rattle of a wagon drew Louise to the window. There was Nate standing beside a stage-coach, his horse tied to the back. The horse was not saddled. Did that mean Nate meant to continue his practice of riding inside?

It meant nothing, she tried to tell herself. He was merely concerned that her health not be the cause of delay.

But she couldn't convince herself that was true. Nor

even that it was only because he wanted to help with the baby.

No, against her better judgment, she believed it meant he wanted to be with her.

She tucked a pleased smile under her heart. Yes, she might be taking this pretend marriage a little too far, but for now she meant to enjoy the pleasure of his company.

The driver sat in his place and said something to Nate. Called him Slim.

"Slim?" she asked as he hurried into the hotel.

He chuckled. "That's what they call me at the ranch."

She studied him openly. "Might it be because you are tall and slim?" She guessed her eyes teased him.

He grinned back at her. "Might be. But it's good to hear Nate from time to time." He strode on by, leaving her smiling at the thought of his nickname. Then she jerked her attention back to the business at hand. She noticed her bags waited by the desk.

"We're ready to leave," he told her.

Kamoose patted Chloe on the head, shook Nate's hand and wished him safe travels. He nodded to Missy, then he turned to Louise, touched his forehead in a kind of salute.

"You are one brave, strong woman," he said, his voice so admiring, she could feel the heat growing in her face. "You will make your husband a proud man."

It seemed certain her cheeks would burst into flames if she didn't get into the cold air quickly. She murmured a thank-you and hurried for the door.

Nate followed more slowly. They reached the steps outside and he chuckled. "You certainly impressed Kamoose and that isn't easy to do. I expect your name will become a legend. The woman who threw herself from a horse rather than let a man capture her and lived to tell about it. In fact, she continued her journey the next day with a newborn baby in her arms."

She couldn't tell if he meant to be admiring, teasing or disapproving and she would not look at him to determine which. She hadn't asked for the admiration of others. Had not sought to earn it. There was only one man she wished would see her as worthy of his admiration and fidelity. And she had promised he would be required to give neither.

Nate took Chloe and held her as he helped Missy and Louise into the coach, then climbed up and sat down beside Louise with Missy facing them. He arranged the robes over them. "Okay, Petey," he called, and the driver released the brake and they jerked away from the hotel. The curtains were not pulled down as yet and Louise peered out at the passing buildings of the fort.

At the gate, they stopped and Colonel Macleod came to the window.

"Have they found him yet?" Louise asked.

"No, but we will. All the best," he said. "Ma'am, I am most impressed by your fortitude. You will be an asset to your husband, your family and your country." He stepped back and saluted as they rolled away.

"Wow," Missy said. "You are a hero, aren't you?"

Louise shook her head. "Of course I'm not. I haven't done anything."

Nate took her hand and smiled at her. "You certainly have. You are brave and strong and courageous." His smile fled. "Just don't take it too far."

She quirked an eyebrow at him.

He chuckled. "You will do whatever you make up your mind to do. Always have. I suppose you always will.

Sometimes it's for the good, but it can also land you in a heap of trouble."

"I landed okay, wouldn't you say?" She referred to jumping off Vic's horse.

"This time. Next time might not turn out as well."

She shuddered. "I hope there is no next time with Vic."

He squeezed her hand. "I think we all share your opinion."

Missy pulled the curtains down over the windows on either side of her. "Pull yours down, too. That way, if Vic is watching for us, he won't be able to see we're in here."

Louise and Nate quickly let down the curtains. It kept out the cold but also most of the light. She settled back, knowing the hours would be long and dull.

Nate's head bobbed. The poor man was tired. She took Chloe from him. "Get some sleep."

"I'm not tired."

She chuckled at the way his words slurred. In a few minutes his head fell to the side and he slept. She leaned into her corner and watched him.

He was a man with a goal. A purpose. She'd like to help him achieve his dream of a ranch. And she knew she could do it. Hadn't she been told three times this very morning that she was strong? An asset to her husband and the country? Would he ever see her as such rather than a responsibility, perhaps even a liability?

He wakened with a start when they stopped to change horses and jumped to the ground where he stretched and yawned mightily.

"Come on down," he said, reaching to assist her. "It's sunny and bright. A day full of hope and promise."

Holding the baby in one arm, both she and Missy stepped outside. She breathed in the cold, fresh air.

"Look at the mountains." He pointed to the west.

She'd been admiring them for days, but today the sun hit the snowy peaks in a way that turned them white and pure. She drank in the sight of them, feeling as if God was very near.

"'Thy righteousness is like the great mountains: thy judgments are a great deep: O Lord, thou preservest man and beast.'" As she quoted a verse she recalled, her heart swelled with joy and gratitude. Then she remembered something she'd neglected. "I meant to purchase a Bible at the fort."

She was still regretting her oversight when it was time to climb aboard again. Once they were settled, Nate reached for his travel bag and pulled out a parcel and handed it to her.

"What is this?"

"Open it and see."

She hesitated.

"Hurry up," Missy urged.

Louise untied the string and folded back the brown paper. "A Bible." She stroked the leather cover, lifted it and felt its weight. She opened the gold gilt pages. "It's beautiful." Her voice caught in the back of her throat. "Thank you."

"I didn't forget."

Their gazes met and held. Did he mean his words as a promise? Or a warning? Likely both. A promise to see her safely to Eden Valley Ranch and a warning their pretend marriage would end there.

She turned her eyes toward the Bible. She would cherish it forever, not only because she could now discover truths about God, but because Nate had bought it for her.

When they parted ways, she would have her memories and this Bible.

They would have to be enough.

Nate was relieved that Louise spent much of the day reading from the Bible he'd bought for her. Only one other thing would have pleased him more. If she'd slept. She had to be tired and immensely sore, though she did her best to hide it.

He smiled as he thought of how Kamoose and Colonel Macleod had saluted her. She certainly deserved the respect she'd earned at the fort. As many of the men said, she was the sort of woman who could handle the challenges of the new West.

Once he'd taken care of the details of buying the place, he'd see if she would like to be part of building a new ranch. He smiled to himself at the thought of Louise and Chloe in the improved cabin on what he hoped would soon be his land.

In his mind he envisioned how she'd make it a real home, all the touches she would add to it. Before he knew it, he'd passed the whole day and they were stopping for the night just before dark. "Our last time to sleep in a stopping house before we reach Eden Valley Ranch."

She grinned widely. "I won't be sorry to sleep in a proper bed night after night, but I also can't say I've minded the adventure of this journey." Her gaze held his, seeking something more. His foolish heart wished she had enjoyed the closeness they'd shared on the trip.

The stopping house was smaller than most they'd slept in; the host somewhat taciturn. But none of that mattered. Tomorrow they would reach Edendale. He'd buy that piece of land and then ask Louise if she wanted to share the future with him.

He took his turn walking Chloe throughout the night and promised himself the first piece of furniture for his cabin would be a rocking chair.

The next morning they rose early and left before the sun broke over the horizon. On the last leg of their journey, he lifted the curtain so they could see the sunrise. Orange and pink and red filled the sky.

Louise leaned over his shoulder. "It's beautiful."

"The promise of a good day and more to come." A future as bright as the sun beckoned.

They made good time throughout the day, with Petey as eager to reach their destination as any of them. It was midafternoon when they approached Edendale. Nate opened the curtains so he could point out the various landmarks. Then the stage rolled to a stop before Macpherson's store.

He jumped down, helped the ladies to the wooden sidewalk in front of the store, smiling at the little bundle cradled in Louise's arms, then turned to help Petey unload the trunks. He meant to go to the livery stables and rent a wagon to take him to Eden Valley Ranch, but a wagon rolled up behind the stage and Buster, the youngest cowboy from the ranch, hailed him.

"Say, are you heading back to the ranch?" Nate asked.

"As soon as I pick up the order from the store."

"We'll ride along, if that's okay."

"Sure thing."

Nate turned and introduced Missy, Louise and the baby. Buster stared at Missy a moment, swallowed hard, then forced his gaze away. Nate grinned, knowing every man in the area would have the same reaction to Missy's beauty. He saw her only as the girl he'd known most of his life, almost a little sister. Compared to Louise, Missy was too fragile looking for his taste.

A few minutes later, they were in the wagon headed toward the ranch. Louise, Missy and the baby were in the back. Louise had insisted she'd be more comfortable in the box than on the hard bench.

Nate sat beside Buster. Several times, he turned around to point out various things.

"The new church. It's almost finished." Blue and Clara had built the pews recently. "We're waiting to find a preacher."

Louise studied the building.

"Back there is where the Mortons run a kind of dining room. They feed travelers and Mrs. Morton bakes goods that Macpherson sells at his store." Suddenly he could think of so much he wanted to tell her. How Cassie had started the business, and she and Roper had worked together to care for four orphaned children, and were now married and parents to those four children. Strange how a child or children had brought so many of the young married couples together. It seemed to apply to him, as well. If Louise hadn't been expecting a baby, if she hadn't needed him to protect her from Vic, if they hadn't agreed to a pretend marriage...well, things would be vastly different. Seemed God had worked everything out to bring Nate and Louise together.

They left the little town behind. Nate turned his attention to Buster. "What's new on the ranch?"

"Boss moved the cows down to lower pastures. We had a couple big storms, but they were all safe." He jerked back. "Say, I almost forgot. There was a man looking for you—Mountain Mike."

"He's here? Is he is town with Rufus?" He should have gone there immediately, but he still had plenty of time to talk to him before he returned to the mountains. First, he had to get Missy, Louise and the baby to the ranch, and make sure Eddie knew about Vic.

"No. He left yesterday. Said there was a bad storm coming and he wanted to be in his own little place when it hit."

The words did not make sense. "Are you saying he's gone?"

"Yup."

Nate stared straight ahead. He saw nothing but the gray fog of disappointment.

"Yesterday, you say?"

"Yup. I saw him ride by while I was out checking the cows. Headed up into the mountains. It's got to be a lonely way to live. I don't think I'd like it. What do you suppose he does? Read, maybe. Play solitaire." Buster shook his head.

Nate stopped listening. Mike had come and gone, along with Nate's chance to buy the ranch.

He had nothing to offer Louise. No home. No future but a hired hand living in the bunkhouse.

His shoulders slumped forward.

There was but one way to change things. He'd go after Mountain Mike. Not tonight. The sun was already touching the mountain peaks, but first thing tomorrow he'd ride after him.

He would not tell Louise of his plans because, until he had something to offer her, there was nothing to speak of.

Chapter Nineteen

Louise couldn't hear all of what Buster said to Nate, but she'd heard enough. Even though it wasn't yet Christmas, Nate had missed the man from whom he wanted to buy the land. It was her fault. She'd delayed him with her needs. She wished she could do something to fix the matter for him, but what?

Before she could even offer her regrets, they turned off the road toward a two-story house. She stared. This was the ranch house? She'd expected something a lot more modest.

Nate turned. "Welcome to Eden Valley Ranch."

She knew he did his best to sound cheerful and welcoming, when he must be full of disappointments and regrets. All because of her.

Missy crowded to her side as they approached the house. "It's big," she whispered. "They must be rich and important."

Nate overheard. "They're very hospitable. You will be welcomed with open arms."

The wagon pulled up to the house and before the wheels stopped turning, the big front door flew open and a young woman with brown hair and brown eyes hurried outside.

"Slim, you're back. And you've brought visitors. Come in, all of you."

Louise tried to think of Nate as Slim, but it would take a little getting used to.

Nate helped Missy from the wagon box, took Chloe and then helped Louise to his side. He led them forward.

"Mrs. Gardiner, may I present my wife, Louise, and her little daughter, Chloe. This is her sister-in-law, Missy."

To her credit, and Louise's relief, the woman didn't reveal any surprise at Nate's announcement. "So pleased to meet you. Please call me Linette. Come in. Come in."

Louise clung to Nate's side as they followed the woman inside. A wide set of stairs led upward. A long hallway passed a number of doors to reveal a stove and cupboards in the far room. Linette led them to the left, where they entered a cozy, warm room, with two green wingback chairs facing a large window overlooking the ranch buildings. Louise looked out the window and tried to take it all in—the row of buildings on either side of a wide roadway, several smaller buildings, two log cabins, a two-story house, a barn and beyond that another two-story house. "It's like a small town," she murmured.

Linette moved to her side. "We've had to be self-sufficient. When my husband, Eddie, first came, there wasn't much available in Edendale. We had to get the bulk of our supplies from Fort Macleod. See the mountains. That's what I enjoy about the view. Soon they'll wear the colors of sunset, then be filled with mysterious shadows. I never get tired of watching their moods." She turned to face Louise. "But enough about me. Congratulations on your marriage to Slim."

"She knows me as Nate," Nate explained.

"Of course. I'll try and remember. I'm sure you'll both be very happy."

Louise murmured thanks, feeling like a fraud. Soon enough everyone would know the truth, but she couldn't deal with the shock of revealing it at the moment. Though perhaps Nate wanted to...

But when she glanced at him, his gaze was guarded and she couldn't read him. It was all she could do not to sigh with a dozen conflicting emotions. Impatience at his impassive exterior. Worry about where she and Missy and a newborn baby would end up. And a long, deep ache of longing for things that always seemed just out of reach.

"Can I see your baby?"

Linette's request thankfully drew Louise from her dark thoughts and she unwrapped Chloe, who blinked in the light and smacked her lips.

"How old is she?"

"Four days."

Linette's mouth dropped open. "That means you had the baby on the trail. My dear, you are a brave, strong woman."

"The baby wasn't due until Christmas Day." Chloe wasn't quite a Christmas baby, but Louise would always consider her the best Christmas gift ever. "I did what I had to do." Slightly overwhelmed, she was grateful Nate stood at her side, near enough she felt his comforting strength.

Linette patted her arm. "You did more than many could do. Your baby is the same age as mine." She went to a cradle in the corner and lifted out a baby. "Meet my son, Jonathan Edward."

Louise smiled at the little boy still sleeping, even though he'd been lifted from his bed.

Then worry crowded every other thought from her mind. "He's much sturdier looking than Chloe. Maybe there's something wrong with her."

Linette chuckled. "Jonathan was a rather large baby. Chloe looks perfectly fine to me. Now, all of you sit down and tell me everything." She fixed her gaze on Nate. "Married now. I wasn't expecting that."

Neither was he, Louise almost blurted out.

"I've known Louise a long time," Nate said. "She was widowed last spring and needed a home. Seems we were meant to be together."

Louise wanted to thank him for making it sound so legitimate, even if every word about them belonging together was false. As soon as she had a chance to speak to him privately, she would inform him he could have the marriage annulled whenever he wanted.

And if pain shafted through her like a lightning strike, she wasn't about to pay it any mind.

"I'll make tea," Linette said.

"Let me help." Louise handed Chloe to Nate and followed her hostess, Missy right behind her.

"Oh, there's no need. But if you want to come and visit, that would be lovely."

Louise would help if Linette allowed it, or visit with the woman. But she would not stay alone with Nate as the word *annulment* burned a hole through her heart, which was plumb foolish. She'd known from the first the marriage was pretend. She hadn't meant to get so comfortable with the idea of being with him as partners, joint caregivers of the baby and so much more she could not admit at the moment.

If she hadn't been the cause of him losing his ranch, she might have asked him to continue the pretend marriage. Maybe even make it real. Her chest muscles tightened, so she couldn't suck in a satisfying breath. She longed to be special to him. Even as he'd always been so special to her from the first day she saw him. The feeling had grown stronger as they'd talked and played together. As they'd shared meals at the Porter home and enjoyed time with the family that had become their surrogate family.

But she had never been anything but another girl. Nate had made that clear when he rode out of her life.

Something flared through her thoughts. He'd tried to convince her to leave with him after the Porters died. Had he cared about her back then and she was so busy trying to keep things from changing that she never saw it?

Had she been the cause of hurting him then?

As well as the cause of him losing his dream now?

Oh, how she wished she could undo all her mistakes.

Linette and Missy had prepared tea as Louise stood around lost in her thoughts. Missy insisted on carrying the tray.

"After all, both of you ladies have new babies. You are probably weak and tired."

Louise laughed at Missy's teasing. "I confess I'm tired, but that's all."

Linette chuckled, too. "No one who has been through what Louise has been through can be accused of being weak."

"You haven't begun to hear all the things she's done." Missy's voice was so full of admiration it brought a rush of heat to Louise's cheeks, especially as they had returned to the sitting room and Nate overheard her comments.

Linette handed around the tea and offered cookies. "I want to hear every detail."

At that moment the outer door in the kitchen opened and closed.

"That will be Eddie," Linette said, her face glowing with love.

Louise lowered her head, unable to face the comparison between Linette and Eddie, and herself and Nate. Her heart felt near to bursting with the secret knowledge of all she wanted—a home, a family and Nate's love.

Eddie strode into the room with a little boy at his side. He kissed his wife on the forehead. Linette took his hand and introduced Louise and Missy and the baby.

She drew the boy to her side. "This is our son, Grady. He's five."

"Almost six," Grady said with some importance. He peeked at the baby, then turned his attention to some toys nearby.

"Welcome," Eddie said. He reached for Nate's hand. "Congratulations."

Again, Louise lowered her gaze and studied her white-tipped fingers that lay twisted together in her lap.

When Eddie sat down to visit, Louise wondered if Nate would reveal the real reason for her arrival. She didn't wonder for long.

"There is a man after Missy and Louise." Nate quickly explained how Vic meant to own the women and sell the baby.

Linette and Eddie both gasped.

"I expect the Mounties will have captured him by now." Nate tried to sound assuring. "But until we hear that's the case, I'd appreciate knowing everyone is watching for the man."

Eddie nodded. "We certainly will be."

Linette got to her feet. "I must finish supper preparations. Slim—I mean, Nate—you will stay and eat with us."

"Yes, ma'am."

Louise looked at Nate then and grinned.

He gave a mocking smile. "You don't argue with the boss's wife," he murmured.

Linette made a dismissive noise. "It will be ready shortly, but first I must feed young Jonathan." The baby had barely made a fuss, while Chloe protested every time Nate stopped rocking.

"Chloe needs to eat, too." As Louise took her baby from Nate, her gaze connected with his. She wanted him to understand she was sorry but feared all her eyes showed was her regret that it was time to end their pretend marriage.

His look told her nothing and she turned away, lest he see how much she wanted him to stay.

She and Linette fed their babies in the kitchen. Linette insisted Louise take the rocking chair while she sat in an armed wooden chair.

Meanwhile, Missy set the table and followed Linette's clear instructions on what needed to be done.

The meal was excellent, roast beef as she had never before tasted, plenty of potatoes, carrots and canned beans that Linette said came from her own garden.

Louise would have enjoyed the meal more if her thoughts didn't whirl around in her head seeking some way to let Nate know she wanted the marriage to last.

As soon as was polite, Nate stood. "Thanks for the meal. Now I'll call it a night. I'll sleep in the bunkhouse with the boys."

"You're more than welcome to stay with your wife," Linette protested.

"I think he's hoping for a good night's sleep." Louise prayed she'd succeeded in sounding a little amused as she followed Nate to the door. Words crowded her mind. Words she ached to have the right to say. *I love you. Please stay with me.* And she didn't mean tonight in this house. She meant forever.

He paused a moment at the entryway, looking down at her. She wouldn't meet his gaze. She understood his reasons for hurrying away. He'd fulfilled his promise to get her safely to Eden Valley Ranch. Now he was angry or at least disappointed that she had cost him his ranch. Though, to be perfectly fair, he had understood he had until Christmas.

He pressed his big hand to the back of her neck like a hug. "Take care of yourself and Chloe."

And Missy, she silently added. Until Vic was captured, none of them would feel safe, though Eden Valley Ranch offered a degree of protection.

He opened the door, stepped outside and shut the door behind him while she stood there rooted to the spot.

His words had sounded like a blessing.

And a final goodbye.

Tears clogged her throat, but she swallowed them. She was strong. Hadn't several people said so? Well, now was the time to be as strong as everyone thought she was, even though she felt as weak as little Chloe.

She returned to the others and helped Linette with the dishes. All the while she answered the woman's questions without having any idea what she said.

"I'll show you to your rooms," Linette said after some

time. She led them to the little hall off the kitchen and showed Missy to one room and Louise to another.

"Oh, there's a rocking chair. Thank you. Chloe thinks she has to be rocking all the time."

"Nate mentioned it. That's why I've given you this room."

"Thank you."

Linette left and Louise was alone with Chloe. Really alone. Nate wouldn't be taking the baby in the night. He wasn't nearby to comfort Louise.

Knowing she would be unable to sleep, she opened her new Bible. Another reminder of Nate.

As she read various passages, resolve grew strong and sure in her heart.

Tomorrow she would talk to Nate. She would tell him that she was willing to make their marriage agreement permanent. She would not tell him she loved him for fear it would cause him to feel obligated to stay with her. No, she'd simply point out the advantages, remind him of his affection for Chloe. If he still wanted the marriage annulled, she would let him go without a fuss. She'd move on. She'd be strong and she'd be—

The tears came so fierce and violent, like a storm of water and weeping. She cried them all out because there would be no crying tomorrow when she talked to Nate.

The next morning, he did not join them for breakfast. She hadn't expected he would. But surely he would come before the morning was out.

She talked, fed the baby, answered Linette's many questions until she was certain the woman knew everything about her, but her mind constantly waited for Nate to appear.

Morning dragged by. She was alternately annoyed—

one would think he might want to check on Chloe at least, or make sure Louise's bruises weren't bothersome—and hurt and angry. Was she to be forgotten so easily?

Finally she could stand it no longer. When Eddie joined them for dinner, she spoke as calmly as she could. "If Nate isn't too busy, could you tell him I'd like to speak to him?" At the very least, they needed to discuss what happened next.

Eddie put his fork down, gave Linette a look full of secrets, then turned to Louise. "He's gone. Didn't he tell you he was going to try and catch up to Mountain Mike?"

The floorboards could have parted and made a way for her to fall through, so great was her shock and surprise. Then a blinding, painful anger left her speechless and drained.

Somehow she made it through the meal. Later, she and Linette nursed their babies. There was something reassuring about seeing Linette with her baby that gave Louise more confidence in her ability to mother this wee helpless child.

"You'll have to forgive Nate," Linette said. "He's not been married long enough to understand he needs to let you know his plans."

"I'm not surprised. I learned long ago that no one stays. Nothing remains the same." But it had never mattered as much as it did now. She should have told him when she had the chance that she wanted him to stay, but she hadn't. Perhaps she'd never get another opportunity.

Linette considered her with understanding and sympathy. "Nothing ever stays the same. Nor should it. Life is too full of opportunities for us to sit back and refuse to move forward."

Louise nodded, unable to say that all she wanted was someone who would not leave her.

Before she could find a reply, Eddie strode in, brushing snow from his coat. "There's bad weather moving in."

Linette's gaze darted to Louise's and then back to her husband.

Louise realized what concerned Linette. "Nate is out there, isn't he? Will he be able to find shelter?"

"I hope so." Eddie did his best to sound reassuring but failed.

Louise thought of the storm they had ridden through on the trail. Blinding snow, freezing. If a man were lost out there... She shuddered.

Her only consolation was to think of the story he had told of making a snow cave and surviving the elements that way.

Lord, God of everything everywhere, please help him find shelter. Don't let him die.

If he froze out there and she'd never gotten the courage to tell him she loved him...why, she'd regret it to her final day.

Nate had lived in the mountains long enough to recognize all the warning signs of a storm. This morning the sun had had a halo around it. The horizon had been gray all morning. He'd even ridden by a rabbit hiding in some brush and the animal had not moved. Even more telling was that Mountain Mike had known it was coming.

Yes, Nate had seen the signs but ignored them. Even when snow started to fall and the wind picked up, he had ridden onward, set on finding the mountain man and buying the ranch from him.

Without a home, he had nothing to offer Louise.

Now the snow came down so heavy, he couldn't see. The wind blew with cruel intensity, making it impossible to stay warm. Impossible to get any sense of direction. There had been little enough trail to follow with clear skies. Now there was nothing. His horse had stopped moving and Nate didn't want to guide him forward not knowing what lay ahead. It could be a cliff with a life-claiming drop. He might never see Louise or Chloe again.

No. He would survive.

He slid from the horse and held tight to the reins. The horse was his only way of getting back to the ranch once the storm was over.

God, show me a safe place.

He stumbled forward, his free hand outstretched, lifting each foot and lowering it gingerly until he knew it hit solid ground.

Something brushed his head. He reached up to feel it. A tree. Trees meant shelter. *Thank You, God.* He eased forward farther. The wind howled above his head but seemed less fierce around his shoulders.

Branches caught at his legs and arms. He must have stepped into bushes. He pushed into them, drawing his horse after him. They were sheltered enough here. He persuaded the horse to lie down, then pulled the bedroll from the saddle. He draped the blankets and groundsheet about his shoulders and head, and sat with his back to the horse. Together they would keep each other warm.

They would survive because he had to get back and tell Louise he didn't want to end the marriage. He wanted it to be real and lasting. He wanted to be Chloe's father, Louise's husband. He loved her.

Why had he never realized it before?

Snow continued to fall until he was encased in it. The

bitter cold seeped into the very marrow of his bones. He couldn't tell if it was day or night or how many hours had passed. It grew increasingly difficult to put one thought after another. The cold was affecting his brain. He could barely stay awake.

It would be so easy to let sleep claim him.

Chapter Twenty

The next morning, Louise rushed from the bedroom the moment she heard anyone moving about. The storm had battered the house all night. She'd shivered through the hours though she wasn't cold.

Nate was out there, perhaps lost and freezing.

She might never get a chance to tell him how she felt. How she'd felt for a very long time, though she had been denying it in her attempt to hold on to the way things were before the Porters died. Now she saw that none of that mattered. They were temporary, as she'd learned. One thing alone had survived the deaths and trouble of her life. Love. It was all that mattered. Love was reason enough to leave the past and go boldly into the future, no matter what lay ahead.

Linette stood before the kitchen stove as Louise stepped into the room.

Louise skidded to a halt. She couldn't force herself to ask the question for which she feared to hear the answer.

Linette smiled gently. "We left lamps in all the windows in case he tried to find his way home, but no one has come or left all night. Eddie will send out men to look for him the minute the storm lets up."

Louise nodded, tears so close to the surface she couldn't speak.

"I'm sorry. I know how difficult this is. But we can only wait and pray. It might comfort you to know everyone on the place is praying for his safe return."

She nodded again. She'd read the Bible throughout the night, finding comfort and strength in the words. Feeling Nate very close, knowing he'd chosen this Bible for her.

She perched Chloe in one arm. "Tell me what I can do to help."

Linette, perhaps realizing it helped pass the time to keep busy, assigned her chore after chore from breakfast right through the morning.

As they ate the noon meal, Eddie stopped with his fork in midair and held up a hand to signal them all. "Listen. Do you hear that?"

Expecting he heard someone on the step, Louise rushed to the window. She peered through the glass, her breath stuck in the middle of her chest. "There's no one out there," she murmured, disappointment consuming her thoughts.

"The storm has stopped," Eddie said, and pushed from the table. "I'll see to getting a search party out." He paused to pat her back. "Don't worry. We'll find him."

"We'll pray," Linette said, kissing her husband goodbye.

Louise returned to her chair, her head bowed. A silent prayer echoed over and over in her head. *Lord, please bring him back safely.*

Somehow, she went through the motions of helping Linette, of talking to Missy and of feeding little Chloe, though tears dripped from her cheeks as she watched the baby. Nate belonged in Chloe's life, too. Even more than Gordie had. Gordie had been a distant husband and would have been a distant father, more interested in his own pursuits than the needs of those around him. She'd known it even before she married him.

She knew now that their marriage had been but another vain attempt on her part to hold on to the things that were over and done with.

At some point, they moved into the sitting room where they could see the ranch below. Linette sat at the window watching, but Louise could not. She sat as far back as possible and tried to avoid looking in the direction of the window.

Linette leaned forward. "Riders coming in."

Despite her intention of not leaping to the window every time a horseman came, Louise jumped to her feet, Chloe in her arms, and hurried over. "Can you tell who it is?"

"Not yet."

Louise squinted as four riders approached. Did one man slump in his saddle? Did two of the men hold him there? "Nate. It's him. He's hurt." She dashed for the door.

Linette caught her before she could hurry outside. "Wait. They'll bring him here." She held Louise back.

Louise's heart lay cold and quivering, unable to function properly until she saw him. Until she could be certain he was—

Her thoughts could go no further.

The hoofbeats came toward the door.

She forgot how to breathe.

Linette released her and pulled the door open. Two men held Nate between them.

Was he breathing?

He lifted his head, saw her, gasped her name.

Her legs turned to pudding. She would have collapsed if someone hadn't caught her.

"Bring him to the kitchen," Linette ordered.

The men helped him stumble down the hall and sat him in the rocking chair.

Louise fell to her knees before Nate. Shifting her baby in her arms, she removed his gloves. His hands were like ice.

Linette had the men remove his coat and told Missy to leave the room as the men removed his stiff jeans and wet shirt. She took Chloe with her and went to the sitting room.

Louise remained. A dozen horses couldn't have dragged her away. She touched his bare chest. "You're so cold."

He mumbled something, but she couldn't make out his words.

Meanwhile, Linette had warmed blankets and handed them to Louise. "Wrap him up. We need to get his body temperature back to normal."

Louise swaddled him from head to toe in the warm blankets, pressing her palms to his chest when she finished.

His eyes found her, full of need and longing that she recognized from the cries of her own heart.

"I'm here," she murmured. "I will always be here."

A smile crossed his eyes.

Linette brought a cup of warm liquid. "This has something in it my Indian friend gave me. It will help."

Louise pulled a chair so close their legs pressed against each other as she sat beside him and held the cup as he sipped from it.

A bit later, Linette touched his neck. "His body temperature is rising."

"I'm fine," he croaked.

Louise didn't know whether to laugh or cry at the familiarity of his words. "That's what I always say."

"Even when it's not true." Color had returned to his face.

She looked deep into his eyes, wanting to tell him something that was very true.

His gaze searched hers. She hoped he saw what she couldn't say with all these people clustered around.

He turned to Eddie, who stood nearby, hovering as if afraid Nate might not make it.

Louise knew he would. She'd seen the flash of fierceness in his eyes.

"You suppose you could get me some clothes?" Nate asked him.

"Buster is bringing you some," Eddie answered.

"Good." Nate sighed and emptied the cup. His fingers rested against hers as she still clutched it, not wanting to lose this bit of contact.

Buster stepped into the room, a bundle of clothes in his arms. He stared at Nate. "You going to be okay?"

"I sure am."

Eddie thanked Buster and took the clothes to Nate.

"If you'll all give me a moment of privacy…" he said. No one moved.

"Allow a man to retain a shred of pride."

"I'll stay," Louise said.

But he shook his head. "I don't want you to remember me at my weakest."

"Very well. Eddie, will you stay?" She couldn't think of him alone in his present state.

Eddie nodded. "I'll make sure he's okay."

Louise reluctantly followed Linette to the sitting room, where Missy rocked Chloe and Jonathan slept in his cradle.

In a moment, Eddie stepped into the room. "He's decent and would like a few minutes alone with his wife." He held the door for her and closed it behind her as she returned to the kitchen.

Nate had never looked so good.

All the words she wanted to say fled her mind.

He pushed to his feet and she hurried to his side, afraid he was too weak to stand on his own. He draped his arms around her and pulled her close.

"When I was out in the storm there was one thing that kept me from falling asleep. Something I needed to tell you."

She clung to him, afraid he would say he wanted to move on. "I have things I need to say to you, as well."

"Let me go first. Louise, I love you and have since we met. I don't want to end our marriage. I want it to be real. Now, I know I have nothing to offer you. But somehow we can make it work. I know we can. If you want to." He held her so close, she couldn't see his face, but she could feel the beat of his heart.

She smiled against his shirtfront. These were exactly the words she wanted to hear. She stayed in the shelter of his arms for the space of two heartbeats, then pushed back enough to look into his face. "Nate, for too long I've tried to hold on to the past when what I really wanted all the time was to share a future with you. I love you. I don't want to end our marriage. We'll work out something. All that matters is we are together."

"Louise, my wife and joy." He bent his head and claimed her lips and the love she freely gave.

She clung to him, unwilling to end the kiss. Only Chloe's demanding cries gave her the strength to draw back.

"Let's go find that demanding child of ours," he said. "I think it will take both of us to raise her."

They joined the others in the living room and Louise took her baby from Missy and sat in the rocking chair. Nate pulled a chair close to them and draped his arm about her shoulders.

Nate watched Louise and Chloe, feeling as if he'd finally reached home, even though he had nothing to offer them but his love. For now it was enough that Louise loved him. Together, they would face the future. He'd be happy to live in a hovel so long as they could be together, but despite what she'd always said, Louise deserved so much more. She'd told him stories of how she and her father had lived in tents, in tar-paper shacks, and she hadn't cared so long as she could stay with her pa. Still, he wanted to give her a proper home.

"Does anyone know what day it is?" Eddie asked.

Linette smiled sweetly. "Christmas Eve Day."

Grady, who played with an assortment of carved animals, jumped up and stared at Linette, his eyes wide with expectation. "It is. Does that mean that tomorrow is Christmas Day?"

Linette nodded.

"Then where's the tree?"

Eddie feigned surprise. "Why, I almost forgot about a tree. I guess we better remedy that right now. Who would like to help me find one?"

"Me. Me." Grady jumped up and down.

"Get your warm clothes on."

The two of them departed.

"I have a few things to take care of for tomorrow," Linette said. Missy followed her to the kitchen.

Nate turned to Louise. "I'm afraid I have nothing for you for Christmas."

"But you do." She stroked his cheek, turning his insides all warm.

"What?"

"You've given me the best present I could ever want. Your love. I need nothing else." She smiled. "Though I certainly appreciate the Bible you gave me." She lowered her eyes. "I'm afraid I have nothing for you."

He chuckled. "You've given me a double present." He tucked his finger under her chin. "You've given me a wife and a child. That's most generous of you." A sudden horrible thought scalded his mind. "Or am I being presumptuous? This is Gordie's baby. Do you want her raised to think of me as something other than her pa?"

She placed the baby in Nate's arms. "Chloe, meet your pa. I know he will love and protect you all the days of your life. You will always be safe with him." She lifted her gaze to him. "Nate, this is your daughter. I give her to you."

He didn't consider himself a man given to tears, but lo and behold, if two didn't trail toward his chin.

Louise wiped them away. "I love you both so much." She leaned toward him so he could kiss her without crushing the baby.

An hour later, Grady and Eddie dragged a pine tree through the door. Eddie brought a bucket of dirt and they set the tree up in the corner next to Linette's chair. They all sat back and enjoyed watching Eddie and Grady decorate the tree. They even popped corn and strung it.

By the time they were done, it was time for bed. Nate thought of returning to the bunkhouse, but he couldn't bear the thought of being so far from Louise.

Eddie grinned at him. "I'm sure no one would object if you want to spend the night with your wife. Linette, could you give them more bedding?"

"I already put more in Louise's room." The two women smiled at each other as if they shared a secret.

"Then I suggest we turn in." Eddie waited for the guests to depart before he lowered the lamps.

In their room, Nate looked at Louise. "I only intend to stay with you and Chloe like we've been doing."

She came to him and wrapped her arms about him, pressing her face to his neck. "I have loved you a long time."

"Sure wish you'd told me," he groused good-naturedly.

"Me, too. But maybe I had to go through all those things to be ready to love and be loved."

"And I suppose I needed to grow up a bit."

They laughed together softly at the pretend regret in his voice.

He spread his bedroll next to the narrow bed and fell asleep with her hand in his.

It was still dark the next morning when Grady called at the top of his lungs, "Merry Christmas. Merry Christmas. Get up, everybody. It's Christmas."

Nate opened his eyes and met Louise's gaze. He smiled, his heart full of joy. "My wife, it is Christmas Day."

"Merry Christmas, my husband." They dressed quickly, and he carried Chloe out to join the others as they watched Grady open presents.

The morning passed in a pleasant glow. One after another, the others on the ranch joined them. Cookie and her husband, Bertie. Cassie and Roper and their four children. Jayne and Seth. Sybil and Brand. From the nearby ranches came Abel and Mercy and the twins, Allie and Ladd. Grace and Ward joined them along with her sister, Belle, and his mother and brother. The newlyweds, Blue and Clara, and her two girls came from town to join the celebration.

They were all in the sitting room, a crowd of noisy children and talkative adults, when a knock came on the door.

"Who could that be?" Linette asked. "Everyone is here."

Eddie pushed to his feet. "Only one way to find out." He pulled open the door. "Howdy, stranger, what can I do for you?"

"I hear you help people."

"We do if we can."

Every eye had turned to the doorway, where a man stood bundled in winter clothes.

"Then perhaps you'd let us spend Christmas with you. Me and these two children." He drew forward a boy and girl. The boy looked to be about Grady's age, the girl somewhat younger, with eyes so big and solemn it made Nate want to rush over and console her.

Linette joined her husband at the door. "You're most welcome to stay here as long as you need. It's Christmas. Please join us."

He introduced himself as Wade Snyder and the children as his niece and nephew. "Annie and Joey."

Linette took their coats and scarves. The children clung to their uncle's side for some time before they edged over to join Grady and the group of children who played in one corner of the room.

Linette, Louise and the other women hurried to the kitchen to take care of the meal. Soon the adults crowded around the table in the dining room while the children sat at the kitchen table.

Louise smiled and ducked her head as if she didn't want anyone to see her joy-filled expression. Nate hoped she was comforted by the evidence she and Missy weren't the only ones seeking refuge at the Eden Valley Ranch. He didn't mind a bit that he was forced to sit so close to Louise that they continually bumped elbows.

Again a knock sounded.

Linette chuckled. "More company."

Eddie opened the door. "Hi, Rufus. Come on in and join the fun."

"Thanks, but I got to get back. Petey and Prudence are home alone and my sister annoys Petey something fierce. I got a message for Slim. Is he here?"

Nate heard his nickname and went to the door. "Howdy."

"Thought you'd come round to see me when you got to town."

Nate didn't see any reason to point out there was no use once he'd heard Mountain Mike had gone.

Rufus went on without Nate's reply. "Mike said to say he was sorry he couldn't wait for you. That man gets real nervous if the thinks it might snow and keep him from getting back to his precious cabin."

"Uh-huh." Did the man come all the way out here on Christmas Day to tell everyone that?

"I told him why you wanted to see him. He said he could take care of it without waiting for you." Rufus pulled a sheet of paper from his pocket. "This here is the deed to the ranch. All signed legal-like. Mike says he'll be back in the spring and you can pay him then. All of it or part. Whatever you can." He handed the papers to Nate, bid goodbye to one and all, and left.

Nate stared at the paper. With unsteady hands he unfolded it and saw the land description and Mike's signature. All it needed was Nate's signature, and he'd add that and get Eddie to witness it.

Eddie clapped him on the back. "Now, *that*'s a Christmas present to remember."

Nate's shock wore off and he laughed, waving the paper over his head. "I just got me a ranch." He stood in front of Louise. "I just got us a home." He pulled her to her feet. "Mrs. Hawkins, you and I have a home of our own." And before she could protest, he kissed her in front of the whole crowd.

As they clapped, the adults gathered around to congratulate him and shake his hand, to wish them both all the best.

He held Louise at his side. He had all the best with or without the ranch. He had Louise and Chloe.

As they returned to the table, Nate could not remember a better Christmas.

Epilogue

"Wait here," Nate said as they stood before the cabin that was to be their first home. He carried Chloe and her cradle inside and put them down, then came back and scooped Louise into his arms.

"What are you doing?" She wrapped her arms about his neck. He could take her anywhere, do anything he wanted, she was that happy to be with him, facing a shared future.

"We've done everything else backward, but I want to do this right." He crossed the threshold and lowered her to her feet but kept his arms around her.

"I have something for you." He reached into his pocket, pulled out a ring and slipped the golden band on her finger. "With this ring I thee wed." His eyes brimmed with love. "Welcome home, Mrs. Hawkins." He kissed her, a kiss full of promise and possibility.

She kissed him back, silently pledging him her love and care for as long as she lived.

Then she turned around in his arms to look at their new home. "It's perfect."

"It sure looks a lot better than it did a few weeks ago."

"We couldn't have done it without help." Eddie had sent some of the cowboys over. The couples had come and washed and scrubbed and repaired until the place was like new.

Missy had helped make new curtains for the windows. She'd announced she wished to stay at Eden Valley Ranch and help Linette, and Louise couldn't find it in her heart to object. At least she'd be safe at the ranch. If only they would receive word that Vic had been captured. The Mounties' assurance the man would be found provided her with a modicum of relief.

Louise had insisted she alone would make the quilt for their bed in the little bedroom. She'd sewn each stitch with love and prayers that God would grant them many happy years and many children.

Nate had made the table where they would share their meals and good conversation at night. She'd discovered he liked reading aloud and she had spent many pleasant hours knitting things for Chloe while he read her books from Eddie's vast library. She looked forward to many more pleasant evenings around this table in the weeks left before spring came and he got busy with cattle.

The sun shone through the sparkling windows, filling the room with rays of light.

One of the rays crossed Chloe's face and she gurgled at it.

Nate went and scooped up the baby, who favored him with a toothless smile.

"She's the prettiest little girl ever." He pulled Louise into his arms. "Looks like her mama."

"What do you mean? I have all my teeth."

They laughed together. Over the past few weeks they had found many things to laugh about.

Most of all, though, they found their love went deep, and each day Louise enjoyed dipping a little deeper into that love.

She lifted her face for a kiss. "I love you, Nate Hawkins," she whispered before his lips claimed hers.

For now and for always.

* * * * *

Dear Reader,

How precious is the birth of a baby. Even in the midst of storms and turmoil, the cry of a newborn evokes tenderness and hope. And what better Christmas gift than a baby? I have a daughter born on Boxing Day. She doesn't think it's a good time to have a birthday, but think about it. Don't all the things we wish for at Christmas—joy and love and peace—promise to come true in the birth of a child?

In this story, I wanted the birth of little Chloe to change the hero and heroine, making them see what mattered in their lives.

This is a work of fiction, but I have used bits and pieces of real life discovered in my research. For instance, Kamoose Taylor, his hotel and his rules are real.

I love to hear from my readers. You can contact me at www.lindaford.org where you'll find my email address and where you can find out more about me and my books.

Linda Ford

REQUEST YOUR FREE BOOKS!

2 FREE INSPIRATIONAL NOVELS
PLUS 2 *FREE* MYSTERY GIFTS

Love Inspired HISTORICAL

LIH15

*Could Hank Chandler's search for a wife lead to
holiday love with schoolteacher Janell Whitman?*

Read on for a sneak preview of
THE HOLIDAY COURTSHIP,
the next book in Winnie Griggs's miniseries
TEXAS GROOMS

"I wonder if you'd mind giving me your opinion on some
potential candidates," Mr. Chandler asked.

"You want my opinion on who would make you a
good wife?" Apparently he saw nothing odd about asking
the woman he'd just proposed to to help him pick a wife.

He frowned. "Not a wife. A mother for the children. I
need your opinion on how the lady under consideration
and the children would get on."

"I see." The man really didn't have an ounce of
romance in him.

He nodded. "You can save me from wasting time
talking to someone who's obviously not right."

"Assuming you find the right woman, may I ask how
you intend to approach her?"

"If you're wondering if I intend to go a'courtin'—"
Hank's tone had a sarcastic bite to it "—the answer is no,
at least not in the usual way. I don't want anyone thinking
this will be more than a marriage of convenience."

"I understand why you wouldn't want to go through a
conventional courtship. But don't you think you and your

prospective bride should get to know each other before you propose?"

He drew himself up. "I consider myself a good judge of character. It won't take me long to figure out if she's a good candidate or not."

"I would recruit a third party to act as a go-between," Janell said. "It should be someone whose judgment you trust."

"And what would this go-between do exactly?"

"Go to the candidate on your behalf. He or she would let the lady know the situation and ascertain the lady's interest in such a match."

"So you agree that a businesslike approach is best, just that I should go about it from a distance."

"It could save a great deal of awkwardness and misunderstanding if you did so."

"In other words, you think I need a matchmaker."

"I suppose. But you *do* want to approach this in a very businesslike manner, don't you?"

Hank nodded. "I have to admit, it sounds like a good idea."

Happy that he'd seen the wisdom of her advice, she said, "Is there someone you could trust to take on this job?"

He rubbed his jaw thoughtfully for a moment. Finally he looked up. "How about you?"

Don't miss
THE HOLIDAY COURTSHIP
by Winnie Griggs, available December 2015 wherever
Love Inspired® Historical books and ebooks are sold.

Turn your love of reading into rewards you'll love with
Harlequin My Rewards